Where You'll Find Him

MEL BOSSA

Published by
DREAMSPINNER PRESS

5032 Capital Circle SW, Suite 2, PMB# 279, Tallahassee, FL 32305-7886 USA
http://www.dreamspinnerpress.com/

Where You'll Find Him
© 2015 Mel Bossa.

Cover Art
© 2015 Paul Richmond.
http://www.paulrichmondstudio.com
Cover content is for illustrative purposes only and any person depicted on the cover is a model.

ISBN: 978-1-63216-930-3
Digital ISBN: 978-1-63216-931-0
Library of Congress Control Number: 2015930656
First Edition May 2015
Printed in the United States of America
(∞)
This paper meets the requirements of
ANSI/NISO Z39.48-1992 (Permanence of Paper).

For the volunteers.

CHAPTER ONE

RUNNING LATE, Wolfe hurried up the stairs to his third-floor office at the YBR center.

Upstairs, he stepped through the entrance doors straight into the chaos of the broad lobby. People were running around, gathering fliers and screaming orders at each other. Wolfe looked around for anybody in management to give him a hand, but of course Yvan was in his office with his door shut.

Quickly, Wolfe gave the new, clueless volunteers directions. "Just keep doing what you're doing," he said, "and I'll be right back."

He desperately needed a glass of water and a moment to cool down before starting the day. It was nine a.m., but the July sun was already scorching Montreal's streets, and his usual pleasant walk to work had left him dehydrated.

At the end of the hall, in his office, his phone was already ringing off the hook.

Pretty soon, he'd have to spend the night at the center in order to actually get anything done.

Inside his office, Wolfe slowly drank some water, going over the list of things he needed Zach and Dominic to pack for the day. He hadn't slept well, but he'd have to make an effort to perk up. Today was Pride Community Day in Montreal, and the board was counting on him to raise some serious funds for the YBR center.

"You look trashed." Zach, his right-hand man and project coordinator, leaned in the doorway, watching him with a sly smile. It was a hundred degrees out there, but Zach was clad in all black. The man was immune to the heat—cool and stunning as ever. "How was your night?" he asked. "Your hair looks like someone slept in it, Mr. Scarecrow."

Wolfe gestured for him to come in while he searched for a pen through the mess on his desk. "My night? Well, let's see, my air conditioner died around two a.m., and I listened to myself sweating all night." He looked up at Zach. "What's up?"

Zach stepped into Wolfe's small and impossibly cluttered office. "You know how this place gets on full moons?"

"That bad, huh?"

"No, man. This is a full moon on *smack*."

"Well, it's Pride week. The season for rainbow madness." The phone kept ringing and Wolfe stared at it in dismay. "Am I the only one who hears it?"

"Hey, look, I need to know who's on at two o'clock this afternoon. 'Cause I have that thing, you know, that appointment I can't miss."

"Oh, right. Yes, I remember." How could he have forgotten? Zach had another doctor's appointment. While his viral load was still under control, lately, his energy was low. "Leave at two," Wolfe whispered. "Me and Dominic will take care of the stand."

"You're gonna stand there all day? In this sun? Man, you're gonna get sunstroke and pass out."

But Wolfe waved Zach off and looked around for some forms he needed to bring today. He could barely see his desk under all the paper.

Everyone needed something from him, and ever since Eric, the center's previous director, had been demoted by the board and quit, two other supervisors had handed in their resignations. Today, all of the organizations in the YBR center, all *four* of them, were under Wolfe's supervision. He was responsible for Talk-Talk, the group discussions program on the second floor, the CPLHIV and its neighbor the Blue Bird Foundation, and the hotline program currently run by Yvan.

He couldn't even remember the last time he'd taken a day off. What he needed was an army of flying monkeys, or pretty soon *he'd* be the one calling a helpline for support.

"Good morning," Clare, the center's lawyer, called out to him from the end of the hall. She walked up to his door and squinted at him. "Is that what you're wearing?" Clare was an adamant civil rights lawyer with a heart as big as her voice. "That T-shirt is too small for you," she said, pushing her old glasses up her nose. The frames were held together with tape. "Way too tight."

Wolfe usually wore dress pants and button-up shirts to work, but today, he'd figured jeans would be best. After all, he'd be out there all day, on the sidewalk, handing out information and condoms in this angry July sun. He was wearing one of the YBR's T-shirts. "It's my size exactly," he argued. "Small."

Clare had a natural authoritative manner that worked miracles for her clients in court. "Remember what's out there today," she said. "All tourists. Mostly Americans who can't handle Canadian beer in the sun, and a lot of horny guys who think you'll help them try on the free rubber for size. Especially if the guy handing the condom out is a cute little blue-eyed boy like you."

Zach strutted back into the office, turning the van's keys in his fingers. "Am I driving or what?"

"Yes, and we should get going." Wolfe picked up his bag, checked his e-mail one last time, and left his office. Zach and Clare followed him.

In the hall, Wolfe grabbed a doughnut out of the box left open on the table. That would be breakfast. "Gimme a second," he said to Zach, heading for Yvan's office.

He poked his head in Yvan's door. "What time are the new helpline volunteers coming in?" he asked, then took a bite of the powdered doughnut.

Yvan looked up from his computer, obviously annoyed at the interruption. "Soon. And you have sugar around your mouth and on your T-shirt."

"Oh." Wolfe dusted himself off. "Thanks."

Yvan was a snobby but energetic guy with years of experience in community work. He was definitely an asset to the center, and Wolfe rarely interfered in his affairs. Yvan managed the helpline, and the recruiting and training of volunteers. However, lately the volunteer turnaround was terrible, and Wolfe knew they'd have to sit down and look at Yvan's program soon.

He was dreading that meeting.

"They're coming in at nine," Yvan said.

"All right," Wolfe said, thinking at the speed of light. There were so many things he needed done while he was away, and no one to pick up the slack for him. Everyone had been with the center longer than he had, and none were keen on taking on more responsibilities from the new guy. Yes, he was still the *new guy*, though he'd been appointed director by the board a year ago. "Okay," Wolfe said uneasily. "That sounds good, but if you could maybe check in with Antonio downstairs about that dinner we're planning for our anniversary—"

"I'm already swamped, Wolfie. Sorry." Yvan smiled tensely and went back to staring at his screen. "Good luck out there today, kid."

"Thanks anyway," Wolfe muttered, turning away from Yvan's door.

Kid.

At twenty-five years old, Wolfe was the youngest director the board had ever appointed. But his two years as a social worker in the gritty streets of East Hastings, the notorious Vancouver neighborhood, had counted for a lot.

"You ready?" Zach tapped his shoulder.

Zach and Wolfe sauntered down the stairs, but on the second floor, Wolfe paused. "Let me just check in with the girls at Talk-Talk, see if they need anything—"

But Zach pulled on Wolfe's arm. "No, if you go in there, they'll keep you for hours."

"But I just need to know if Astrid needs—"

"Wolfe."

"All right. All right."

Zach dragged him down the last flight of steps. Again, at the Committee of People Living with HIV door, Wolfe slowed down. "I know Antonio needs to talk to me about his ratios—"

"You know how much that damn booth is costing us by the hour?"

"No, no, you're right."

Zach tossed his head to the door. "Come on, Wolfie, let's go save the world for a little while."

Wolfe followed Zach down the stairs and out into the back parking lot. The YBR building was in Montreal's gay village, blocks away from the action of Sainte-Catherine Street. It had once been a Catholic school, then abandoned, and later turned into a community center during the early days of the AIDS epidemic. Today it housed the whole of the YBR's nonprofit organizations. The center was close enough to be in the middle of things but far enough from the bars and club scene to provide privacy for the people who frequented the center.

"Everything loaded up?" Wolfe opened the back door of the van. "Let me just do a quick spot check."

Zach settled into the driver's seat, turned the engine on, and rolled down his window. He leaned his tattooed arm on the sill. "Take your time."

Already, Wolfe could feel the heat cooking him. He scanned the backseats. Everything seemed to be in order. He jumped into the passenger seat and pulled his seat belt on. "Okay, I'm ready."

Zach shot him a glance. "Yeah, sure? You don't wanna check the tires or oil or maybe see if the neighbors need anything?"

"Don't tempt me. Now roll your window up and turn on that AC, please."

"No can do." Zach drove out of the parking lot with a screech of tires. "It's broken, like my heart."

Wolfe laughed. "Ah, the joys of nonprofit work."

Zach glanced over at him with a smile. "We really do live it up, don't we?"

IN THE bedroom, Gaspard grabbed the sunscreen off the commode and rubbed more on his face and arms. Decades ago, when they'd all been in their twenties, his buddies had poked fun at his obsession with sunscreen, but now that the big 5-0 loomed around the corner for all of them, Gaspard was glad he'd been so paranoid about the sun back then. He'd managed to slow the hands of time a little.

Yet, as young as he looked, time was catching up with him every day. More reason to go out there today and try to stir something up before he turned into a hermit.

"Oh, you look great," Malena said as he walked into the living room. Malena was still in her pajamas, lounging on the couch. She definitely needed to get a job offer soon. "I like your hair like that. You look like you just rolled out of bed or something."

"Really?" Alarmed, Gaspard checked the mirror in the hall. "Well, that's not good." He combed his fingers through those rebellious strands he'd never really been able to tame since he was a boy. He was thankful he still had a head full of thick, blond hair. "I don't even know why I'm going out there today anyway," he half lied, smoothing his hair down.

"You mean out in the *world*?" Malena motioned for him to come closer. She looked lovely with her hair tied up in a bun. "You haven't been out all week," she said, watching him with those vivid hazel eyes he adored. "I come home from job-hunting, you're on your computer. I go to bed, you're on your computer."

"I have clients, remember? I'm not retired yet."

But Malena was right; he did spend way too much time on his computer. He was lonely and putting off work, wasting time online. "It looks really hot out there," he said, changing the subject. "It's gonna be crazy. There's gonna be too many people out. And the heat makes everybody wild—"

"Listen to yourself." She turned the volume down on the television and gave him that look he knew too well. "You said you wanted to break down some of the gates that held you in all of your life. You moved us here, downtown, to be closer to everything. To the action. To people. But we've lived here for six months now, and all you ever do is work on your book and those awfully boring software programs—"

"Those boring programs pay the bills. And I'm trying to be more outgoing." Gaspard was looking out at the street. Their new apartment was on the ground floor of a four-unit building, on University Street, steps away from the McGill University campus and beautiful Mount Royal. It was a busy and restless neighborhood. He still couldn't get used to the noise at night, with all these student houses around him. He slept with earplugs and the windows closed, with the AC turned up full blast. But this place was perfect for Malena—she was walking distance from almost every job interview she'd had so far. He liked the idea of having her working so close by. "It's just such a change," Gaspard said, watching groups of people, all young, walk past his window on their way up to Mount Royal.

"Yes, it's a change from living in a five-bedroom house in the burbs, I'll admit, but remember how miserable you were in that house after Curtis and I left for university, and Mom started sleeping over at Karen's place more and more—"

"No, I know, and you're right." Gaspard stepped away from the window and looked at his wise daughter. She was so brilliant. So level-headed. At least he'd done something right in his life.

"Look, Dad, you gave Mom your best years, but you're still young, and it's not too late to start living again." She tossed her chin up at the door. "Go. Take a walk through the gay village. Be bold. What's the worst that can happen?"

He hesitated, looking at the front door. "I'm forty-nine years old. The world is a different place now."

"It's just a walk, Dad. Not like you're going to a strip club or hiring a male escort—"

"Malena, please, you're not helping."

"Oh, Dad, don't be such a prude."

"I'm not a prude. Just not comfortable talking about this with you."

Ever since Malena had completed her degree in gender studies, she was more and more at ease with discussing issues he still thought should stay private and behind closed doors. That was the problem with her generation. They dissected human sexuality as though they were performing an autopsy on romance. It made him uneasy, but regardless of her forthrightness, Gaspard was immensely grateful for Malena's open mind and support. Ever since the divorce, Malena was, in many ways, his only and best friend.

"Anyway," she said, smiling at him from over the couch seat, "this is better than going to a bar full of twenty-year-old kids, right? There's going to be tons of people walking around, and all kinds of stands there. There's going to be some information desks, and you can get a tan and an education all at once."

An *education*? No, he didn't need an education. He needed to connect with someone. To feel alive again. Or just to be seen. He'd even settle for being noticed. Eye contact from across the street could do the trick. Anything to confirm he still had it in him to attract some kind of attention.

"Oh by the way," she said, "I'm having dinner at Cory's tonight."

Gaspard wasn't surprised. Malena had been seeing Cory almost every day now for two weeks. "It's getting serious with him, then?" he asked, grabbing his keys.

She bit her lip and shrugged. "Maybe."

"When do I get to meet him?"

She didn't answer his question. "Call me later" was all she said.

Gaspard stared at her for a moment. "Thank you, by the way. For being so supportive."

"Dad, you've supported me all of my life." She turned her attention back to the television. "You're still *supporting* me right now.

What kind of a woman would I be if I didn't show you a little gratitude?"

He didn't know what to say.

"Go," she said, waving him off again. "Before you change your mind."

Gaspard looked out at the busy street. "Here I go."

"And remember," she called out from the cool apartment. "You're not *old*, you're successful and experienced!"

AT THE YBR stand, Zach tore open the last box of fliers they had. He wiped his brow with the back of his hand and looked over at Wolfe. Zach seemed a little on edge. Lately Wolfe couldn't help wondering if Zach had really won his battle against substance abuse. Was he still using?

"We're gonna run out of these by one o'clock," Zach said, piling up more fliers on the table. "We're gonna need another box."

Wolfe opened a fresh bottle of water. "There's a lot more people this year," he said before drinking again. He'd gone through four already. Nothing seemed to quench his thirst. He'd tried staying in the shade under the stand's awning, but the heat was engulfing anywhere you stood.

Zach grabbed the bottle from Wolfe's hand and drank from it greedily. The crowd had thinned a little, and they were enjoying a short break. "When Dominic comes back," he said, "I'll ask him to go get more fliers and rubbers at the center."

"Where is he, anyway?" Wolfe helped Zach with reorganizing the stand a little.

"I don't know, but I'm not enjoying the way he's been disappearing on us all morning."

"Yes, I know… and I'll talk to him about that."

Dominic was a volunteer. He wasn't paid a dime to be there. Wolfe was discovering how difficult it was to manage the volunteers who offered their time to him. What could he say to Dominic? *Work harder or I'll fire you?*

"And notice how Dominic only talks to the cute guys?" Zach shot him a side glance. "Meanwhile, I'm answering about ten different people all at once."

"Are you sure you're okay? You look a little wired."

"I'm fine, and remember the rule."

The rule was, only Zach could decide when he needed a breather. He didn't want anyone's concern or advice. He never spoke of his HIV status. Even when he'd gotten very sick last year, he hadn't complained about the nausea and extreme fatigue. They'd all watched the weight fall off him, expecting and fearing the worst. But Zach had made it through.

"Okay… forget I said anything." Wolfe looked away at the busy street. It was a circus out there. This stretch of Sainte-Catherine Street was closed to cars all summer and turned into some kind of queer Land of Oz. Everywhere Wolfe looked he saw bare skin and tight jeans. People were definitely on the prowl today.

"Hey," Zach said, leaning into his ear. "Sorry I snapped. I'll take a break in a minute." He nudged his shoulder. "Don't worry about it. Anyway, I'm leaving in an hour."

"That's all I needed to hear."

"I don't like leaving you alone with Dominic," Zach said after a moment. "He's pretty useless."

"I'll be all right." But in truth, Wolfe was exhausted already. They'd spent the last three hours greeting people, answering questions, handing out pamphlets and condoms, explaining the various services the YBR offered the community. Public relations was key to his job, though he didn't enjoy that part much. He was always begging for funds.

"You know," Zach said, "you're gonna have to start looking for some decent help. You're on your last leg, Wolfie."

Wolfe caught sight of Dominic across the street, chatting it up with a young man on a bike. "There he is," Wolfe said, pointing him out to Zach. "Go get him, please."

Moments later, Zach returned with Dominic.

"Sorry, Wolfie, I lost track of time," Dominic said. "What can I do here?"

Wolfe realized he'd be stuck with Dominic all day, unless he sent him out there instead. He decided he'd rather man the stand alone than listen to Dominic comment on every guy's appearance for the next five hours. "Here," he said, handing Dominic more fliers and a registration sheet. "Just take a walk and pass these out. You know, talk to people. You seem to be good at that. Try to get us some donations."

Dominic seemed thrilled. This would give him an excuse to randomly hit on anybody. "I'll get you so many donations, you won't even know what to do with the money," he said, walking away.

Zach stretched his arms and yawned. He was clearly bored with everything already. "I should get us some lunch, right?"

"I could eat something, yes."

But before Zach could leave, another crowd gathered around their stand, and Wolfe tried sorting out the potential donors from the lurkers but couldn't turn anyone away. He could never tell who could be a real supporter or a future volunteer.

Zach leaned in closer to Wolfe's ear. "Look over there," he said. "The guy in the pale blue shirt there."

Wolfe scanned the crowd and immediately spotted the man Zach was referring to. The first thing he noticed was the man's very blond hair. "What about him?" Wolfe asked nonchalantly, but his curiosity was piqued.

"He keeps looking over here. I think he walked past our stand ten times already. You didn't notice him?"

"No, I never noticed." Wolfe looked at the man again. He was fit, dressed casually but impeccably in dark blue jeans and pale blue shirt. He was tall, probably a little over six feet, and wearing dark sunglasses. Handsome maybe. It was hard to tell from here. Besides, a man's best feature was his eyes, Wolfe had always thought, and he couldn't see the man's face at all. The blond stood looking into a storefront, but though his eyes were hidden behind those dark glasses, Wolfe knew the man was glancing toward his stand every few seconds. "You should get us something to eat," Wolfe said, turning his attention to Zach again. "Before you go, if you don't mind." He took his wallet out.

"Oh, here he comes." Zach winked and stepped back. "Good luck. He looks like he's got some dough. Maybe he's the big fish we've been searching for."

When Zach had walked off, Wolfe grabbed the last stack of pamphlets and began arranging them in neat piles. Anything to look very busy and serious. He didn't glance up but knew the man was standing at his table.

"Hi," the man said. His tone was friendly, but nervous, and his voice was deep.

Wolfe looked up and met the man's arresting blue eyes. He hadn't been prepared for such beautiful eyes, and he was frozen for a moment. The stranger had hooked his sunglasses on his shirt and was smiling at him.

He had a very classy look. An impossibly sexy smile.

"Hello," Wolfe said, his voice jumping a little. "How are you?" He made an effort to appear cool and professional. Maybe Zach was right. Maybe this guy was exactly the type to write out checks to charity. He was a man in his forties with a certain air of power about him.

"Well, I'm hot." The man was suddenly embarrassed. "No, I don't mean, me as in *me* me," he muttered. "I mean, the weather is hot."

Wolfe immediately changed his mind about the man. Maybe he was looking for support or information instead. "You should have some water." He took a bottle out of the small, flooded cooler. "Here… on us."

"No, I couldn't. With the economy the way it is, people aren't giving as much as they used to, I bet."

This man was getting more interesting by the second. He had an aura of a man who lived a healthy, carefree existence only the rich could afford. Wolfe had spent the first part of his life around guys like this. All of his father's country-club friends had this man's look. "We can manage a bottle of water or two," he said, changing his attitude.

"Well, in that case, thank you." With a charming smile, the man accepted the water and twisted the cap off. He drank and looked down at the fliers. "You're a community center?"

"Yes, we are." While the man read the information kit, Wolfe stared at his attractive face. Why was this man here today? He wore an expensive watch. Designer shoes. Didn't seem to be the type to frequent or even be interested in a queer community center. "We offer many different services under one roof," Wolfe explained, going into fund-raising mode. "We also hope to reopen a shelter for young adults soon. It was closed down last year for lack of funds."

The man looked up. His eyes were full of zest and kindness. He actually seemed genuinely interested in the YBR. "And a helpline, I see."

"It's more of a support line. We don't offer any help really. Just listen to people."

The man frowned a little and stared at the flier. "I didn't know there were people who still listened these days."

"We also run all kinds of discussion groups through Talk-Talk, and house both the CPLHIV and Blue Bird foundation. The foundation raises and manages funds for queer people over the age of sixty-five living alone or needing help at home."

"And the CP… what does that stand for?"

"Committee of People Living with HIV."

"Oh, I see."

Before they could talk about anything else, more people gathered at the kiosk, and Wolfe had to give them his attention. He hoped the man wouldn't leave and was glad to see he stayed by the stand, reading the material, clearly waiting for him to be finished with the crowd. Maybe it wasn't support or information the man was looking for, but a chance to speak with him alone. Wolfe's heart raced as he noticed the blond's eyes following his every gesture.

Was this man interested in *him*?

This guy was close to his father's age and clearly successful. Why would he be interested in someone like him? Wolfe suddenly felt insecure. Here he was, standing behind a plastic table, handing out pamphlets for a community center, wearing sneakers he'd gotten at a thrift store over the weekend.

"Chicken wrap for you," Zach said, returning with lunch. He put the brown bag on the stand. "And one Arizona green tea." He didn't waste a second and instantly locked eyes with the blond man. "Hi there," he said, reaching his hand out to him. "I'm Zach."

Wolfe hated himself. Why hadn't he introduced himself to the man first?

"Hi, how are you?" The man shook Zach's hand, but his clear blue eyes were on Wolfe. "I'm Gaspard, by the way," he said, winking playfully.

"I'm so sorry," Wolfe babbled. "I never even introduced myself. I'm Wolfe. Wolfe Byrne." He shook Gaspard's hand and checked for a wedding band.

There was no ring, but that never meant anything.

"*Gaspard*," Zach said before biting into his sandwich. "French, I suppose?"

Gaspard only smiled and picked up a flier. "Can I have one of these?"

"Absolutely." Zach said coolly. "Rubbers are in here." He grinned, pushing the box toward Gaspard. "Help yourself."

Gaspard stepped back a little and quickly looked away from the condoms. "No… that's okay." Shyly, he glanced back at Wolfe. "But thanks," he muttered.

Wolfe glared at Zach. This man wasn't the type to grab a handful of rubbers.

"So," Zach said, losing the clever grin. "What brings you here today, to *Pride*'s Community Day?"

"I thought it would be nice, you know, to meet some of the amazing people who are trying to help."

Zach looked over at Wolfe. "We do our best, don't we, Wolfie?"

"Well, I think it's fantastic," Gaspard said, his eyes meeting Wolfe's again. "Thank you. Both of you." He hesitated. "Have a great day, and thanks for your time."

"Say something to him," Zach whispered to Wolfe as Gaspard slowly moved away from their stand. "He's leaving. His *money* is leaving."

Wolfe pulled out a stool and unwrapped his sandwich. "He wasn't here to donate." He bit into his wrap, watching Gaspard make his way through the crowd, going east. Who was Gaspard, anyway? He was very attractive but slightly insecure. Charming in an awkward way.

"Maybe not, but with the way he was looking at you—"

"You're wrong, Zach. I think he just wanted to stop and talk to someone."

"Are you kidding me? A guy like that? He doesn't need to make a new friend. Man, the guy's obviously loaded and probably has a hundred friends. Not to mention lovers he can fly to Paris on a rainy day. I know the type. Trust me."

Wolfe drank some cold tea. "Never judge a book by its cover. He seemed lonely or something."

"Lonely for a nice piece of young ass like yours."

"You're so cynical." Wolfe shook his head at Zach. "And you made him feel uneasy with the whole condom thing. That wasn't cool. He's from another generation; you know better than to shove rubbers in his face."

"I'm sorry, okay?" Zach grabbed his bag in the corner. "I gotta take off. You, you be careful out here and don't take shit from nobody." He went around the table but stopped and widened his eyes at Wolfe. "Oh, don't look now, but someone's coming back for you."

Gaspard was indeed walking back to the stand.

Excited, Wolfe busied himself with anything his nervous hands fell on.

AT THE corner of Papineau Avenue, Gaspard stopped and looked over his shoulder at the crowd.

He had to turn back. He couldn't risk never seeing Wolfe Byrne again.

Gaspard slowed down and took a moment to think. Wolfe was young. Very young. And the man probably had a boyfriend. A husband even. Gay men were getting married now. Adopting kids. If he went back to Wolfe and asked him out for a drink, the young man probably would think he was a creep. An old pervert or something.

But before Gaspard even knew it, he was standing at the YBR booth again.

Wolfe was busy with a trio of girls. The dangerous-looking, dark-eyed boy named Zach was nowhere to be seen. Instead, another man, this one heavier and sweating profusely, was behind the table, sipping iced coffee through a thick straw. "Hey there," the man said. "Can I help you?" His name tag read *Dominic*.

Gaspard pretended to be interested in the literature on the table. "Just browsing, thanks."

After a while, Wolfe finally looked over at him and Gaspard's heart started to pound. Wolfe was extremely cute; short, well built, with soft chestnut hair he'd combed to the side and very pale gray-blue eyes. His boyish face could turn serious at a moment's notice, despite the dimple in his cheek. This wasn't a young man who'd be easily impressed, Gaspard suspected. Dominic sipped his drink louder and tossed his head at Wolfe. "You wanna talk to him, I guess."

Gaspard flipped through the pamphlet for the tenth time. He was beginning to know it by heart. "Yes, when he has a minute."

"Wolfe is busy. He's the director."

Wolfe was the director? That explained his seriousness. Then certainly Wolfe wasn't *that young*.

"What do you need? Maybe I can help you." Dominic leaned in to talk to him.

But before Gaspard could answer, Wolfe stepped closer. "Could you get us more water, please?" Wolfe asked Dominic, putting money in Dominic's hand. "I'm so parched."

Dominic reluctantly walked away to the nearest convenience store. "But, Wolfie," he called back, "if a tall brown-haired guy in a red T-shirt comes by, tell him I'll be right back."

"Sure," Wolfe said. Then he looked back at Gaspard and smiled. "Well, hello again."

"Your stand is really busy." Gaspard tried to build up his courage. "I've been walking around for a few hours, and yours is the most frequented."

"Really?" Wolfe remained guarded still.

"Actually," Gaspard quickly replied, hoping humor would break the ice. "You and the free-lemonade stand with the shirtless bartenders are killing out here."

This time he actually made Wolfe laugh. "Oh, those guys. Well, they don't play fair."

Wolfe's crystalline laughter gave Gaspard a jolt, and he came closer to the table. "You have a nice laugh."

Wolfe seemed to tense and his smile faded. "Thanks," he muttered.

Not too fast, Gaspard told himself. *Not too fast.* "I forgot to ask you, what does YBR stand for, anyway?"

Wolfe looked down at his T-shirt. "What do you think it stands for?" He smiled again and looked up into Gaspard's eyes. He was on and off. Open and guarded all at once, like a door swinging in the wind.

Gaspard stared at the T-shirt. "YBR... *Youth... Boys... Rescue?*"

"That's pretty good, actually. That's the best guess I've heard so far."

"Yeah? So, do I win anything?" Immediately, Gaspard regretted his words. That line had been cocky and contrived. A poor combination, indeed.

"Nope, you don't. Sorry." Wolfe picked up a T-shirt from the pile and raised it up to him. "But we sell them. Want to buy one to help the cause?" His beautiful smile was gone again. "Or was there something else you needed here?"

The ice in Wolfe's voice caused Gaspard to step back. "No, I... I was just curious about the name." He'd blown it here. "Well, thanks again." He'd been too eager.

Wolfe slipped his phone out of his pocket. It was typical of his generation, Gaspard thought. He was using it as a shield, a decoy, or a wall. "Have a good day," Wolfe said, looking down at his phone.

Gaspard knew he was being turned down politely. "Take care," he said, stepping back. "See you around maybe."

"Yeah, see you." Moments later, another group of people had gathered around Wolfe's table.

And there was nothing left for Gaspard to do but go home.

CHAPTER TWO

IN THE YBR's stuffy conference room, Wolfe sat across from Yvan, trying to keep their conversation from derailing. Things were getting very tense between them, and if he didn't mind his words, Yvan would storm out and possibly quit on him. "Let me crack the window open a little more," Wolfe said, looking for an excuse to stand and take a moment to regroup. "It's hot in here."

"Leave it closed or you'll ruin the AC."

Everything was an argument with Yvan. Since Pride Day three weeks ago, things had gotten worse between them. Every time Wolfe asked him for anything, no matter how nicely, Yvan bit his head off.

"Yeah, maybe you're right," Wolfe said. Regardless of what Yvan thought, he was not against him. He just wanted to find better ways to make the system work. Wolfe tried to stay focused. He'd been at the YBR since seven o'clock this morning, and today being Thursday, the hotline would be open until 10:00 p.m. He'd be home by midnight, if he was lucky. "You know I appreciate everything you've done here, for the face-to-face outreach program and—"

"Yeah, the program I developed and put in place, all by myself, when you were still popping zits in BC."

"See, this is what I mean, Yvan. This attitude you have with me—"

"Attitude?" Yvan's jaw clicked. "I don't have an attitude problem. You're the one who's constantly on my case. Never satisfied with anything I ever do. Always wanting more. When Eric was here, things were very different—"

"Of course they were. He didn't care about expenses. You guys were getting your meals catered at the center's cost. You were using cab coupons for personal trips—"

"But we worked our asses off!" Yvan glared at him. "Oh, what the fuck do you know, anyway? I don't even know why I bother explaining those days to you. You're from another planet. You were in diapers when I was being arrested for doing the very things you take for granted today. Your fucking generation. You're all ingrates."

Wolfe had heard all that before. Maybe Yvan was right. But it was irrelevant now. He'd been hired to do a job, and the board expected results from him. "Yvan," he said, more softly. More carefully. "I'm sorry if I made you feel like I don't appreciate your work around here, but you have to understand, when I was hired, this place was literally on the brink of closing. The budgets were so off, it took me six months just to clean the numbers up. And you know they closed the shelter for lack of funds and staff, but I wanna get it running again. People depend on us. They need this place to stay open, and when I'm on your case, it's only—"

"Look, I know, Wolfe. I know all that." Yvan sighed, shaking his head. "I've been around the block, all right? And I saw this coming. As a matter of fact, I've been waiting for it, I suppose. It used to be, community work was the only place a guy like me, a dreamer, a loner maybe, somebody who wasn't cut out for big business, could make a place for himself. But nowadays, big business is everywhere. You kids are coming out of university with a degree in social studies or whatnot, wanting to turn our sacred places into profitable, bankable organizations." Yvan paused and stared into Wolfe's eyes. "But the dream is over the minute you bring cash into the equation. You start having to answer to committees and boards, and us dreamers start counting our hours, wondering why we didn't go to business school instead of working eighty hours a week for less than forty thousand dollars a year."

Wolfe was struck by Yvan's words. He'd never seen it quite that way before. Sometimes he forgot he wasn't a director in a bank. This was an LGBT community center. He had to remind himself why he was here in the first place. "I wish I could tell you things will go back to the way they were, but I can't. The government is broke and always looking for excuses to shut us down."

"And I'm too old to change my ways, kid." Yvan looked around, and his eyes filled with tears. "I think it's time I found another dream."

"No, don't say that—"

"Wolfe, I've been thinking about it for months now, but I just didn't have the guts."

"Don't quit on me. On us."

"I'm sorry." Yvan reached out and squeezed Wolfe's shoulder. "I know I'm leaving you high and dry, but you'll find someone to fill my old shoes. Consider this my resignation."

Wolfe jumped out of his seat. "Please, Yvan, let me talk to Jacques, or the chairwoman, and see if I can get you some kind of raise or time off—"

"No, Wolfe. No. I'm done, kiddo." Yvan stepped back to the open door. "I'm moving to Cuba in the winter. Fernando misses his family, and I'd like to grow old someplace warm where capitalism isn't a religion."

Wolfe followed Yvan out into the broad hall. He caught Clare and Zach backing away from the door, both of them pretending they hadn't been eavesdropping. "Yvan!" Wolfe shouted, but Yvan had closed his office door already. Wolfe rubbed his hair back, looking around at the various faces watching him. "That's just great!" he yelled.

He bolted for his office. That was it. That was the last straw. He was done. To hell with this place. He'd quit too. They didn't pay him nearly enough to take this kind of abuse. He could barely afford his student loans or rent on this ridiculous salary anyway. No, he'd take Yvan's advice and get a real job. He'd go into sales and make a six-digit salary by the age of thirty. His parents would finally be proud of him. No more "bleeding heart Wolfie."

Wolfe fell back in his chair and stared out into space.

Who was he kidding? This was his life. Community work. Helping people. *Queer* people.

Zach walked in without knocking and shut the door behind him. "What happened? He really quit?"

Wolfe hadn't cried since that time he'd thrown his clothes into a suitcase and left his ex-boyfriend Sawyer in the middle of the night. But his nerves were raw from exhaustion and stress, and angry tears were coming now. Determine not to break down, he swallowed the huge sob threatening to reduce him to a blubbering mess.

All this before noon.

"Wolfie… come on now." Zach stooped down to him. "Don't fall apart on me now." With warm hands he brushed Wolfe's hair back from his forehead. "Yvan couldn't take this place anymore. It happens to the best of us. It's not your fault."

"I'm tired of all this shit." Wolfe wiped his nose with his sleeve. "I don't even know why I came here, to this crazy, dirty city—"

"Montreal takes some getting used to, but you have to kind of *embrace* it, you know? Not be such a square about it. And you know very well why you came here." Zach put his hand on his knee. "Hm? To start again. To make your contribution."

Zach was a man who lived with a time bomb ticking under his skin every day. Not yet thirty years old, but already so wise and toughened. Wolfe felt a little ashamed of his pitiful outburst. "I know you're right, Zach. But I miss my friends, my family. I miss having a life."

"When was the last time you went out for a drink or met up with some friends?"

"I know. I guess I've just been using work as an excuse to avoid seeing how empty my life is here."

"Hey, you have me." Zach slapped Wolfe's shoulder. "I hope that counts."

Wolfe let his guard down and grabbed Zach's hands. "Of course it counts. Of course it does. I'm sorry. I'm being silly—"

"Silly?" Zach laughed. "Only a guy from British Columbia would use that word."

"What am I gonna do if Yvan really does quit?"

"The board's gonna replace him. You don't have to worry about that."

"I don't want the board to make that decision. I wanna find someone who fits here and knows what our real mission is." Wolfe realized he was going to have to find Yvan's replacement and show the people here he could build a team and keep it together. "I should be the one responsible for putting the right people in the right positions."

"That sounds kinky." Zach winked. "Look, in the meantime, I can help you out with the helpline and outreach program."

"No, you already do too much around here. I'm abu—"

"I don't mind." Zach rose and ran a quick hand through his black hair, looking down at him. "I like being around you… I mean, I like working here." He turned for the door. "You gave me a chance when no one else believed in me. Remember that."

It was true; none of the other places Zach had tried before the YBR had risked hiring a recovering addict fresh out of rehab. It had taken a lot of convincing on Wolfe's part, but his own experience with addicts and recovery had finally won the board over. "Anyway," Wolfe whispered, staring at Zach's shoulders, "it's a decision you never make me regret."

Zach glanced over his shoulder at him but didn't say anything.

STEPPING OUT of the shower, Gaspard heard his phone ringing somewhere in the apartment. He quickly towel-dried himself and jumped into his jeans. He looked for his phone under the newspapers on the mantle, but he'd missed Curtis's call.

He hurriedly called him back.

"Hey," Curtis answered. "Did I catch you at a bad time?" He sounded tense again.

Gaspard promised himself he'd be calm and patient and not ruin another phone call. "It's good to hear your voice."

"How you been, Dad?"

"Great. You?"

"Fine."

"What's new?"

"Nothing... you?"

"Not much."

They'd covered everything.

Then, "Listen, Dad, I gotta ask you for a favor again."

Gaspard caught his own tense expression in the mirror over the mantle and stretched his neck, trying to relax. "Sure, what is it?"

"Well, the thing is, Cassie, the girl I told you about, the one I'm seeing, well, she's got a real sick grandma up in Ohio, near, um, I don't remember the city, anyway... she's dying. Cassie's been real close to her all these years, before she moved to New Orleans, and she really needs to see her old grandma before—"

"How much?"

"Well, it's a round trip and all, and I'd like to go with her, 'cause she's gonna need my support. I mean, you raised me right and—"

"How much?" Gaspard held the phone tight. Curtis was becoming an amazing liar. His stories were more and more complex. He'd gone off to Louisiana on a scholarship last year, and had done one semester at Tulane, but then he'd met this girl. This Cassie. Everything had started to fall apart after that. "Just tell me how much you need, Curt."

"A thousand outta cover it."

"Are you registered for the fall semester?"

Curtis sniffed. "Yeah."

"How are your grades?"

"Good."

"Your mom would like to see you."

"I'll come up there for Thanksgiving."

"The American or Canadian one?"

"I don't know. The first one on the calendar."

Gaspard went to the window and looked out. It was a beautiful day. "She misses you. So does Malena."

"How is Mal, by the way?" Curtis sounded distracted. "Still looking for a job?"

He was losing his son. His little boy. He hadn't seen Curtis's face in over a year. "Are you in trouble down there?"

"No. Dad, I told you, I'm fine."

What could he say to him without pushing him further away? "Look, Curtis, I know the divorce rattled you kids and I know you're angry with me—"

"I'm not angry."

"Or upset—"

"Dad, I gotta go. Will you wire the money today? Or tomorrow?"

"Your mom loves you. She's still the same woman who raised you and took care of you when you were sick and—"

"She's a dyke and you're a fag. Do you know what that feels like, Dad? Do you have any idea? Look, I don't hate you and I don't hate her, and I don't even waste time thinking about it anymore. But I don't know who raised me and I don't know who you two are, so please, just wire the fucking money and leave me alone."

Gaspard bit into his knuckle. "You can't talk to me like—"

"Yes I can. You lied to me all my life. Look, I gotta go. I have somewhere to be."

He'd have to give the boy more time. More time to heal. To cope. To understand. "I love you, Curt."

"Yeah.... Bye."

The line went dead, and Gaspard looked at his car keys hanging on the wall. It was time he paid Meredith a visit. It was time they had a talk about their son.

GASPARD DROVE up his old driveway and parked the car behind Karen's Jeep Wrangler.

Karen. The woman who'd stolen Meredith's heart away. But she'd held back a long time. Karen had loved Meredith for years without ever confessing her feelings, out of respect for their marriage. The two women had been best friends before Karen had finally come clean.

All through their marriage of thirty years, Gaspard and Meredith had had a common understanding. They were both bisexual and from the time they'd both come out to each other in their late twenties, they'd set up rules and followed them religiously. They'd always been decent about their encounters with other people. Never slept around. They were allowed to kiss other men and women, but that was where they'd drawn the line. However, in the last years before their separation, the innocent flirting they'd agreed on, and the "kissing only" rule, had not satisfied Meredith anymore. She and Karen had started their affair.

There was no use thinking about all this now. It was the past. That life was over.

Gaspard looked up at his old home: it was a gorgeous brick house with wooden shutters and a double garage, and he remembered how they'd struggled to make the mortgage payments every month in the beginning. They'd almost lost the house twice. Then finally Meredith had gotten her degree and built her client base, while he'd started making a name for himself in his field. By the time they'd reached the age of thirty, they'd both had thriving careers, she as a child psychologist and he as a software engineer.

They'd had a nearly perfect life in those days.

Gaspard stepped out of the car and took a moment to look at the front yard. Meredith had done a truly amazing job with the landscape. The maple tree and oak tree they'd planted at each of their kids' births now stood tall and furnished, shading half of the front yard. Time had flown by so quickly.

At the front door, Gaspard knocked and waited.

Moments later, Meredith greeted him. "You didn't get any traffic, then." She pulled him into the cool and elegant entrance. She'd made some subtle changes around the house. It seemed somewhat more feminine. "Look at you," she said, frowning at him. "You're as devastating as ever."

"You look great too," he said, taking a good look at his ex-wife. She'd cut her dark brown hair a little. It reached her shoulders now. She wore a simple gray shirt over blue jeans. "You really do."

"God, come here. Gimme a hug. I missed you, Gatsby." She was the only one allowed to call him that. It was a nickname she'd come up with when they'd first started dating in high school. "How you been?" She hugged him tight and released him but kept his hands inside hers. "How's Malena?"

"She's doing great. I promise."

Malena and her mother had not been on good terms since the divorce. Meredith had taken a lot of the blame for the breakup. Maybe he'd allowed the kids to think Meredith was the initiator of their separation. But in truth, he'd stopped paying attention to their marriage in the last years. He'd been coasting along, confident it would last forever.

"I really wish I could give her a call and get her to come over here."

He squeezed her small hand. "Give it some time."

"Come into the kitchen. I made some sangria. The way you like it, with plenty of cloves."

"Sounds good." He looked around. "Where's Karen?"

In the kitchen, Meredith was rummaging through the huge stainless steel fridge. "She went out to get a few things for our dinner party tomorrow."

"Dinner party…. Oh." Gaspard sat at the very table where they'd shared all their meals together until Curtis had moved out four years ago. He remembered putting a phone book under the kids' diapered bottoms when they'd been too small to reach their plates. They'd had many conversations here in this kitchen. Halloween parties. Christmas brunches. Easter egg hunts. They'd argued here over idiotic things. Things that didn't matter now.

"Here you go." Meredith set a full glass of Sangria before him and pulled a chair out next to his. She raised her glass. "Cheers."

"Cheers." Gaspard drank a good amount, hoping the alcohol would help soothe his nerves. "Are you really doing all right?"

She fiddled with the corner of the tablecloth. "Yeah, Gatsby, things are good."

"You're happy?"

She looked at him. "Most of the time."

"That's good, then." He drank some more.

"You?" She touched his hand. "What have you been up to?"

"Working, and brainstorming about the book. Settling into the new place—"

"I'd love to see it. It must be great living in the midst of all that young energy. So different from here. I look around every morning and it seems all our neighbors are getting old. And then I think, 'I'm the same age.'"

"Well, fifty is just around the corner."

"Don't remind me." She tapped his hand. "So have you met anyone?"

He frowned and looked out the wide kitchen window. The garden was unbelievable. "You must have enough vegetables here to provide for the whole neighborhood."

"Yeah, it's nice. But don't change the subject."

He glanced over at her. "It's not the same for me, Merry. I don't have your charm and trusting nature. I'm a loner, you know that. And when we split, I lost all of my friends—"

"That's not true. You just stopped calling them after I left."

"Maybe you're right. You were always the social one." He took another sip of the cool drink. "But it doesn't matter, because all our friends are straight and married and I just don't fit in anymore."

"You never really did." She winked and sipped her drink. "Remember how Bill and Stephen freaked out when you announced you were gonna stay home and take care of the kids while I finished my degree?"

He remembered all right. Back in those days, his decision had not been a popular one. But those four years of working from home and raising the kids had been the best years of his life. "They used to call me Mr. Mom."

"Yeah, but look at our kids now. Look at how well they turned out."

He thought of Curtis. How could he tell her about his concerns without worrying her too much? But they'd never kept any secrets from each other, so Gaspard explained the last months to her, sharing his doubts about what Curtis was really doing down there in the Big Easy. When he'd said it all, he watched Meredith's face, anticipating her reaction. He could tell from the look in her eyes that this time, her years of training were no match for her fear.

"I want him to come home," she said. "Do what you gotta do, Gaspard, but I want my son to come home." She grabbed his hand. "Promise me. I can't bear the thought of him miles away doing God knows what. He's so hurt. So angry. I'm not willing to lose my baby boy over a selfish decision I made."

"It wasn't selfish. It was about telling yourself the truth."

"It was selfish, Gatsby. And I don't want Curtis to pay the price. Go get him if you have to. But I want him home. I'll take care of him after that."

Knowing their son, there was no way Gaspard could convince Curtis to do anything. Especially now that Curtis was in love and tasting freedom for the first time. "I'll do my best," he said, giving Meredith a reassuring smile. "Please don't worry."

As they talked about other things, their conversation reminded Gaspard of better days, when he'd believed his life would always be the same. When he'd imagined they'd grow old together and become grandparents. It was over now, and thirty years of Gaspard's life had gone by. Sometimes his new freedom weighed on him, but he didn't want to go back to the past. He yearned for a new experience. A new love to share.

He remembered how even in the earlier years of his marriage, his desire for men had haunted his picture-perfect dreams of marital bliss. Back then, he'd wake up at night, in a cold sweat, with his heart beating furiously, thinking of beautiful men like the one he'd passed by in the street over the weekend, the one whose green eyes had followed him for two blocks. Those nights, Gaspard would wonder how long he could tame that side of himself. He'd never crossed the line Meredith had drawn for them, but in his mind, he'd made love to thousands of men. His bisexuality had caused him anxiety all through his life, but Gaspard was determined to accept it now and find peace in this duality.

In the entrance, Gaspard and Meredith hugged again. "Take care of yourself," Meredith said in his ear. "I love you, you know that. Please be good to yourself, Gatsby."

He leaned away from her, desperate to keep it together. "I'm trying," he said, opening the front door. He could smell rain in the air. A thunderstorm was coming. "You should shut your windows. It's gonna be pouring out here pretty soon."

"You always had a good nose for forecasting the weather." She smiled and leaned on the doorway. "I'm glad you came by today," she whispered, her smile fading. "Let me know about our son. Let Curtis know I'm thinking of him and hoping he'll call."

"I always tell him so." He stepped down to the driveway. "Take care, Merry."

"Hey, wait." She walked down to him. "Are you doing anything tomorrow night? Because we have that dinner planned, and I was thinking maybe you'd like to come."

All his old friends would be there. He couldn't imagine it.

"It could be fun, right?" She nudged his arm. "Like old times."

"Except you're going to be sitting there with Karen and I'll be alone."

She stepped back a little. The wind picked up and rattled the leaves in the oak tree. "You could bring someone."

"I don't have anyone to bring." He looked up at the clouds. "You should go inside. It's gonna rain."

She held herself, watching him.

"Go," he said and opened his car door. "I'll call you soon."

"Oh, Gatsby, you were always too sensitive for your own good." She waved and smiled sadly at him. "Good-bye, darling."

As he drove off, Gaspard could still see her standing there, staring out at the street with her faded smile like a shadow on her face.

CHAPTER THREE

WOLFE LOOKED down at the résumé on his desk. "You worked for the Open-Hands Center downtown?" He glanced up at the man sitting across him.

The man, whose name was Richard, blew his nose loudly and shrugged. "Yeah, that's right," he said, stuffing the used tissue into his sleeve. He was Wolfe's second interview today. Late fifties, thin, well-dressed, with dark, somewhat malicious eyes. Something about the man felt off. "For five years, son."

Son?

Wolfe shot Zach a look of disbelief.

Zach, who was assisting him in the interview process, leaned in closer to the desk. "So," he asked the man, "you must know Nancy, then?"

"Nancy, yeah, of course I know her. I worked for that bitch for two years."

Nancy, a *bitch*? Nancy knew everyone in the field and had saved his butt many times since he'd started at the YBR. Wolfe had nothing but respect for her. "Well," he said, looking over at Zach, "I appreciate you coming down here to meet us, Richard." Discreetly, he tapped his pen twice on his lip, giving Zach the signal.

Game over.

Immediately, Zach stood up and offered his hand to the man. "We've got a few more people to see, but you should hear from us soon."

Richard looked at them with rodent-like eyes. "That's it?"

"Yes, that's all for now." Wolfe hated this part. Hated it. "Thank you so much for your time."

When the man understood and left, Zach shut the door behind him and whistled. "Who says that? Who calls his ex-employer a *bitch* in an interview?" He plopped down into the seat across Wolfe's desk and made a face. "Tell me. Explain it to me. Who are these people, man?"

Wolfe laughed, but it was a desperate laugh. "I don't know anymore." He rubbed his face with both hands. "I have no idea where to look anymore. The graduates want the high pay. The old-timers want things to be the way they were at the last place they worked, and everybody else is either taken or insane."

"So who's next up for the grilling?"

Wolfe looked down at his list. "A girl. Hm, nice change. Recently graduated. No experience except for some volunteer work for Greenpeace and, um, telemarketing."

"Greenpeace, huh. What else?"

"Well, no experience is sometimes a valued asset in a place like this. And it says here she's got a degree in gender studies. That's interesting, no?"

"I don't even know what that means. *Gender* studies?" Zach stretched his long arms over his head. He was already bored with the process, jumping out of his skin. "Do you want me to stay for this one too?"

Wolfe looked at his watch. "No, they'll need you in a minute down at Talk-Talk. Astrid asked if she could borrow you for the afternoon."

"Is that what I've become around here? A commodity?"

"A very *valued* commodity." Wolfe smiled. "I forgot to tell you this morning. Sorry."

"Astrid hates me."

"No one hates you. How could they possibly?"

Zach stepped back to the door. "You owe me one, Wolfie. I hate going down there to the pit."

The pit was Talk-Talk's secret name among the guys upstairs. The Talk-Talk girls were headstrong feminists with razor-sharp tongues. Gay men were their favorite targets—after straight men, of course. But Wolfe got along with them fabulously.

"I owe you more than one," Wolfe said, winking. "I'll share my dessert with you later."

"Oh, well, dessert, wow." Zach walked away into the lobby.

Moments later, an attractive brunette wearing a green wraparound blouse appeared in his open door. "Mr. Byrne?" She had a very nice voice and a beautiful smile. "Am I too early?"

Green was his favorite color. Wolfe immediately liked her clever hazel eyes. He straightened in his seat. This could be it. This could be the one. "No, please come in." He rose and shook her hand. Her fingers were a little cold, probably from nerves. "I'm Wolfe. *Mr. Byrne* reminds me of the evil boss in *The Simpsons*." She laughed and he was charmed by her laughter. "Please have a seat." Wolfe went around the desk and picked up her résumé. "Ms. Augustin, right?"

"Yes, but just call me Malena." She settled into her chair. "If you don't mind, of course."

For a moment, he wondered if he'd seen her before. "You look familiar," he said, trying to think of where he could have met her. He saw so many people in a week.

"Really? I don't think we've ever met before."

"No... probably not." He sat behind his desk and went back to business. "Let's see, I'm going to ask you the typical boring questions, but then I'd like to run through a few scenarios with you, if that's okay. Sort of like role-playing."

"Shoot. I love those."

He definitely liked this girl. "Here we go, then," Wolfe said, hoping he'd be offering her a job by the end of the hour.

GASPARD WENT to the kitchen to check on the spinach lasagna—Malena's favorite dish. He stuck the plate back in the oven, shut the door with his thigh, and hung the mitts back on the handle. Anxious, he stood in the living room for a while, watching the muted television.

Malena had phoned him earlier and screamed out, "*I got a job!*"

She hadn't given him any details yet, but he couldn't help thinking of all the changes to come. Very soon, she'd see no need to live with her old man anymore. No, she and Cory, the boy he had yet to meet, would probably want to move in together.

How he wished Malena wouldn't go down the hard road he and Meredith had. Times were harder now. A couple couldn't live off one salary anymore. How would she and Cory survive in the real world? Cory was still in school.

Trying to relax, Gaspard turned the television off and picked up a magazine. Meredith was right; he was the worrier in the family. There was no need to be so tense. He still had some good contracts and investments to get the kids through the next years of financial turmoil.

If Curtis didn't drain his savings account first.

"Hey, I'm home," Malena said, walking in. "Oh, it smells so good in here!" She slipped her purse off. "What are you making?"

"Your favorite."

She threw her arms around his neck. "Thank you, Daddy." She leaned away from him, holding on to his hands, the way her mother always did. "I'm so happy…. You have no idea how amazing this job is gonna be for me."

"Let's go in the kitchen and you can tell me all about it."

In the kitchen, they stood by the oven, drinking red wine, and Gaspard listened to the details of her new employment. Malena was going to be responsible for managing, recruiting, and overseeing the training of volunteers for a nonprofit organization in a community center. They were willing to give her a chance, even without any real experience in the field. She would have a trial period of three months, but this job was her dream come true. A place where she could eventually put her degree to use by building a program to assist young transgender people in need of support and resources.

"And the people there," she said with excitement. "They're all so passionate and committed. Nothing like the people at that dreary telemarketing place I used to work at."

"This is very different. This is community work." Gaspard set his glass down on the counter. "So how's the pay?"

She scrunched her nose.

"Under thirty?" he asked.

"A smidgen over." Malena took another sip of her wine. "My degree counts for something." She grabbed his hand. "But, Dad, I really don't care about the money. You know I've never been motivated by cash. I really wanna do this. I wanna be part of something bigger than me. I wanna be part of the YBR."

"Wait… did you say the YBR?"

"Yeah, you know the place?"

"Um, no, I don't think I know it." Gaspard slipped the oven mitts on. "Let me check this."

But he hadn't forgotten about Wolfe Byrne.

How could he? Ever since the day they'd briefly met, Gaspard had caught himself thinking of the young man with the serious eyes and guarded smile. In the evening, he'd lie in bed and fantasize about Wolfe. He'd imagine calling Wolfe up to ask him out for a drink. Maybe even dinner. It was a wonderful fantasy.

But that was all he'd ever been allowed to have... *fantasies.*

"That looks delicious," Malena said as he took the deep dish out. "I'm starving."

"Good, 'cause there's enough for an army."

"You always make a little too much."

Gaspard set the plate down before them. "Well, I guess it's a force of habit. I cooked for four people for twenty years."

"Do you miss it?"

He wouldn't ruin this moment with his melancholy. "No," he lied. "I love my life today as much as I loved it then."

"Really?" She dug a fork into the smoldering pasta. "I'm so glad to hear that. Sometimes I worry about you."

He poured more wine into their glasses. "You shouldn't worry. I'm fine. I'm free. I'm looking up."

"But you're alone, and now that I'm gonna be working all day, and sometimes evenings, what are you gonna do all by yourself?"

Gaspard looked into his glass and back at her young, open face. "Don't know," he said. "I'll figure it out, but tell me, with all this work, when are you going to have time for Cory?"

"I don't know, but I'm sure he'll be supportive." She didn't sound too convinced.

He decided not to risk spoiling her mood. "Hey," he said, "by the way, what does YBR stand for, anyway?"

"Oh, it's kind of cool, actually. The woman who founded it was named Dorothy, and she had this obsession with the movie *The Wizard of Oz.* So, when she was looking for a name for the center, she thought of her childhood, of the times she'd dreamed of walking hand in hand with her friends, you know, down the yellow brick road."

"The *yellow brick road* center."

Was Wolfe Byrne the young wizard behind the curtain? The one who made everyone's wishes come true?

"You should see the guy who runs it," Malena went on. "He's so young, yet so grounded. I was really impressed with him. I think we're gonna get along."

"Well, how young is he exactly?" Gaspard asked, hoping Wolfe was in his thirties.

"I couldn't believe it, but he's Curtis's age. Twenty-five years old and already running this huge place. He's making such a difference in the community, and I'm inspired by him."

Gaspard tried to hide his shock. She couldn't be talking about Wolfe. *Twenty-five*?

That was twenty-four years between them.

Wolfe Byrne was his son's age.

She frowned. "What's wrong? You have a funny look on your face."

He shook it off. "Really?" he said. "I'm fine."

What did it matter how old Wolfe Byrne was? It wasn't as though he'd ever had an actual chance with the beautiful young man anyway. This settled the matter for good. He was actually relieved. He could stop thinking of Wolfe once and for all. Or he could think about him all he wanted but keep Wolfe up there, locked up in his mind, caged in with all of the other fantasies he'd never be allowed to experience.

Gaspard raised his glass, thinking of his daughter's dreams coming true. He'd had his own chances in his youth, but it was her turn now. "Congratulations," he said. "I'm proud of you."

WOLFE PUT his empty bowl in the sink and glimpsed at the time on the microwave clock: ten p.m.

Friday.

He was dead tired, yet he knew he couldn't sleep. Not right now, anyway. He was still too wired from the day's work. He opened his fridge and looked for something sweet. The shelves were pathetically empty, and it wasn't from lack of money, but time. He rarely shopped for food and ate everything on the go. On the bottom shelf, Wolfe found three Stella Artois beers, and twisting the cap off a bottle, he went to the living room and settled himself into the mismatched cushions on the couch. He picked up his phone.

He drank his beer slowly, wasting time online, taking BuzzFeed quizzes for a while.

What kind of superhero are you? If you were a dish, which one would you be?

When he felt a little slow from the beer, he went to get another one. On the couch again, he checked his personal e-mail and wrote his mother a quick note.

> *Hi Mum,*
>
> *Doing very well here. Busy, as you know. How's Pappy doing? Hope you're enjoying the beautiful weather over there. I bet your rose bushes are unbelievable.*
>
> *Thank you for the money order, but please, Mum, you don't have to send money. I'm doing all right. And ask Dad not to send me any more shirts!*
>
> *Say hello to Xander and everybody.*
>
> *Here's a picture of me at the Pride Community Day. Thought you'd like one. The guy next to me is Zach. We work together. Don't freak out over his tattoos and dark clothes. No, he's not a killer :-)*
>
> *I love you,*
> *Wolfie*

After he sent the e-mail, he spent the next half hour watching videos of his nephew's third birthday on his brother's Facebook page. They all looked well and happy. He was glad to see their faces, but gladder to be miles away.

After the second beer, he checked Sawyer's profile and, smiling bitterly, scrolled down his ex-boyfriend's page for clues as to what Sawyer was up to these days. Same old, same old. Yes, Sawyer was still living the good life, hitting the trendy spots on weekends and bragging about it on Mondays.

A little drunk, Wolfe stared at his ex-lover's face. What had he seen in those cold green eyes? He'd been so infatuated with Sawyer. So deeply in love. At least, he'd believed it was love. Thinking about it now, he knew better than that.

Had he really ever been in love? Real love. The kind that flowed both ways, freely and smoothly. The kind that made life worth living.

Wolfe threw his phone on the couch. That's all he ever did when he was home; fiddle on his stupid phone and wait for sleep to come, thinking of ways to keep the YBR open. Then he'd wake in the morning, relieved it was time to go to work.

But he missed being touched.

Wolfe pulled a blanket over his legs and stretched out on the couch. Drifting to sleep, he listened to the ticking of the clock in the kitchen and tried not to think about work.

CHAPTER FOUR

GASPARD PARKED the car in front of the YBR center and looked out the passenger window at the building's facade. It was an impressive three-story building, probably built in the early 1800s and not much retouched over the years. It didn't look like a community center at all. More like an old presbytery or Catholic school. The only sign it was neither of those was the very subtle banner hanging over the first-floor window.

Yellow Brick Road Center. Welcome to all.

Gaspard's heartbeat picked up a little. He'd had too much coffee this afternoon. He turned the engine off and sat there with his clammy hands clutching the wheel. He waited a few minutes for Malena to come out. She'd been coming home later and later every day, exhausted but elated. Every evening, she'd sit at the kitchen table and eat whatever he put before her. Then he'd listen to her recount the madness of her days at the center. She was overwhelmed but optimistic. She usually went on and on about the people she met and the friends she was making. Gaspard felt he knew them all already. Malena had a soft spot for Zach. Her face lit up every time she spoke of the man. It was always *Zach said this*, and *Zach did that.*

She hadn't mentioned Cory much this week.

After ten minutes of waiting in the hot car, Gaspard tried Malena's phone. Maybe she'd forgotten he was picking her up this evening.

"Hey, Daddy," she answered. "Where are you? I thought you were picking me up."

"Oh, I'm in the car. In front." He sat up, tensing. "I thought you'd come out."

"No, no, I want you to meet everyone. I told them you were coming up."

Sweat pooled under his arms. "I don't know, Mal, I'm a little shy to come up—"

"Dad, come on. Don't be shy. They're all so nice, and I really, really want you to meet Wolfe!"

Gaspard looked out the window at the building again. "Sure, why not."

"I'm on the third floor."

"Yep." He hung up and sat back in his seat, blowing out a long breath. Wolfe probably met dozens of people every day. How could he remember a face out of all the others he'd seen on that busy Pride Community Day?

Gaspard climbed out of his car and up the large stone steps to the front door. On the first floor, he paused and looked at the glass door on his right. This was the Blue Bird Foundation and the CPLHIV offices. He gazed up at the narrow and twisted staircase before him and began his climb up. On the second floor, he stopped to read the sign on the door. *Talk-Talk*. Under the Talk-Talk sign were the words *Emerald Center*, but they were faded and half scratched off. This was the shelter Wolfe had mentioned.

On the third floor, Gaspard paused again and took a moment to catch his breath. He wasn't too winded, but his nerves were making his breath short. He slipped his sunglasses off, hooked them on his shirt, and ran a hand through his hair.

Seconds later, Malena stood in the door, looking at him. "There you are!" She grabbed his arm. "Come. Come!"

He was reminded of her first day at school. "Yes, I'm coming," he said, dragging his feet.

They stepped through the door into a large vestibule full of tables, chairs, and rows of shelves overloaded with books, binders, and papers. People were walking back and forth, and Gaspard recognized the dark-haired boy named Zach.

"Zach," Malena called out to him. "Come here for a second."

Zach squinted at Gaspard. "Hey, wait a second, I know you."

Malena looked back and forth from Zach's face to his. "You know my dad?"

Zach's expression changed. "What, your *dad*?"

"Yeah, this is my dad, Gaspard." Malena swung Gaspard's arm. "I know, he looks so young, huh?" She frowned and turned her eyes to Gaspard. "You know Zach?"

"No," Zack quickly said before Gaspard could even answer. "I thought he was someone else." Zach reached his hand out to him. "Nice to meet you, sir."

Gaspard shook Zach's long, fine hand and gave him his warmest look. He was grateful for this young man's presence of mind. "Pleasure," he said, holding Zach's hand. "I've heard so much about you."

Malena looked thrilled. "Yeah, I keep babbling about you guys to my dad." She beamed with pride, standing between them. "Zach is our project coordinator, and he's everybody's best friend here. Whenever we need anything, he's the man. Right, Zach?"

Zach was staring into Gaspard's eyes with a clever smirk. "That's right," he said, holding Gaspard's stare. "But really, the main squeeze around here is Wolfe." He looked over at Malena. "Has your *dad* met him yet?"

"No, we were just on our way to his office."

"Well, I'm sure he'll be happy to meet your *father*." Zach winked at Gaspard and turned away for one of the offices at the back. "Come see me before you leave," he called out to Malena. "I need to go over the Graffiti for Change Project with you."

"He's so cool, huh?" Malena nudged Gaspard's arm. "He's like Dallas from *The Outsiders*."

"Who?"

She pulled on him. "Let's go say hello to my boss."

With his stomach lurching, Gaspard followed her to the first office on the left. The door was open, and inside, clad in a fitted gray suit, Wolfe stood by the window with his back to the door, looking at something across the street. He was on the phone.

"He's busy," Gaspard whispered, stepping back. "I'll meet him some other time."

"He's always busy." Malena knocked on the open door and coughed. "Hi, Wolfe."

Wolfe turned around and smiled at her, but his cheeks darkened slightly when his eyes met Gaspard's. He covered the mouthpiece with his hand. "Just a second," he said over his knuckles. "I'm almost done."

"Sure," Malena said, dragging Gaspard into the office.

Wolfe was quick to hang up. "Hi." He searched Malena's face for an answer. "Well, I see we have company."

"This is my father. Remember, I told you he was coming up today?"

Gaspard debated running out the door, down to his car.

"Dad, this is Wolfe, my boss." Malena looked at both of them.

"Hello, pleased to meet you." Nervously, Gaspard extended his hand over the desk, but for a moment, Wolfe only stared at it.

Then at last Wolfe shook his hand. "It's very nice to meet you," he muttered.

Malena clapped her hands and laughed. "This is so great," she exclaimed. "I love this!"

Gaspard couldn't help laughing at her excitement.

"Malena," Zach said, poking his face in the door. "Do you have a minute, please?" He shot Wolfe a subtle look that Gaspard caught. "I need her in my office for a quick second."

Malena looked at all three men. "Sure, I'll be right back, Dad."

In the door, Zach moved to let her by. When she was out of earshot, he looked at Gaspard. "Well now, this is very interesting," he said. "You don't look a day over thirty. Unbelievable."

After Zach had left, Wolfe stood behind the desk and laughed anxiously. "I'm a little surprised," he said, running a hand through his hair.

"You remember me."

"Yes, of course I do. And I also remember how rude I was to you." Wolfe's eyes warmed a little. "I felt bad about it the whole day."

"No, I shouldn't have pestered you. You were busy. You were working—"

"And you were just being nice." Wolfe looked over Gaspard's shoulder into the hall. "Now I understand why Malena's such a sweetheart."

"Well, her mother had a lot to do with that."

"Your wife?"

"Ex-wife." Gaspard touched the back of the chair. "I'm divorced."

Wolfe cleared his throat, watching him closely. He was guarded again. Hard to read.

"Malena is very happy here," Gaspard said, trying to keep the conversation going. "She feels at home."

"That's very good to hear. She's a joy to work with." Wolfe smiled again. He had many different smiles, and all revealed a different side Gaspard yearned to know better. "It was nice seeing you again," he whispered, "Gaspard."

Hearing Wolfe speak his name gave Gaspard a thrill. "Yes, it was." He tapped the chair, stepping back to the door. "I'll leave you to your work." If only he could pause the world for one moment and have a minute alone with Wolfe, he'd know what to say and do.

Wolfe held his gaze. "I'll see you again, I hope."

CHAPTER FIVE

ANOTHER WEEK had gone by, and Wolfe was quite satisfied with the progress he'd made in the last few days. With Malena's help, he'd been able to delegate some of his work and concentrate on more urgent matters. He was to meet with the board by the end of this month. His main goal was to keep the YBR open and convince Jacques—the president—and his trustees to reopen the Emerald shelter on the second floor. He'd been working on this for months.

Glad the day was over, Wolfe set the alarm on the YBR's first floor and stepped out of the center. Outside, he found Dominic, Zach, and Malena talking with Astrid on the sidewalk. He'd done a good thing by hiring Malena. What she lacked in experience she made up for with joy and curiosity. He really enjoyed her company and found himself drawn to her. They'd begun having lunch in his office this week, and somehow, she'd managed to get under his armor. Women had a way with him, he'd noticed. Wolfe had opened up to her about his current anxieties regarding the center's future and even shared some personal information with her. She reminded him of his best friend he'd adored in high school. A girl he'd lost contact with.

But of course, every time Malena winked at him from across the hall, he couldn't help thinking of her father.

Father.

Wolfe still couldn't believe that one.

"Hey, finally, there you are." Astrid saw him coming down the steps. "We were just saying that maybe we should go up there and check up on you."

"Well, here I am. I crawled down the last flight of steps, but I made it out."

For a few minutes, they shared stories of their day. After a while, Malena checked her phone. "Oh shoot." She hooked her purse on her shoulder. "My dad's been texting me. I should go. He worries."

Zach took a drag from his cigarette. "As he should. A nice girl like you shouldn't be hanging out with the likes of us."

"What makes you so sure I'm such a nice girl, Zach Mackay?" She pinched his arm and laughed. She'd started flirting with Zach at work, but Wolfe wasn't surprised: everyone flirted with Zach. Even Clare.

"Ouch." Zach rubbed his arm and shot Wolfe a conspirator's glance, then looked back at Malena. "So *how* is your sexy dad doing, anyway? Man, he's definitely a DILF."

"A what?"

"Shut up," Dominic said, frowning at Zach. "Have some respect."

"No, what's a DILF?"

Wolfe had no idea what Zach was talking about, but he decided not to ask.

"Come on, Zach." Malena was looking from face to face. "Educate this nice girl. What is a DILF exactly?"

"Trust me, you don't wanna know," Dominic said.

"Now *I* wanna know," Astrid chimed in. "And that's saying something."

"A DILF, ladies and gentlemen," Zach said ceremoniously, "is the abbreviation for a *dad I'd like to fuck*."

Malena shoved Zach hard. "Hey, that's my dad you're talking about!" She laughed and shook her head at him. "That's just wrong."

Wolfe was very uncomfortable. "As enlightening as this conversation is," he said, stepping back to the street, "I really need to go home and collapse on my couch."

"Me too." Astrid blew them all a kiss. "See you guys." But her stare lingered on Zach's face. "Have a good weekend," she told him, her tone serious. "Try not to destroy too many people's innocence." She looked over at Malena, obviously meaning her. "You know what I mean, Zachy boy?"

Zach gave Astrid a sardonic grin. "I'll do my best."

Dominic took Malena's arm. "Come on, let me walk you to the metro."

"Good night, Wolfie," Zach said, stepping back to the street. "Try not to be too good and decent."

"Me?" Wolfe laughed. "Get out of here."

When Zach had left, Wolfe set out in the opposite direction, but as he walked away from the center, out of the corner of his eye, he saw a black car slowing down next to him. The car pulled up to the curb, and Wolfe immediately stiffened, all of his defense mechanisms kicking in. He hadn't thought about the assault in Vancouver for a long time, but in a flash, that night came back to him.

In his mind, he could see himself lying on the sidewalk, in front of the halfway house he'd worked at, bleeding from the nose and mouth.

They'd left him there for dead that night.

The car stopped, and Wolfe peeked into the front seat, ready to tell someone off or run.

But in the driver's seat, Gaspard waved at him. "Hi, I'm looking for Malena," he said over the sound of the radio. "I've been trying to call her all night, and I just got this feeling—"

"She left a short while ago." Wolfe realized he was shaking a little. The panic had gotten the best of him.

Would he ever get over that night?

"Hey, are you all right? You look a little spooked."

"Yes, I'm fine." Wolfe forced a smile. "Sorry, we kept her late again." Calmer, he leaned into the window. "But Dominic, a colleague, walked her to the metro."

"Oh, I didn't know guys still did that." Gaspard unlocked the side door. "Were you on your way home?"

"Yes. Yes, I was." Wolfe looked down the dark street and back at the car. He was still frazzled.

"Do you want a ride?"

"Oh, I can walk."

Gaspard leaned in and opened the passenger door. "I know you can, but please, let me give you a ride home."

This was a chance to be with Gaspard alone.

Awkwardly, Wolfe climbed into the car. "I'm ten minutes from here. It's a short walk."

Gaspard turned the radio down and put the car in gear. "No problem."

They rode up the street, but though he tried to be talkative and interesting, Wolfe was too affected by Gaspard's presence, by the very scent of his cologne, to make conversation. They were mostly quiet, and once in a while, Gaspard would look over at him. Every time their eyes met, Wolfe enjoyed the little jolt of pleasure.

It wasn't very long before they reached his place, and Wolfe was disappointed the ride had been so short.

"Well, here you are." Gaspard turned his sexy blue eyes on him again. His smile made Wolfe hot. "Thank you for letting me take you home," he whispered.

"I'm the one who should thank you." Wolfe unfastened his seat belt and hesitated. He should at least give Gaspard his card. Or something. He pulled out a card from his wallet. "I should give you my card, you know, in case you need to reach me or Malena—"

"Yes, that would be great." Gaspard took the card from his hand. "Thanks so much."

"Okay… well, good night." Wolfe opened the door and stepped out. He shut the door and leaned into the window, waiting for a cue. Would Gaspard ever call him?

Or was their age difference a problem for him?

"Thanks again," Wolfe said, in no hurry to leave that car door.

"You're very welcome, Wolfe." Gaspard put his hand on the stick shift. "Good night."

"Good night." A little disappointed, Wolfe walked up to his door and glanced over his shoulder: Gaspard was still there, waiting for him to be safe inside his apartment before driving away. Wolfe waved at him one last time and stepped inside his home.

Smiling, he leaned up against his door and sighed.

Gaspard was definitely old school.

LATER IN bed, Wolfe sat up, trying to read the time on the clock. It was a little past one a.m., and his phone was ringing. Could it be his mother calling about his grandfather? His grandfather had been in intensive care for the last three weeks, recovering badly from a kidney operation.

Wolfe pulled the blankets off and checked his phone on the nightstand. Zach was calling him. At one a.m.?

Something must be wrong.

Wolfe answered quickly.

"Hey there," Zach said in a low voice.

"What's up?"

"You were sleeping, right?" Zach's words were slurry. He was definitely on something. "I was just sitting here thinking about stuff and... I shouldn't have called you."

"No, it's okay. I was still awake," Wolfe lied. "What's happening?" He tried to sound calm but didn't know what to expect. He never knew what Zach was thinking or going through. How could they be friends when he didn't even know what kind of life Zach led outside the YBR?

"I'm all right." Zach coughed. It sounded as though he was smoking something. "Hey, you know, in the last days of November, when the streets are full of leaves and dirt, and everything looks dead, and then you wake up one morning and God's pulled a white blanket over everything? You know, like all the ugliness is gone. Like magic." He paused. "Well, Wolfie, you're like that white sheet covering death."

Speechless, Wolfe stared at the curtains moving in his open window.

"Anyway, that's my poetry for the night, ladies and gentlemen." Zach cleared his throat. "Um, are you still there?"

"Yes...."

"I'm not in love with you or anything, so you can breathe."

"I know that," Wolfe quickly replied, sitting up a little more. "I wasn't thinking that."

"Good, 'cause I'm not. I'm just going through a phase. I do that. It's a bad habit I can't break. I get infatuated with my new friends."

Wolfe fiddled with the sheet, trying to figure out what to say. He decided to confront Zach once and for all. "Is that why you called me in the middle of the night? To tell me you're infatuated with me, but not to worry, because it'll pass?"

"I detect frustration in your voice."

"I'm not frustrated, Zach... I'm confused."

"And I'm HIV positive."

Wolfe bit his lip. *Damn.* "Look, Zach, I'm sitting here with my heart in my mouth, wondering what kind of bomb you're gonna drop on me—"

"That's not why I called you, man." Zach sighed. "I'm just trying to tell you something. Or maybe I'm trying to tell myself something."

"Are you still using?" Wolfe had to know.

"That's what you wanna talk about? That's your concern right now?"

"No, well… yes, I think—"

"Oh okay." Zach's voice had an edge to it. "Fine, Wolfgang, you wanna piss-test me tomorrow morning?"

"That's not fair."

"No, what's not fair, sir, is the way you just turned this whole fucking conversation around."

"It's important to me, Zach," Wolfe said as softly as he could. "You're my friend and I care about you. And you're also my employee, I mean—"

"Yeah, and you have this upper hand on me 'cause of your status and your everlasting sobriety."

"Should I apologize for my sober living? Should I also feel ashamed for having my health?"

Zach was quiet for a moment. "No."

"I know you've been struggling lately, trying not to slip off the tightrope you walk every day, but I'm here, Zach. I'm really here for you." Wolfe stopped, a little overwhelmed.

"You mean that. I know you do."

"Yes."

"Are you attracted to me, or what?"

Wolfe ordered himself not to answer. Was he? Maybe, yes, a little.

But before he could answer, Zach spoke again. "Just give me your speech about friendship and professional relationships."

"It's not a speech…. It's the right thing to do, for both our sakes."

"Because we'd never work, you and me."

"I can't say for sure, but are you willing to risk—" Wolfe stopped, not wanting to say the wrong thing.

"Am I willing to *risk* infecting you?"

"It's not only that. And you know it."

"It's me. It's everything that comes with me."

"No—"

"It's all right. I know what you mean, and honestly, I don't think I could handle being with a West Coast square, anyway. No offense, but your white bread toast wouldn't mesh well with my Jack Daniels pancakes."

Wolfe shook his head, smiling. "How 'bout we try being better friends to each other?"

"I could try that."

"I'd like you to open up to me a little more. Tell me what's going on in your life—"

"Yeah? Well, right now, I'm working for this cute little guy at this place called the YBR and—"

"Shut up."

Zach laughed. "I'll see you Monday."

"You're gonna be okay?"

Zach was serious once more. "Sorry I woke you up. Go back to sleep."

After they said good night and hung up, Wolfe fell back against his pillows and sighed pitifully. He turned to his side and pulled the blanket over his ear. Curled up, he tried to go back to sleep.

The tension had finally broken between him and Zach, and their fun flirtation was over. It was for the best, he told himself, but that didn't lessen the sting.

CHAPTER SIX

WOLFE LOOKED down at the large collage spread out on the table. "This is wonderful," he said, taking in as many details of the artwork as he could. He glanced up at Astrid and Megan, who were waiting for his reaction. "This should be somewhere everyone can see."

"That's what we thought," Astrid said, coming around the table to him. "But the thing is, if we put it up like this, it's going to get damaged with time, and the whole point of this collage was for the group to express resilience in the face of adversity."

Wolfe finally tore his eyes away from the collage. Talk-Talk had started a new discussion group for people between the ages of eighteen and twenty-five recovering from the effects of high-school bullying. It was a trial group, and the board wasn't too keen on it. However, Wolfe believed in it. And this amazing collage of pictures clipped from fashion magazines was their work. The message was clear and he endorsed it fully. "Tell you what," he said, making a spur-of-the-moment decision. "We'll have it laminated and hang it up on that wall right there." He pointed to the back wall, the one directly facing the entrance. "As your mission statement."

Astrid shot Megan a look and widened her eyes at him. "The board will never okay that expense. Laminating something this size is gonna cost quite a chunk of change, my friend." She ran her fingertip across the bottom corner of the work. "In the hundreds."

"I'll make sure it gets done, okay?" He was going to have to pay for it himself. "You all deserve it, Astrid. I'm so impressed with the work you do here."

"Yeah?" Megan stepped closer. She was fairly new at the YBR but extremely dedicated. "It would be great if you could attend one of our meetings." She looked at Astrid for approval.

He'd come down to Talk-Talk's office many times to introduce himself to the people who stopped by during the day, but he'd yet to sit through a session with any of the groups. "Sure, why not. Which group? What time?"

Astrid quickly answered him. "I think you should attend the discussion group for assault victims. That's the one with the highest attendance anyway, and the most heated discussions. You'd really get a sense of what we do."

Wolfe's face felt hot. He cleared his throat, looking around. "Just send me a little reminder on that." Of all the discussion groups, she'd chosen the one he'd prayed she wouldn't. "I'll definitely do my best," he said, stepping back to the door. He congratulated them again, promised to take care of the collage, and then left, heading up to his office.

He was going to have to find a way out of that promise. He couldn't imagine sitting in a room full of assault victims. He didn't want to talk about that night.

Upstairs, Wolfe bumped into Malena. "Hey, there," he said, slowing down.

"Hi, Wolfe." Her eyes were a little red.

Had she been crying?

"Everything all right?" he asked her.

She nodded, but was on the brink of bursting into tears. "Are we having lunch?"

"What's wrong?"

"Ms. Augustin?" An older man in red glasses was approaching them. He was a new volunteer. "Could we get a short break? I'd like to make a call, if that's okay."

"Come by my office at lunch," Wolfe whispered to Malena and squeezed her arm. "We can talk then."

For the rest of the morning, he was buried in work and completely forgot about Malena's troubles. But when she poked her face in his door at noon, Wolfe was immediately concerned again. "Come in," he said, half rising out of his chair. "What's going on?"

She appeared calmer and put together. "Cory broke up with me," she said, slumping into the chair across his desk. "He hates my job. Said I love it more than I do him."

This sounded familiar. Wolfe remembered all the fits Sawyer had thrown over the time he'd spent "trying to save people who couldn't save themselves."

"How are you holding up?"

She shrugged. "Right now, for the time being, I don't think I'm ready to feel guilty about devoting all my hours to my career."

She was a wise girl. She'd be all right. "That's a brilliant answer," Wolfe said, wishing he'd had that kind of self-worth back then. "That kind of attitude is going to save you a lot of grief, trust me."

"I'm only twenty-two, right? I have time for everything." She opened her lunch bag. "Anyway, Cory criticized me, but meanwhile, he's in school and studying ninety hours a week." She took out a container full of strawberries and offered some to him. "And I don't wanna end up like my dad and mom. They sacrificed so much in their twenties. For what? They're not even together anymore, and now my dad is alone and doesn't even know how the dating world works anymore. Not to mention the gay dating world."

"Is there a difference?" He handed her a napkin. "Dating is dating."

"I don't know... maybe." She gave him a sad look. "I worry about him. He's so alone."

The mere mention of Gaspard sent a little thrill through Wolfe. It was annoying and pleasurable all at once. "How is your father, by the way? Aside from being alone." He took a few bites of his wrap, hoping she wouldn't catch his blush.

"Oh, he's all right, I suppose. He's working on his book and still has some consulting contracts with the firm he works with. He mostly stays home, and sometimes we have dinner together."

"A book?" Wolfe looked over Malena's shoulder.

Zach was coming down the hall.

"Yeah, it's a book on the software program he developed for managing customer databases and sale leads." Malena glanced over her shoulder, and her face reddened. "Oh, hi, Zach," she said, tucking a strand of hair behind her ear.

Zach stood in the doorway. "May I join you two?"

"I thought you didn't eat lunch," Wolfe teased him. "I thought you smoked it."

"I'm changing my ways." Zach entered the office and pulled out the last chair. He put a Tupperware container on the desk. "Doc says skipping meals isn't doing me any good."

Malena shot Wolfe a worried look.

Wolfe's stomach tightened. "How was your appointment yesterday?"

"Fine," Zach said, opening his container. Whatever he was having smelled delicious.

"Did you make this?" Malena was checking out Zach's lunch. It was rice and aromatic vegetables tossed with some kind of meat. The whole thing made Wolfe's mouth water.

"Yeah, last night." Zach looked at both their shocked faces. "What? I can cook."

Wolfe laughed. "Let me have some of that."

They sat around his desk and shared the rest of their lunches. Zach and Malena seemed more and more fond of each other, and sometimes, Wolfe noticed Zach's eyes lighting up when she spoke. After they'd cleaned up and complained about eating too much, Malena gathered her things and stood. "Hey, Wolfe," she said, pausing in the doorway, "I was thinking, do you wanna go out for a coffee tonight?" She looked at Zach. "And you could come too," she added, her gaze riveted to Zach's face. "If you want to."

Zach and Wolfe exchanged a brief look. "I can't tonight," Zach said, smoothing his hands down his black jeans.

"How about you?" Malena looked at Wolfe expectantly. "Just for an hour or so. I think I could use the company."

How could he shoot her down? She'd just been *dumped.* "Yes," Wolfe said a little uneasily. "We could do that. I should be done here around seven or so."

"Great! I'll see you later, then."

GASPARD TRIED Curtis's phone again, but his call went straight to voice mail. He left another message and tossed his phone on the coffee table. He hadn't heard from Curtis in three weeks, ever since he'd wired him money for that fictitious trip to Ohio.

Meredith was getting more and more frantic about it, and Gaspard had sworn he'd get this all sorted out soon.

On the couch, he stared at his dark reflection in the television's black screen. He'd been reading this evening while listening to the hockey game on the radio. Malena was going to come home late. She was out having drinks with Wolfe.

He couldn't forgive himself for being jealous of his own daughter. That was absolutely despicable of him.

But he was.

He was insanely envious of her.

Gaspard checked his phone in case he'd muted it by mistake. No missed calls. It was nearing ten p.m. He'd been up early this morning, for his usual run up the mountain, and the fatigue was gaining on him. Maybe he'd go to bed before Malena came home. She was twenty-two years old. Did he really have to wait up for her?

As he gathered his book and phone, Gaspard heard the key in the door and turned to see Malena walking in. "Hey, Dad," she said, slipping her purse off. She opened the door wider, looking out. "Come in," she told someone out there. "Just for a second."

Seconds later, Wolfe hesitantly stepped into the entrance. "Hello there," he said, clearly uncomfortable with the situation. "I... I thought I'd take a cab with her. Just to make sure she got here all right."

"Mal, you okay?" Gaspard asked, walking up to them.

"She's fine," Wolfe said, helping Malena to stand. "Easy now," he told her.

"I just need to go to the bathroom." Malena stumbled away and down the hall. "I'll be right back," she called out and shut the bathroom door behind her.

"I apologize," Wolfe said, looking down the hall. "We just had a few drinks, but the last one was a vodka cranberry, and it sort of knocked her out—"

"She's got a real low tolerance for alcohol. Like her mother." Gaspard gave Wolfe a reassuring smile. Wolfe looked good enough to eat in his white shirt. "Don't worry about it. She's tired. She's a little upset."

"I know. We talked about Cory, and I think it helped." Wolfe was obviously nervous, checking the hallway every other second. "Well, I think I should go. You can take it from here, I'm sure." He smiled and ran a hand through his hair.

The gesture sent a fireball through Gaspard's veins. He wanted to run his fingers through Wolfe's soft brown hair. "Let me call you a cab—"

"The metro's steps away." Wolfe walked back to the door. "But thanks, and um, well, good night." He looked down the hall again. "Tell her sweet dreams for me."

He couldn't let Wolfe walk away again.

Desperate to keep him here, Gaspard clutched the doorframe, his mind racing to find something to say. Something to keep Wolfe at his side for one more minute. "Hey, wait," he said as Wolfe started walking down the street.

Wolfe turned to him and stood by the sidewalk. "Yes?"

Gaspard checked the hallway for a sign from Malena—she was still in the bathroom. He hesitated between checking up on her and going to Wolfe. But he heard her retching loudly in the washroom, and it sounded terrible. She'd never done anything like this before. "Oh, I think she's sick," he said, quickly running back into the apartment.

Wolfe followed him inside.

Gaspard knocked on the bathroom door. "Honey? Malena? Are you all right?"

"I'm okay," she said in a very clear voice. Had she really been vomiting? "Just give me a minute. You guys just talk a little. I'll be fine."

"Open the door."

"I'm fine, Dad! I'm gonna take a shower. Did Wolfe leave?"

"No, I'm right here," Wolfe said, leaning closer to Gaspard's shoulder. Gaspard could feel Wolfe's body near his, though they weren't touching at all. Wolfe's cologne was subtle, but the scent turned him on and made his head swim.

"I'm sorry, Wolfe," Malena called out. "Thanks for walking me home. If you're thirsty, have some water or something. Dad, *offer him something.*"

"Don't worry about it," Wolfe whispered to Gaspard. Then he came closer to the door. "Good night, Malena. I'll see you Monday."

Seconds later, Wolfe was on his way out again.

This time, Gaspard didn't hesitate. He'd go insane tonight, in that cold bed of his, thinking of all the things he could have said or done to let Wolfe know he was interested in him. Interested in his life. In who he was. "Do you like steak?" he asked Wolfe.

That was all he could manage. That idiotic question.

Wolfe seemed to freeze up. "Yeah... I do."

"I mean, I used to go to this fantastic steakhouse in the Old Port, well, I'm not even sure if it's open anymore. It's been so long—" Gaspard stopped, completely lost in his own muddled words. "Look," he whispered, taking a small step in Wolfe's direction, "what I'm trying to say is, would you like to have dinner with me?"

He'd done it. It was done.

Wolfe looked at the bathroom door and back to Gaspard's hot face. "Dinner... like a date?"

What had he just done? "More like dinner between friends," Gaspard quickly said, trying to save face. "I thought maybe that could be nice. I guess I'd like to get to know you a little better."

Wolfe looked over at the bathroom door again. The shower was running. "What would Malena think of it?"

Gaspard sighed. "I blurted the question out without much thought, and I'm sorry if I made you uncomfortable."

But Wolfe came closer to him. "Can I be honest with you?" His blue eyes were warmer and friendlier now. He was such a beautiful man.

"Please," Gaspard said, regaining his composure. "By all means."

"I swear I'd love to have dinner with you, but I'm your daughter's boss and I just couldn't blur the lines like that." Wolfe held his breath for a moment. "Believe me, Gaspard, I'm sorry."

"So what you're saying is, maybe, in other circumstances—"

"No, that's not what I'm saying at—"

"Oh... I'm sorry, I thought—"

"Would you let me finish?" Wolfe chuckled softly. "What I'm saying is, *definitely*, in other circumstances."

The word *definitely* had never sounded so sexy before.

"Gaspard, look, I hope you don't take this the wrong way, but Malena worries about you. She says you spend a lot of time alone and working, and believe me, I can relate to that, but there's no reason for a man like you to be alone." Wolfe came a little closer still, glancing at the bathroom door again. The shower had stopped running. "You have so much going for you."

"You think so?"

"Oh yes."

Gaspard felt more confident. "I know she worries, but I'm just sort of figuring things out right now."

"Do you have any friends? Or people you used to hang out with before you were married?"

"Before I was married? I don't even remember that time. That was almost thirty years ago. Can you believe it? You weren't even born when I was getting married." He regretted bringing up the age thing, but it was there between them, and he wouldn't dismiss it or deny it.

"Actually, I wasn't even in my parents' plans."

"Hey, watch it there." Gaspard laughed. "Are you sure I can't change your mind about dinner?" He gave Wolfe his sexiest grin. "No?"

Wolfe climbed down the three steps leading to the street but turned back. "I don't know," he finally said, from the sidewalk, "but tell you what, you should *definitely* keep asking."

With those last words, he walked away.

In the door, Gaspard shut his eyes for a moment, overwhelmed with excitement. He'd ask Wolfe out to dinner until he said yes. Or the world ended. Whichever came first.

"What are you doing standing there?" Malena tapped his shoulder. She was in her pajamas and appeared to be completely fine.

"I was saying good-bye to Wolfe." Gaspard shut the front door. "You seem much better."

"Yeah, the shower helped." She looked around the living room, obviously lying. He knew her too well. "So, what did you guys talk about?"

He looked her straight in the eye. "Were you faking it?"

"No... what? Of course not, Dad."

Gaspard held Malena's clever stare and took a chance. "I asked Wolfe out to dinner."

"Yeah? What did he say?"

"He said he wasn't sure how you'd feel about it."

"He did, huh. That's funny."

"Why's that funny?"

"You guys are so clueless. I've been bragging about you to him for a month now. And then I come home and brag about him to you." She pinched his side. "Why do you think I do that, Dad?"

"Wait... what are you saying here?"

She turned for the hall, heading for her bedroom. "I'm saying it's about time! Jeez!"

CHAPTER SEVEN

CROSSING THE short hall to him, Antonio, head coordinator at the CPLHIV, offered Wolfe his hand. "If it isn't el directorio himself," he greeted Wolfe, pumping his hand vigorously, pulling him into his office. "Come in, please." Antonio gestured for him to sit down.

But Wolfe couldn't stay very long. "No, thanks, I just need to talk to you for a minute." He looked into the CPLHIV's small offices: Janice was hard at work on the phone, and Claude was in his office, counseling someone. "Actually, I'm here about Zach," Wolfe said, shutting the door behind him.

Antonio nodded seriously. "Bad news?"

"I don't know." Wolfe was worried. It was Monday morning and Zach hadn't shown up. Then, finally, at 11:00 a.m., Zach had called in sick, telling Wolfe he had a terrible migraine and had to stay in bed. "He didn't come in this morning, but that's not what worries me." Wolfe looked at Antonio's kind and round face. "I feel like he's pulling back from us. From this place."

Antonio was a treasure for the YBR. Without him, the place wouldn't have been the same. He'd dedicated the last fifteen years to the committee. Wolfe trusted and admired him. "I don't know what to tell you, Wolfe. You know he won't come down here. Not like I didn't try."

Zach wanted nothing to do with the CPLHIV and avoided it at all costs. His refusal saddened Wolfe. This place had so many resources he could use. The committee offered counseling and legal advice, with a few more services. But most of all, they offered people living with HIV what they needed the most: support and up-to-date information on the newest breakthroughs in research and every alternative health regimen out there.

"I know you tried," Wolfe said. "But do you think maybe you could talk to him again?"

"Yeah, sure, but you gotta understand, not everybody deals with it the same way. If the man doesn't wanna talk about it, he just doesn't wanna talk about it."

Wolfe thought of his own refusal to deal with his demons. Why couldn't he let Zach be? "Sometimes," he said, quietly, "I get the feeling Zach pushes people away only to test their commitment to him, and I wouldn't want him thinking I don't care."

"Yes, but be careful with that, or you'll be overcompensating, and the more you do that, the more he retreats. It's a game that can leave you both with nothing but space to cover."

Wolfe took a moment to process what Antonio had said. How many times had he chased people away because of his fear of losing them? "So what should I do?"

"As his boss, or as his friend?"

"Both, I guess."

"Let him ride this out to the end. If you don't, he'll never know how strong he is or what he's capable of."

"That's pretty scary. We are talking about Zach Mackay here." Wolfe had no idea what Zach's limits were. "But, yes, I get it."

"Now as his boss, if he misses too much work, you're entitled to say something." Antonio came around the desk and put his big hands on Wolfe's shoulders. "You're gonna be okay, Wolfe. I've been around, you know, and you've got what it takes."

Those kind words moved Wolfe, and he tried to hide that fact as best he could. "Thanks," he muttered, walking back to the door. "I do appreciate it."

"Anytime." Antonio walked him out to the stairs. "Hey, about that anniversary dinner…. What's happening with that?"

Every year, all YBR volunteers, past and current, were honored at a celebration dinner, and many looked forward to the evening. It was a time to socialize and get to know the new recruits, and a way to keep in touch with the ones who'd left and only appeared each year at this dinner. The meal was catered and prizes for attendance and dedication were handed out. This traditional evening had been going on for the last fifteen years.

"Are we having the same guy cater this thing?" Antonio asked. "Because my cousin just started a restaurant, and she wouldn't mind helping us out. Could get a good price from her."

Wolfe had no idea how to tell people the dinner would be canceled. Another budget cut the board was seriously looking into. He'd been racking his brain trying to find a solution. "It should be sometime in October," he lied, buying a little time. "I'll let everyone know as soon as I have a date. And I'll keep your offer in mind, of course." He hated having to be so sneaky. But he was meeting the board next week and would fight them on this decision.

After Wolfe thanked Antonio again, he climbed up the stairs to his office, but on the second floor, Astrid stopped him as she exited Talk-Talk for her lunch break. "Oh, I'm glad to bump into you." She squeezed his arm. "Thank you so much for the amazing job on the collage. It looks great!"

Laminating the huge poster had cost him quite a bit, but Wolfe promised himself he'd never tell Astrid the money had come from his pocket. "You're very welcome." He took a step to the stairs. "Have a good lunch."

"How did you get Jacques and his minions to okay this?"

"It wasn't that difficult." He'd lied to two of his employees in the last minute alone.

"Well, you are just something else, Wolfe Byrne." Astrid winked and stepped down a few stairs, on her way to the first floor. "Oh," she said, stopping and looking up at him, "you're coming on Friday, right? For the group discussion."

Wolfe tried not to cringe. "Absolutely."

"Good. They're a great group of people. You'll be impressed with their strength."

"I'm sure I will." He hadn't been able to get out of his promise to attend the group discussion on Friday. He had no clue what that would be like.

A little overwhelmed with everything, Wolfe walked up the rest of the stairs to the third floor. There, Malena caught up to him. "You're back," she said, grinning. "I was just going to have lunch. Wanna share?"

They sat at his desk, and he watched her eat. His stomach was too upset for food, so he sipped his cold tea instead.

After a while, Malena put her fork down and gave him a strange look. "So… I heard you and my dad had a nice talk the other night."

He'd been wondering if Gaspard had mentioned anything to her. "Why do you ask?"

"Oh, I don't know." She slapped his hand. "Why did you turn him down?"

"He told you?"

"We talk about everything. We're tight like that." She took another bite of her lunch. "Does it bother you?"

He wasn't sure what he thought of all this. But he hadn't been able to get Gaspard out of his mind all weekend. How could he be attracted to a man twice his age? Sawyer had been five years older than he was, and even that small difference had caused tension between them sometimes. But twenty-four years? A divorced man with two grown kids? A man who'd spent almost thirty years living with a woman?

"Malena," he said, "shouldn't I be asking you that question instead?"

"It's not my business who my dad dates."

"I'm your boss—"

"I know… but I really don't see the problem with that."

Wolfe leaned back in his chair. "Are you for real?"

"Look, Wolfe, all I'm saying is, if you wanna have dinner with the most generous, caring, intelligent, and honest man in the world, then you go right ahead. Who am I to stop you?"

CHAPTER EIGHT

WOLFE WALKED around the empty third floor, making sure everything was shut down and properly locked. Everyone had gone, and because Zach hadn't come to work today, he was the only one staying late tonight. He didn't like seeing an empty chair in Zach's office. He'd missed him dearly today.

Pausing at the entrance door, Wolfe looked back at the YBR's broad and dark lobby.

If only its walls could talk, the YBR would have countless stories to tell. Stories of hardship and loss, but of joy and friendship as well. He was blessed to come here every day, though the task was sometimes almost more than he could handle.

He'd have to fight harder for this place. He wouldn't let them shut the center down. He'd do whatever the board asked him to do. Whatever it took.

Outside, the air was chilly, and Wolfe turned the collar up on his jacket, heading for his street. He passed a coffeehouse he liked and decided to treat himself to a latte. He had loads of work to do. His presentation to the board was coming up fast, and he wasn't satisfied with what he'd put together so far.

At the counter, Wolfe ordered and looked around for a place to sit. He found a spot in the corner by the window and glanced around the small place, catching a few men looking his way. He quickly settled into his seat and picked up a random paper from the table. He certainly didn't want to talk to any of these guys. With surprise, he realized just how suspicious and antisocial he'd become since moving to Montreal.

Flipping through the paper, Wolfe listened to the conversations around him and tried to live in the *now*, as Zach often said. *The now.* What did that mean, exactly?

Inside his jacket, his phone rang, and Wolfe pulled it out. "Hello?" he answered, softly, turning a little to the window so as not to disturb the other customers.

"Hi… it's Gaspard."

Wolfe stiffened in his chair, turning to the window yet a little more. "Hi, how are you?"

"I'm great. You?"

"I'm fine. Just getting off work now."

"*Now?* It's nine p.m."

Wolfe laughed. "I know. I'm terrible."

"Of all the adjectives that come to mind when I think of you, that would be the last one I'd ever use."

Gaspard was a charmer. "Well, thank you," Wolfe said, feeling better than he had in a long time. "So what are you up to?"

"Nothing. Just sitting on the back porch, looking at the sky and wondering if you'll have dinner with me."

Wolfe's heart leaped. "Is that so?"

"What do you say, Wolfe, will you?"

"I'd love to," he whispered. He wanted to. He really did. He hadn't understood until now just how much he wanted to spend time with Gaspard. "That would be really nice, actually."

"Thursday, seven o'clock?"

"Okay."

"I'll pick you up at work?"

Wolfe caught sight of his reflection in the dark window and saw he was smiling from ear to ear. "Yes, absolutely."

Finally, he was going to have a moment alone with Gaspard.

AT LAST, Zach put the final page down on the desk and looked at him. His expression was hard to read, as always.

"Well, don't torture me." Wolfe laughed nervously. "What do you think? It's complete shit, isn't it?"

Zach had been reading his presentation.

He leaned in and kissed Wolfe's forehead. "It's fucking amazing," he said. "I could almost shed a tear right now." He wiped an imaginary tear.

"Are you playing with me?"

"No, Wolfie. I mean it. It's perfect. It's heartfelt but professional. It's got substance, and yet it doesn't feel too weighed down with numbers and statistics." He slapped Wolfe's shoulder. "You nailed it. Right on the head."

"You think so?"

"You worked so hard on this, didn't you?"

Wolfe rose, gathering his papers. He had tons of work to do before the end of the day. "I did, and I hope it pays off. There's nothing else I can do but go in there and give it my best."

Zach walked him out. "Thanks for everything," he said as Wolfe passed him in the door. "And you know, for not busting my balls about missing a couple of days this week."

Zach had missed three days of work, but this morning, when Wolfe had seen Zach's face, he'd been too relieved to give Zach a speech. Zach hadn't elaborated on the reasons behind his three-day absence but had given Wolfe a doctor's note, as the board requested.

Migraine and rest was all the note said.

"I'm glad you're feeling better," Wolfe said in the hall. "We really missed you here… I really missed you."

"It's good to be back," Zach whispered. "Hey, listen, what do you say we go out for a drink tonight?"

Wolfe thought of Gaspard. Of their first date this evening. "Actually, I'm gonna be leaving around seven tonight. I'm going out to dinner with Gaspard."

Zach's expression immediately changed. His smile turned into a straight and hard line. "Malena's old man?"

"What? I like him. He's nice."

"Didn't say he wasn't." Zach looked down at his feet. "All right, we'll do it some other time." He turned away and went back into his office. At his desk, he stared at his computer screen.

Wolfe hesitated by the door. "I'd really like to do something with you tomorrow or some other time. And we could see a—"

"Wolfe." Zach was still staring at his screen. "Can you give me a little time to process this?" He glanced up at him. "All right?"

Wolfe stepped away from the door, into the hall again. Couldn't he have kept his mouth shut?

But Zach called out to him. "Hey, wait a minute. Come here for a sec."

"I shouldn't have just dropped it on you like that," Wolfe said, nearing the door again. "I'm sorry."

Zach put his hand up. "I'm a bastard, born and bred, okay?"

"You're not. You're not a bas—"

"I am, Wolfe. And I want you to have a great time tonight. You deserve it."

"Now I feel even more guilty. I think I prefer it when you're a jerk to me."

"Yeah, I know," Zach said, smirking. "You're a little sick that way."

GASPARD PUT his hand over his glass. "No, thanks," he said to Malena. "I've had enough. I'm driving, remember?" He looked at his watch again.

Time was dragging on.

"Would you try to relax?" Malena sipped her wine, watching him. "You're gonna have a wonderful evening, Dad."

They sat in the living room, passing time. Malena had come home early this evening, and he was grateful. "I don't know if this is a good idea anymore," Gaspard said, turning his empty glass in his hand. He'd been waiting anxiously for this evening all week, but now he suddenly wished he hadn't been so bold as to ask Wolfe out. He wondered what kind of company he'd be to Wolfe tonight. He set his glass down. "I should have asked him out for a drink instead. It would have been much easier than dinner."

"Why are you so nervous? Really? I can't understand it."

"Malena, I really appreciate your willingness to be open-minded, and I love the fact that we can be so close, but on the other hand, I'd really like you to see it from my perspective."

"I am, seeing it from your *perspective*." She was clearly not happy with his remark. "And I don't see why dinner with a good-looking and decent guy has you falling to pieces." She blushed. "Sorry."

"No, it's okay. I don't know why I'm this nervous… but I just am. I keep thinking of where I was in my life when I was Wolfe's age. And you know, that was around the time I came out to your mother." They rarely discussed this. "I was twenty-nine years old. Curtis had started kindergarten, and every time I picked him up at school, I stayed longer and longer to speak with his teacher." Gaspard remembered Sean, the kindergarten teacher, fondly. He was a beautiful man with slanted green eyes and hands that flew when he spoke. "While Curtis played with his friends, Sean and I talked…. It was hard pulling away from that fence, Malena."

"Sean, that was his name? Did you have an affair with him?"

"God, no." Sean had called him once, at home. Had wanted to see him outside of that schoolyard. Had wanted to share a moment with him. "I was way too scared."

"Of what Mom would say?"

"No, we'd talked about our desires openly that year, and she was very supportive of my 'queer longings,' as she called them, but she'd also set some rules, and I agreed to them all."

"The 'kissing only' rule."

"You know about that?"

"Mom told me." Malena took a sip of her wine. "She regrets it, you know. She says, had she known how all this would end, she'd have done it differently. Not set so many limits for you both."

"We were young. We had a family. Sleeping around didn't seem like a good idea at the time. And I don't regret it."

"But you missed out on opportunities, while she—"

"They weren't opportunities, Mal, they were *men*. Men with hearts and hopes and feelings. And I was married with two small kids. What could I offer them?"

"I'm talking about sexual encounters."

"I was never into that." Gaspard was uncomfortable talking about this. He'd reached his limit. "Can we change the subject?"

"Dad," she whispered, taking his hand, "did you ever think that maybe you're attracted to Wolfe because he's about the age you were when you were forced to stop living fully? That in some way, you're still twenty-five years old in your mind?"

She was a smart kid. He'd never really looked at it that way. "Maybe, but I'm not in my twenties anymore. And tonight I'm gonna be sitting across from him, and the waiter is probably gonna think I'm taking my son out to dinner."

"Are you so afraid of what people might think?"

"I'm *very* afraid of what people might think, yes."

"But you taught me and Curtis to be fierce and self-assured."

"I just wanted you two to be everything I wasn't."

"Dad!" She gripped his arm. "Don't say shit like that. You're a spectacular person."

"I'm glad you think so, honey." He looked at the time. "I gotta go." He rose, but his knees were a little weak. "What am I doing?" he said under his breath. "What am I really doing here?"

She stood and put her hands on his arms. "Clear your mind for one second, okay? Now tell me," she said with a serious expression. "Do you like him? I mean, do you *really* like him?"

The image of Wolfe's face flashed behind his eyes, and Gaspard felt electrified. "Yes... I really like him. He's intelligent, kind, reserved. Somewhat mysterious—"

"And cute. Very, very cute."

"That he is."

"Remember, Wolfe isn't your typical twenty-five-year-old guy. I don't know, Dad, but something tells me the man has gone through a lot."

Gaspard knew this to be true. He remembered Wolfe's tense expression when he'd pulled up alongside him that night. How apprehensive he'd seemed to get in the car with him. Gaspard had a feeling something bad had happened to him, and the very thought of someone hurting Wolfe made him angry. He realized just how protective he was of him already.

"Now listen to me," Malena said, opening the door wider for him. "This is the way out to freedom. And Dad, that's where you'll find him."

WOLFE SIPPED his Irish coffee, his blue eyes catching the light.

Mesmerized by his beauty and countenance, Gaspard watched him, forgetting the bustling dining room around them. He could only see Wolfe.

Nothing else existed anymore.

Every one of Gaspard's fears had been unfounded. They'd had a great time. Wolfe had enjoyed the food and not been so guarded with him tonight. Conversation was easy with him. They'd laughed a lot, which he hadn't been prepared for. Wolfe was quick-witted and had kept him interested all through dinner with stories of his years as a recovery counselor in Vancouver. Gaspard was impressed with Wolfe's life experience. In college Wolfe had chosen an accelerated program and graduated a year and a half early. Because he'd worked all through his studies and volunteered for various nonprofit organizations, he'd landed a position as a counselor in a busy downtown shelter right after graduation. His commitment and devotion had quickly gotten him noticed by his older peers, and Wolfe had been given more responsibilities. At the age of twenty-three, he'd been well known in his field and sought out by all. Then the YBR had come looking for him, and Wolfe had jumped on the opportunity to test his abilities. He'd left Vancouver and taken a chance on something new in Montreal. The man was half Gaspard's age, yet had lived such a rich life. Not only was Wolfe level-headed and sensitive to those around him, he was also very bright and ambitious—full of passion.

Wolfe's intelligence was a major turn-on. His intelligence, yes, and his sensual mouth. Gaspard couldn't keep his eyes off Wolfe's lips. Would he get the chance to kiss him tonight?

Feeling a little tipsy, Gaspard drained the last of his strong coffee. They'd definitely have to take a walk. "Are you ready to go?" he asked Wolfe, who was finishing the last of his crème brûlée.

Wolfe leaned back in his chair with a sigh. "I can't even imagine putting anything else in my mouth tonight." He cringed. "Oh God, I can't believe I just said that." He was blushing from ear to ear.

Gaspard decided not to tease him about it, lest he embarrass him even more. "Do you mind if we take a walk? Maybe down by the riverfront?"

"I was hoping we would." Wolfe had regained his cool composure.

They headed down to de la Commune Street, walking under a deep indigo sky. The night was starless, with only a sliver of a moon cutting through the clouds. It was a cool August evening, the way Gaspard loved them, and they walked for nearly an hour to the clock tower and back. All along, Gaspard played tour guide for Wolfe, giving him a brief history lesson on Montreal. Wolfe was curious and attentive to details, asking about buildings and street names, constantly pointing things out as they walked. Wolfe had a different way of interpreting the world. While Gaspard looked at life as one would a canvas, seeing the whole picture first, Wolfe seemed to take in the smallest details before stepping back and seeing the complete picture. When Wolfe spoke of his friends or family, he often began by telling Gaspard about the little things, such as his mother's love for roses, before mentioning the greater things, like her recent battle with cancer.

Gaspard felt as though he was being led, not in leaps but in very small steps, into Wolfe's world, and it was a world he wanted to live in.

Up until now, his own world had been black and white, and for the first time in his life, Gaspard felt he was seeing his life in living color.

At de la Commune Street, they stepped off the sidewalk, and Gaspard pulled Wolfe away from a huge pothole. "Watch it," he said. "Those things are deep enough to swallow a truck."

Wolfe moved closer to him, and Gaspard didn't let go of his arm. They were walking up a narrow street, to the parking lot where they'd left the car, with no one around to see them. Boldly, Gaspard reached down for Wolfe's hand and folded his fingers over his. Without a word, they walked with their hands locked together. Wolfe's was warm and strong inside his, and Gaspard was sad to have to let it go, but they'd reached a more crowded street, and he didn't have the courage to cut through a crowd holding hands with another man. The moment he let go, he felt the all-too-familiar shame. Wolfe had moved away from him and was walking steps ahead.

At the lot, Gaspard retrieved his car keys and found his car. Inside the car, he waited until Wolfe had settled into his seat, then turned to look at him. "Back there, you know, I should have held your—"

"I had such a good time," Wolfe said, cutting him off with a smile. He put his hand over Gaspard's on the wheel. "Thank you."

"It's late… I guess I should drive you home." It was nearing midnight. Wolfe had to be up early for work.

"That would be the reasonable thing to do, yes." Wolfe put his seat belt on and stared out the window. "I've got a big day tomorrow."

"Anything special?" Gaspard drove out of the lot. He'd heard enough stories from Malena and Wolfe to know that a day at the YBR center was never anything but a *big day*.

"The usual," Wolfe said, chewing on his thumbnail again. "But then I've got this thing I can't get out of with the Talk-Talk girls."

Gaspard drove, glancing over at Wolfe from time to time. He noticed Wolfe's expression was a little tense. "Sounds important."

Wolfe shot him a quick look. "Yeah, well, Astrid and her colleagues want me to attend a group session. You know, to get an idea of what they do, and I'm really nervous about it, actually."

"A group session? Like therapy?"

"Yes, sort of. This is for people who were physically assaulted and need to talk about it." Wolfe looked out the window again.

At a red light, Gaspard turned to him. "And you're nervous about it." Wolfe was trying to tell him something; he could feel it. "Because of the subject matter or just the idea of a group discussion in general?"

Wolfe looked down at his hands on his thighs. "Because of the subject matter," he whispered.

Gaspard hesitated, but then put his hand on Wolfe's hand. "Okay… I see." Had Wolfe been assaulted? There was a pale scar near his eye, and Gaspard had noticed a thin line where hair didn't grow along the back of his head. But he wouldn't ask him. No, he'd let Wolfe bring the topic up.

Wolfe didn't say anything else about it. As they made their way to Wolfe's home, they talked quietly, mostly about Gaspard's book in progress. Wolfe was curious about Gaspard's work and seemed genuinely interested, which was quite a change from most people. Software engineering wasn't exactly a fascinating or seductive topic. He'd never wooed anyone by discussing computer hardware and system requirements.

"So," Wolfe said, "you have a degree in computer science or IT?"

"No degree. Remember, I started my career in the early nineties. Back then, the game was open. Since I was a kid, I've had a knack for taking things apart and putting them back together. The toaster. The radio. Remotes. My sister's Easy-Bake Oven." Gaspard laughed, glancing over at Wolfe. "Later, we got our first computer at home so Meredith could do some research, and while the kids went down for their afternoon nap, I'd mess around on there. It was easy for me. I just understood it. The language of it. I took a few classes and started helping out friends. Soon enough the word spread, and I had my own little network-consulting company for a while. I made the move to small business in the late nineties, and by the time the famous year 2000 came around, I was snatched up by the big leagues."

"Wow, that must have been exciting at the time. To be in the middle of all that new technology. The effervescence of it all."

"I enjoyed it a lot." Gaspard turned the corner of Wolfe's street. "But things have changed now. Everything is quieter."

"Boring?"

"Yeah, a little. Thus the book. Keeps me challenged." They reached Wolfe's place, and Gaspard parked the car. He unfastened his seat belt. "But the book also keeps me cloistered."

"You don't see many people in a day," Wolfe said, unfastening his seat belt as well. "And I see too many.... What's your background, then? If not computer science?"

"You wouldn't believe it if I told you."

"Try me."

"It's a long time ago."

Wolfe tapped his knee. "Come on, tell me."

Gaspard stared at him for a moment. "All right, well, when I was eighteen or nineteen, before I got married, I wanted to be a dancer."

Wolfe was clearly shocked. "A dancer? As in, a *dancer*?"

"I told you, you wouldn't believe me." Gaspard hadn't spoken about his childhood aspirations for years. "I was really good at dancing. I wasn't allowed to take any classes or anything, but my sister took modern dance classes and she'd show me. We'd run off to the soccer field near our house, and when there was no one around, she'd be Ginger and I'd be Fred."

"How sweet is that." Wolfe grinned. "Honestly."

"I gave it up after my dad found out about our little excursions." Gaspard remembered the look on his father's face that day. A look of shock. Disgust. But most of all, a look of disappointment Gaspard had not been able to forget.

"I'm sorry," Wolfe said softly. "Did your sister become a dancer?"

Gaspard thought of Gisele's face. He couldn't remember the details of it anymore. "She died just before her twentieth birthday. She was visiting some friends up north, at their cottage near a lake. They partied pretty hard and went for a boat ride. She wasn't wearing a life jacket."

"Gaspard, that's terrible. I'm sorry I even brought all this up."

"It's okay. I think about her every day but rarely get a chance to talk about her."

"What was her name?"

"Gisele."

Wolfe spoke very gently. "Did she look like you?"

"Yeah, she did actually. Some people thought we were twins."

The car was their shelter now, and he could feel a connection with Wolfe. The outside world had melted away beyond the windows. "We were very close," Gaspard whispered. "Gigi understood me completely.

I think, in some way, she was the only woman who's ever really understood me."

"And your wife... I mean, your ex-wife?"

"Meredith? I don't know. She could read me well. And she knew how to reach me and motivated me, but—"

"But there was a place in you she couldn't reach."

"Yes, something like that."

They were silent.

And Gaspard ached to kiss Wolfe, but he hadn't kissed a man, or anyone for that matter, in too long. He'd ruin it. He'd be too eager or not eager enough.

Wolfe leaned back a little, breaking the spell. "I should... I should get to bed."

"Yes, okay." Gaspard popped his door open and climbed out of the car. What did a gay man of Wolfe's generation expect these days? Was it romance and a long courtship? Or dinner, followed by breakfast in bed? Before Gaspard had reached the other side of the car, Wolfe was already climbing out. He'd have to stop treating Wolfe like a woman. Or was it all right to be a gentleman to another gentleman?

"Good night," Wolfe whispered, walking backward to his front steps. The street was vacant and quiet. "Unless, maybe, you wanna come in for a few minutes?"

Gaspard followed Wolfe but froze on the first step, his mind racing with a thousand different possible scenarios. He'd been fantasizing about Wolfe for weeks. And now he was here, right here, inviting him into his house, but Gaspard couldn't take another step forward. He'd spent the last twenty years making love to men in his mind....

But could he really be any good at it?

Wolfe stood in his doorway, watching him closely. "Are you okay?"

He'd come clean. "Wolfe," Gaspard said, still standing on the first step. "This is actually my first date with a guy. Well, with anyone really, since my divorce, but more importantly, this is my first date with a gay man."

Wolfe cocked his head. "Who told you I was *gay*?"

Gaspard felt the blood drain from his face. "I... I... thought—"

"Gaspard, relax, I'm just messing with you." Wolfe reached down and touched his hair. He chuckled. "I'm sorry."

"You had me going there for a second."

"Well anyway," Wolfe said, serious again, "you were really charming and interesting tonight, so first date or not, I had an amazing time with you."

"What happens now?"

Wolfe frowned a little. "Hm, I don't know," he said softly, leaning in. "A kiss maybe?"

"Yeah?" Gaspard stepped up, closing the distance between them.

"Oh yes," Wolfe said, smiling and pulling him close.

Gaspard kissed Wolfe with restraint, but when he felt Wolfe's velvet tongue in his mouth, he gripped his neck and kissed him deeper and harder.

He didn't know how long they'd been kissing when Wolfe leaned back with his eyes full of fever and his soft brown hair disheveled as though he'd been caught in a windstorm.

Gaspard's body reacted to Wolfe in a way he hadn't been prepared for. The lust he felt surprised him. It was real. It was tangible. He was outside of his head, feeling the desire, no longer imagining it.

Wolfe ran a hand through his hair. "Well, I certainly didn't expect that. You're full of surprises, aren't you?"

"Come here." Softly, enjoying the taste of his mouth, Gaspard kissed Wolfe again. This was easy, yet so thrilling. He kissed his lips, his nose, his neck. The scent of Wolfe—clean and green—made his blood pound. He could have kissed him all night.

"Come inside now," Wolfe breathed against his mouth, pulling back a little, yet holding on to him.

It was too fast. They had so much time still. "Not tonight." Gaspard stepped down. "Is that okay with you?"

Wolfe bit into his lip, narrowing his eyes. "Will you call me?"

"Are you serious? I'll call you tomorrow, as soon as I open my eyes." He brought Wolfe's hand to his mouth and kissed it, staring up at him. "I promise…. Now go to bed."

When Wolfe had entered his apartment, Gaspard stared at the front door for a while.

From this moment on, he knew he would divide his life into two distinct times. One was the time he'd lived without knowing of Wolfe Byrne's existence, and the other had just begun tonight.

CHAPTER NINE

"I JUST wanted to do a decent thing for a stranger." The woman, whose name was Natalie, stopped and shook her head, clearly reliving her attack. "But that decent thing ended up costing me an eye." She still wore an eye patch she touched every few seconds. "Sometimes I think it was all a nightmare. I never thought something like that would happen to me."

They all had their own version of the same nightmare, Wolfe suspected. And while Natalie took a moment to gather her thoughts, he shifted uneasily in his plastic chair, drinking the rest of his cold coffee.

"Um, well, I'm finished," Natalie said, after a while. "If anyone else wants to speak, please go ahead."

"Thank you, Natalie," Astrid said, gazing around at the group. Eleven people were seated in a circle in this small, stuffy room, and Wolfe made a mental note to get that window fixed. No matter the cost.

"I'd like to say something." Another woman, this one older than Natalie and wearing a flowered summer dress, raised her hand. "Does anybody here feel like it's their own fault? Because that's what keeps me awake at night. That thought… I keep seeing myself lying on the kitchen floor, cowering, not even trying to fight back. I wonder if that encouraged my attacker." She shut her eyes for a second. "I don't know. I just don't know."

Wolfe couldn't take much more of this. He'd been here for forty minutes already. He'd done what Astrid and Megan had wanted. Now, he needed to get out of here. He moved in his seat, trying to catch Astrid's eye.

But she was listening to the woman with interest and didn't look at him.

"I feel like that sometimes," someone said. It was the cute, bearded young man to Wolfe's right. "I mean, all I did that night was try to protect my face the whole time. That's all I kept thinking. 'Not my face.'" The man laughed quietly. "Or maybe it was my brain I was protecting. Or my fucking vanity."

Embarrassed laughter went around the room, and Wolfe seized that opportunity to stand and extend his good wishes to everyone. He quickly shook hands with a few people and said good night.

"Excuse me," Astrid said to the group as he walked away to the door. "Give me a minute." Seconds later, she touched his shoulder. "Wolfe?"

He froze and turned around. "Thank you so much for inviting me—"

"We still have twenty minutes or so left to the discussion."

"I know, and I'm sorry, but I really need to get back to work before I call it a day."

"I appreciate you coming, and would you be so kind as to give us your thoughts on tonight's experience, maybe next week?"

His *thoughts* on tonight's experience?

He never wanted to be in a room full of victims again for the rest of his life. He'd heard the same story told over and over again tonight. He didn't belong here with these people. They were still living their nightmare. They seemed to be stuck in its net like flies. The violence had clipped their wings, but he wanted no part of that.

What was the point of talking about something you wished had never happened?

"I'll send you a little note, absolutely." Wolfe stepped back to the door. "Thanks again, Astrid."

"You know, Wolfe, a lot of people would say these people are victims, but after you hear their stories, you realize they're *survivors*. There's a big difference there." She stared at him unflinchingly. "Don't you think?"

To him, the word *survivor* meant nothing else but *not dead*. But he kept that to himself. "Yeah, I think so." His voice was not as strong as he'd have liked. This whole evening had managed to weaken him. He had things to do. He couldn't feel this way. "Have a good weekend," he whispered, walking out.

Glad to have escaped that room, Wolfe climbed up the steps to the third floor and went straight for his office there. He clicked into his e-mail and dove into work again. It was nearing nine o'clock, and he hoped to be out of the YBR by ten.

"What are you doing up here?" Zach stood in his doorway. "I thought you were down in the pit, being roasted."

Wolfe looked up. "I left early."

"I don't blame you." Zach cleared his throat. "So, we're still going out tonight or—"

"Oh, right." He'd completely forgotten. They'd talked about going for a bite or coffee together. "Tonight, hm."

"*Hm*. Is that what I get from now on? *Hm*. Or maybe a *huh*?"

"Stop it." Wolfe laughed, locking eyes with Zach. "I'm just all over the place, and I'm sorry—"

"How was it last night?" Zach plopped down in the chair across from the desk. "Come on, Wolfie, I'm dying to know, okay? Really, tell me."

How could he explain his excitement every time he thought of Gaspard's face? That was his little secret for now. He didn't want to share any of it with anyone. Because he didn't even know what *it* was yet. All he knew was, every time he thought of Gaspard, he was happy. Insanely and terrifyingly *happy*. "We went for steak and a walk in the Old Port."

"Sounds nice." But Zach yawned.

"Then I chained him up and drank whiskey out of his belly button."

"Are we still friends?"

"Yes."

"Good. How 'bout I come by your place tonight and we chill out together?"

Wolfe hesitated, not quite sure what Zach considered *chilling out* these days.

"We'll listen to music and have a couple of beers." Zach was insecure again. "No?"

How could he get to know Zach if he constantly kept him out of reach?

"You mean *tea*, of course. Sure, why not." Smiling, Wolfe waved him off. "But now you have to leave me alone. I have a lot of work."

"I'm gonna head out anyway. I'll meet you at your place around ten thirty."

When Zach had gone, Wolfe stared out into the empty hall for a few minutes, thinking of the presentation he'd have to give next week. Of the shelter he desperately wanted to reopen. The volunteer dinner in October he couldn't imagine canceling.

Then he thought of Gaspard's kiss and his heart leaped.

Trying to concentrate, Wolfe returned his attention to his daily reports, but his cell phone rang, and he took it out, checking the caller ID.

It was Gaspard. Every time he thought of him, Gaspard seemed to be doing the same.

"Hi," he answered. "How are you?"

"I'm fine, but I figured you were coming out of group session, and I really wanted to know how it went."

"Oh, I left the group early, actually." Wolfe spun his chair around to face the window. There was an enormous tree growing on the other side of the street, and he could just see the crown of it from his window. It was the only green around the YBR, and it soothed him to look at it. He missed the West Coast. Missed the beaches. The mountains. The vastness of it all. He liked watching that lonely tree.

"And how was it?" Gaspard asked. "You didn't like it?"

"It was, well, it was like sitting in a room full of mirrors, I guess." Wolfe became aware he'd just admitted something crucial to Gaspard. And he'd done it with such ease. "I didn't enjoy it at all. I couldn't wait to get out of there."

"How are you feeling now?"

Wolfe hadn't even taken the time to assess his own feelings, but now that Gaspard was asking, everything came to the surface. "Weird. Shaken. Sickened."

"That's not good. Not good at all."

Why was he talking about this with Gaspard? Gaspard had enough of his own problems to deal with. "Hey, I'm okay," Wolfe said. "Don't worry about me…. How was your evening?"

"Not so good, either. I was on the phone with my son for more than an hour, and I think maybe he's gonna come home. I'm not sure what's going on with him, exactly." Gaspard sighed. "The girl he was seeing, turns out she's married, and now the husband is back, and Curtis is kind of stuck in this big mess down there—"

"That sounds intense. So he's not in school anymore?"

"No. So let's just say I'm not sure where my money was going."

"Gaspard, you need to stop sending him money right n—" But Wolfe stopped, regretting his quick reply. How could he tell Gaspard what to do? This man was a father. "Never mind," he said, "you know what to do better than I do."

"No, no, you're right. I just need some time to get my head around this."

"Do you think he's using or—"

"Drugs? I've thought about it. But he's not the type. He really isn't."

Wolfe refrained from saying anything, though his experience had taught him there was no such thing as "types" when it came to addiction. "I wish I could ease your mind," he said instead.

"I'm more afraid of how his mother will react when she finds out Curtis is out of school and sleeping with a married woman."

"Yeah, that doesn't sound too good." Wolfe thought of his own mother. She was the type to worry when he changed his cologne. "Are you gonna tell your ex-wife?"

"Of course. Meredith and I share everything." Gaspard was quiet for a moment. "I was wondering if maybe I could see you again tomorrow? Unless, you have too much work?"

"I'm not much of a cook," Wolfe said, his heart speeding, "but if you come to my place, I can try and surprise you."

At last, there was a smile in Gaspard's voice. "That sounds fantastic. I can't wait to see you again. I really can't."

WHEN WOLFE hung up, Gaspard leaned back into the couch, completely overcome with excitement and panic.

He'd forgotten how euphoric the first stages of dating could feel. The very thought of Wolfe's smile caused him palpitations and sweaty hands. The idea of being alone with him tomorrow, in his apartment, made him sick with lust and fear.

What did Wolfe see in him? How long could this wonderful dream really last?

Gaspard sat up, determined not to ruin his mood with worrying. He'd done enough of that in the last days.

He heard Malena giggling in her bedroom and couldn't help listening a little more closely. She'd been on the phone for the last half hour, talking to someone.

Minutes later, Malena came out of her room and walked by him, heading for the kitchen.

"Are you hungry?" he asked her, standing. "I can warm up some of the leek soup."

"Dad, stop it. You're always doting on me. I can warm up my own soup. Plus, I don't want soup. I want ice cream." She walked away.

Gaspard followed her into the kitchen. "Who was that you were on the phone with? A new friend?"

"No, I was on the phone with Zach." She plucked a box of ice cream out of the freezer and scooped a chunk of cookie dough ice cream into a bowl. "He's been calling me after work. We've been talking a lot lately."

"You mean Zach from the YBR?" Gaspard felt a chill run through him.

"What?" She licked the spoon, squinting at him. "You don't like him?"

Of all the people Malena could have gotten close to, Zach was definitely not on top of Gaspard's list. "I don't know him very well, but he seems a little complicated, let's put it that way."

"Complicated is fascinating." Malena dove the spoon into the ice cream.

"He's going through a lot." During their first and only date, Wolfe had spoken about Zach, and Gaspard had quickly understood that Zach was much more than an employee to Wolfe, but also a friend. Wolfe seemed worried about him lately. Concerned for Zach's health.

"I know that." Her stare iced over as she brought the spoon to her lips. "He's told me everything."

"Okay, well, that's good. I'm glad he's being honest with you."

"He's a splendid man, Dad. He's just very careful, and can come across as a bit of a jerk, but deep down inside, Zach is just a scared little boy who's never really known love. He's been tossed from foster home to foster home most of his life. He's trying to get his life together."

Gaspard made every possible effort not to let his utmost concern show. "When you say he's told you everything, do you mean *everything*?"

"If you're hinting at his HIV status or his recovery from heroin addiction, then yes, he's told me about all that."

He was surprised at the coolness of her tone. "Why do I feel like you're thirteen again and I'm the enemy trying to dissuade you from watching *The Exorcist*?"

"Because I don't want you to judge him. Because I like him. I like him a lot, actually."

"You know I don't judge people by their past. And I certainly don't judge people by a virus they carry in their blood, even if it's a potentially *life-threatening* virus, but I'm your father, Malena, and there's a limit to my compassion when it comes down to you."

"I know... I know that." She reached for his hand. "Look, Dad, we're not... *you know*. We're just friends. He makes me laugh. And I make him feel good about himself. He says he's never had a friend like me."

"He's got Wolfe."

"It's not the same." She seemed to want to say something else but only moved the ice cream around in her bowl.

"Do you have feelings for him?"

"For Zach? I don't know... maybe. But he's gay, so that settles it."

"You know, he could be bisexual, Mal."

She shrugged. "I think he has a thing for Wolfe anyway."

"Oh, I see."

Malena squeezed his hand hard. "Hey, don't worry so much. Look, if you'd seen the smile Wolfe had on his face all day, you'd put any concern you have out of your mind. It's obvious he's crushing on you *big-time*."

How could they be discussing this so naturally? "He is?" Gaspard couldn't help asking anyway.

Malena put her empty bowl in the sink and winked before walking away. "Oh yes. I saw a doodle on a notepad in his office."

"What did it say?" Gaspard swallowed hard.

She pushed the door with her hip. "He drew a heart there, and inside, he wrote, 'Wolfe Augustin.'"

"My last name," Gaspard breathed.

"Yep, looks like he married you this week."

She left him standing there with his mouth open.

CHAPTER TEN

WOLFE AND Zach sat side by side on the couch, with the radio playing in the background.

Finally, Wolfe was unwinding from his long day at work. He took a sip of his tea and looked at Zach. This was the perfect opportunity to speak to him about more personal issues. "So, how have you been lately? I don't wanna pry or anything, but I was wondering how your—"

"The radio," Zach cut him off, smiling over the rim of his cup. "How nineties of you. I didn't know people still listened to the radio."

"It helps me learn French," Wolfe said, putting his cup down. "I have it on all the time when I'm home."

"Your French is pretty decent for a West Coast guy." Zach leaned back in the seat. "Do people bother you about your accent?"

"Depends on the area." Wolfe had yet to get used to the politics of language in Montreal. In some neighborhoods, speaking English was a political affront to francophone people, but in others, downtown, for example, it seemed to be the language of preference. Tension surrounded the issue of language, and he'd soon realized it was better for him to pretend he was American instead of Canadian. "Let's just say I didn't hang my Canadian flag in the window this year."

Zach laughed. "Yeah, I get it. But I'm half and half, you know, so I can blend in with the frogs and the blokes. My mother is a blue-blooded descendant of a loyalist family, and my dad was a separatist half in love with René Lévesque. He grew up in the east end. Trust me, there were some bitchin' fights in my house around election time." He drained his tea and reached for his pack of cigarettes on the coffee table. He lit a cigarette—his third in the last hour—and blew out the match. "Well, at least until the good folks at the Youth Protection Department got me out of there."

"I didn't know you smoked so much," Wolfe said gently. "You should take it easy on the —"

"Gimme a break, Wolfie, all right?" Zach's eyes flared up. His mood had darkened so quickly.

Wolfe had noticed just how volatile Zach was becoming lately. He never knew how to handle him these days. "Yes, okay," Wolfe said. "But the thing is, I worry about you, and people at work are concerned that maybe—"

"Have I done anything out of line at work?" Zach sniffled and crushed his cigarette into the cup Wolfe had given him to use as an ashtray. "You got some complaints about me or something?"

"No, of course not. That's not what I'm saying."

"Then what are you saying?"

"I don't know," Wolfe whispered, looking up at Zach's tense expression. "I just... I care about you, and though I play this supportive-friend role very well with you, inside, I'm freaking out. I keep thinking the worst. That you're gonna go back to using. That you're gonna get sick. That you're gonna lose everything you've worked so hard for and I won't be able to help you, because you keep me out of reach all the time, and that's why—"

"Hey, hey," Zach said, softly. "Easy now." He moved closer. "Don't get so worked up over me. It isn't worth it."

"See? This is exactly the type of shit you say that makes me feel like you've given up already. It gives me this sick, cold feeling in my gut, and I feel like you've sealed yourself up in this invisible cage I can't even touch. I just need you to tell me what you're going through. Just talk to me, that's all."

Zach sat with his elbows on his knees, staring at the black television screen. "You want me to talk to you?"

"Yes."

"About what?" Zach shot him a look full of fury and pain that cut Wolfe's air. "Huh? What do you wanna hear, Wolfe? You wanna see me coming apart here? You wanna take a tour around Zach's fun house? See the freaks I keep on leashes inside my head? No, man, I don't think so." He looked back at the screen, at his own face. "I really don't think so."

"You show me yours, I'll show you mine," Wolfe said, turning to face Zach. "Go ahead, Mackay, lay it on me."

Zach glanced over at him. "You don't quit, do you?"

"I'm a compulsive control freak with abandonment issues. So, no, I don't quit."

Zach smiled sadly, shaking his head. "Fine, but you go first."

Wolfe loosened his tie. It was time he told someone about that night. "Okay… I will, then." He'd tell Zach everything. He *needed* to tell him about the assault. "Two years ago, I was walking out of the halfway house I used to work for, a shelter for young adults. My first real job in the field. It was Friday night, and Sawyer and I had plans to meet at a club we loved. We hadn't done that in a long time, so I was excited about the evening ahead, wondering what kind of night it was gonna be." Wolfe could see himself on that porch. Under the broken light they never bothered to fix. He remembered how cool the evening was and what the air smelled like.

"You don't have to do this," Zach whispered, putting his hand on Wolfe's knee.

"I turned the key in the lock and checked that the door was properly locked. My phone rang, and it was my boss, Debra. I told her I was on my way home and everything was okay. The house was closed for the next two weeks. We had a leak in the basement. I was wondering what I was going to do with my time off. And as I stepped down to the sidewalk, out of the corner of my eye, I saw two dark figures coming at me. I turned to look at them. I knew most people in the neighborhood. And they all knew me. I recognized one of the guys and called him by his name. *Aaron*. Aaron's eyes were glassy, and he had that smile I'd seen so often on the streets. It was the smile of someone who'd made a decision and wouldn't go back on it. My instincts told me to walk away, but I'd been trained to always take that step forward. I said something—I don't know what—but it didn't matter. It didn't matter what I said. They were laughing. Asking for money but in a very noncommittal way, like they didn't care one way or the other if they got it. Then it was a blowjob they wanted. Or someone's phone number, a woman I worked with, and then it was meth. By this time, I knew I was in trouble, but I tried to be cool, you know, to show them I thought they were human, and I wasn't like the people out there—"

"Fucking addicts." Zach's dark eyes were like hot black stones. "Never trust an addict, right?"

"To this day, I don't know why he hit me so hard and for so long. When they picked them up later that week, Aaron didn't even remember that night. Didn't remember punching the side of my head, right on my left ear, pushing me down, kicking me in the ribs, the face."

Zach was watching him, his face pale. "Jesus," he whispered. "I had no idea."

"Anyway, Aaron pled guilty and so did his friend, and that was that. They went straight back into the system, but this time, it wasn't juvenile hall, but real time in jail, and six weeks later, I was back at my job, back in the streets." Wolfe still felt sick every time he thought of those two young men in jail.

They were in there because of *him*.

"How bad were you hurt?"

"Two broken ribs. A concussion. Bruises all along my side and a black eye." Wolfe took a sip of his tea and cracked a semblance of a smile. "I was no longer the prettiest face in East Hastings, I'll tell you that much."

Zach didn't smile. He just stared at him intensely. "So two addicts beat you up and leave you on the sidewalk for dead, and two years later, you hire an addict fresh out of rehab as your right-hand man?"

"Yeah, well, I liked the shirt you had on that day," Wolfe said lightly, though his heart was still beating hard from the confession. From reliving that night.

"Don't joke, Wolfie. Why on earth would you do that? Why would you take that chance with me—"

"I don't know… I just knew I had to give you an opportunity and maybe in doing that, I'd give myself the opportunity to heal."

Zach leaned in, coming very close. Too close. "Your heart is like a cathedral," he said, touching Wolfe's chest. Zach leaned in closer, as if to kiss him, but Wolfe came to his senses, and with great effort stood up. "Excuse me," he muttered, stumbling away. "Bathroom."

"Are you okay?"

"Yeah… I'm fine." Inside the bathroom, he turned the faucet on full blast and splashed cold water on his face.

If only Zach wasn't so attractive.

But he'd have to send Zach home now. Wolfe looked up at his face in the mirror. He'd do the right thing. No matter how sexy Zach was, he wanted Gaspard.

That thought struck him.

He hadn't felt this way for so long. Decided. Committed. Sure of something. It was clear to him now: he wanted to give Gaspard all of his attention, and he'd do everything he could to not mess this up.

Wolfe wiped his face and looked at the door. He'd be frank but gentle with Zach. He stepped back into the living room.

Zach grabbed his pack of cigarettes from the coffee table. "Do you mind if I have another one?"

"No, go ahead." Wolfe sat down. "Can we talk for a second?"

"Look, I know what you're gonna say, okay? So you don't have to look at me like that."

"Are you angry? Do you think I shouldn't have invited you over?"

Zach wouldn't say anything. He sat facing the table, smoking furiously. Wolfe stared at him, waiting. Finally, Zach put his cigarette out and stood. "I'm gonna get going."

"Zach, please—"

But Zach put his hand up. "It's all right, okay?" He gathered his combat boots by the door and pulled them on, but didn't lace them up. "I'll see you Monday."

He couldn't let Zach leave like this. What if he did something reckless tonight? "Listen to me," Wolfe whispered, daring to come a little closer. "I know I've been sending you mixed signals. I know I have. And you should hate me right now—"

"Stop it. Just stop it." Zach leaned his head back on the door, sighing. He looked Wolfe straight in the eye. "You did nothing wrong, all right? Nothing. I played the game too."

"Zach—"

"Just let me go." Zach turned and opened the door. "Good night, Wolfie."

"Where are you going?" Wolfe ran down the three steps leading to the street and took hold of Zach's arm. "Huh? Where are you going?"

"Not your fucking business. Where I go. What I do." Zach pulled away and walked off. "As long as I punch in Monday and do my work, you have nothing to say about what I do with my nights."

Wolfe stood barefoot on the sidewalk, defenseless against Zach's anger. But he wouldn't run after him. "You're right!" he screamed out instead, watching Zach walk away. "Go! Take your revenge on the world! But you're only destroying yourself in the process, and the world doesn't give a fuck about you!" He didn't care if he woke the whole neighborhood with the scene he was causing. "But I do, Zach! *I* care!"

But Zach kept walking and, deeply hurt, Wolfe turned back for his apartment.

CHAPTER ELEVEN

WOLFE WAS locked up in his bedroom, on the phone with his mother. He'd been in there for the last ten minutes. To pass time, Gaspard walked over to Wolfe's bookcase in the living room to see what he'd spot on the crowded shelves. He saw some gay classics there, such as Isherwood and Baldwin, but the bulk of Wolfe's book collection was mostly nonfiction, consisting of college manuals on psychology or substance abuse, and an array of textbooks dog-eared in various places. Between manuals, Gaspard found a wrestling figurine.

He dropped it as though it had burned his hand.

Instantly, a memory of Curtis, eight years old, playing with the same figurine came rushing back, making him sick. Quickly, Gaspard put the toy back on the shelf and shook the nasty memory off.

He couldn't think about Donny, their neighbor, and what the boy had done to his son. Upset, Gaspard picked a picture frame off Wolfe's desk, hoping to push the horrible feelings back into the recesses of his mind. He looked down at the picture, a snapshot of Wolfe and another man standing on a trail, surrounded by tree trunks the size of houses. The sun was in their eyes, and they were grinning at the camera. The other man had a protective arm around Wolfe's neck and seemed to be pulling him near when the picture had been snapped. They looked positively radiant and perfectly matched. Both men were of the same height. Had the same hair color. And that same dazzling smile.

"Oh," Wolfe said, stepping out of the bedroom, "that's a terrible picture of me, but my brother Xander looks amazing in it. That's why I keep it there."

"That's your brother?" Gaspard looked at the picture again. Of course this was the brother. "Where was this taken?"

"Redwood National Park." Wolfe's voice wavered, and Gaspard noticed his face was as pale as snow. "We took a trip there before Xander got married." Wolfe stared at the picture in Gaspard's hand. "Yeah…," he whispered, and nothing more.

"Wolfe?"

Wolfe glanced up at him, but his eyes were vacant. He seemed to be somewhere else. "More wine?" Wolfe finally asked, walking away to the kitchen. Something was wrong. From the moment Gaspard had walked into the apartment, just a little less than an hour ago, he'd been trying to figure out why Wolfe seemed so distant with him. Wolfe wasn't the same as he'd been the last and only time they'd had dinner together. He appeared preoccupied and a little frazzled.

Gaspard followed into the kitchen and found Wolfe standing up against the counter, staring at the tiled floor. "Do you wanna talk about it?" Gaspard asked, carefully approaching him.

At the sound of his voice, Wolfe looked up. He was obviously upset and trying to hold it together. "My grandfather passed away," he said flatly.

"Wolfe, I'm so sorry—"

"No, it's okay. It's okay." Wolfe looked around the kitchen, then back at Gaspard. "I'm fine. He was very old, and he lived such a wonderful life. I should be so lucky to live the life he did."

"Were you close to him?"

"When I was younger, yes, I was. But we sort of grew apart when I came out, although he wasn't completely closed off to the idea of me being gay, just uneasy around me, and I guess I was in that phase where I wanted everyone to celebrate my coming out, etc."

"The etc. part is pretty hard."

"Yeah, I suppose it is. Anyway, his funeral is this week, and my mother wants me there. She's absolutely adamant about it."

"How long has it been since you've been back home?"

"Two years this October."

Two years was a long time not to see your son. Gaspard thought of Curtis. He wouldn't let his son slip away from him. He'd let Curtis down before, but he wouldn't allow it to happen again.

"Problem is," Wolfe said, "I can't just pick up and leave for BC. Especially not this week. I'm meeting with the board on Tuesday. I can't cancel—"

"I'm sure your bosses would understand. This is a death in the family."

"No." Wolfe shook his head, frowning. "No way. I'm not gonna risk losing the YBR for a family who only pretends to give a shit about me to keep up appearances." He looked down into his glass, his cheeks reddening. Clearly, he was embarrassed about his outburst.

"Is that how you feel?" Gaspard suspected this was a highly sensitive and potentially dangerous subject for them to be discussing so early in their relationship.

"Yes, that's how I feel. They're kind to me just to put it in my face. To show me just how selfish I am to pursue what *they* deem to be a silly, low-paying, degrading job in a city they think is the rectum of the world."

"Why did you leave?" Gaspard came closer, touching the back of Wolfe's hand.

"Because I couldn't stand who I was when I was around them anymore. Because we were always bickering about every single decision I ever made. Because my mother couldn't go a day without calling to check if I was still alive, and because after I was assaulted, it got so bad with my family that I couldn't even heal… I couldn't step outside of my Gastown home for a pack of gum without having to take my phone with me. And my ex-boyfriend didn't help. All Sawyer ever did was complain about my family, my anxiety attacks, and my inability to stand up to anybody he judged unworthy of him." Wolfe paused, staring into Gaspard's eyes. "That's why."

Gaspard slipped the glass out of Wolfe's fingers and held both of his hands. "Listen to me," he said, coming very close.

"What?" Wolfe was clearly irritated, still tense and wired with emotion.

"You're burning the chicken," Gaspard whispered and winked.

Wolfe stared at him with surprise. "Is that all you care about? Food?" He pinched Gaspard's waist and walked over to the oven, then pulled open its door. "The chicken is fine, by the way." With a smirk, he shut the oven door. He was definitely in a better mood, or at least trying to be. "Have some bread if you're so hungry."

Gaspard tipped his head to the kitchen door. "Why don't we go sit in the living room?"

They stepped into the living room, and Gaspard looked around for a paper and a pen. "Do you still have that thing they call paper around here? Or do you write everything on this?" He pointed to Wolfe's laptop.

"Why?"

"I have an idea, that's all."

"And you need to write it down in case you forget it?"

"Yes, because at my age, the memory isn't what it used to be." Gaspard rolled his eyes at Wolfe. "No, kiddo, I don't need to write anything down. Just hand over a pen and a piece of paper, and I'll show you what I do when I'm struggling with an overloaded program that needs to lose a few pounds of useless information."

Wolfe eyed him suspiciously. "What?"

Playfully, Gaspard patted the couch. "Let me take a look at your database."

Wolfe laughed and brought him a sheet of paper and a pen.

When Wolfe sat next to him, Gaspard couldn't stop himself from kissing him. "Now," he whispered, leaning back, but still hungry for Wolfe's mouth. "Let's break everything down. Your schedule. Your priorities. Your support network. Your midterm and long-term goals with the YBR—"

"You don't have to do this. This is work."

"I want to." He wanted to help Wolfe. Wanted to do everything he possibly could to lessen his workload. But more importantly, he needed to get closer to Wolfe. To understand his world. "It won't take but an hour or so. And I'm really good at this. This is what I do, in so many ways."

Wolfe nibbled on his bottom lip, obviously debating.

"Bring the wine, some bread, and let's get to work." Gaspard patted Wolfe's knee. "Come on."

Wolfe finally conceded. He rose and looked down at Gaspard with tenderness. "Okay… I'll play along."

"You won't regret it."

"So far," Wolfe said, his tone shy, "I haven't regretted a single moment spent with you, Gaspard."

ON THE narrow back balcony, Wolfe moved the small patio table off to the side and rearranged the two garden chairs for Gaspard and himself. But he didn't feel like sitting just yet. He needed to get a few good gulps of air and clear his head a little. While Gaspard was in the washroom, Wolfe stood leaning up against the wrought-iron railing, looking out at the narrow courtyard he shared with the other tenants. It was quite neglected—a testament to the busy lives of his neighbors, all young professionals or full-time students.

But next summer, he'd do something with this small green space. He'd lead the way, and maybe his neighbors would follow.

Why was he thinking about this now?

Gaspard was right: He *did* spread himself too thin. He had this unproductive tendency to project himself into the future and take on imaginary responsibilities that only weighed him down in the present. They'd talked about all of this in the last few hours, and Wolfe had been impressed with Gaspard's perceptiveness. Gaspard had made Wolfe draw up a list of all the things or people he felt responsible for. Wolfe was shocked at the length of the list. He really did need to allow people to be more accountable for themselves at work and in his personal life.

"Oh, it's nice out here," Gaspard said, sliding the door shut behind him. "Indian Summer, I guess."

Wolfe took the glass of water Gaspard offered him. "Thank you. How did you know I was thirsty?"

"I don't know. I just figured you would be."

Gaspard was always thinking of him. Guessing his needs. All evening, he'd helped Wolfe with dinner, work, cleaning up. Gaspard had listened to him, encouraged him, made him laugh.

But it was almost one a.m., and the evening was coming to its end. In the last hour, Wolfe had tried reading Gaspard more closely. Would he spend the night? They'd kissed a few times, and on the couch, Gaspard had even allowed Wolfe to put his hand between Gaspard's thighs, but every time the heat rose between them, Gaspard had discreetly pulled away.

"What are you thinking of?" Gaspard asked. "You're in another place right now. You do that a lot. Just sort of drift off."

"I do? I'm sorry... I was just thinking about tonight. How great we get along."

"We do, don't we?" Hesitantly, Gaspard touched a strand of Wolfe's hair. He liked to do that, Wolfe noticed. "It's getting late."

Wolfe shivered and glanced back into the dark, forbidding apartment. "Yeah," he said in a quiet voice. "I should probably get some sleep too."

"I had a really good time tonight."

"We'll do this again soon, I hope." The banal words came out of his mouth, while inside, he screamed for Gaspard to stay. "Let me get your jacket." He slid the patio door open and stepped inside. His open bedroom door was a dark mouth waiting to swallow him whole.

Inside, Gaspard gathered his phone and keys. His movements were nervous, and he seemed to be uneasy. "Um, well, thank you so much for dinner and—"

"Gaspard," Wolfe said without thinking. "I don't know how you'll take this, but it's late, and maybe, if you wanted to, you could stay here, with me. I mean, I just wanna—" But Wolfe paused, calming down. "What I'm saying is do you wanna sleep here?"

Gaspard was unsettled. "Sleep here?"

"I mean *sleep*, as in the act of closing one's eyes and nodding off." Wolfe smirked, trying to be bold and brave.

"In there, in bed, with you?"

Clearly, this was a hundred miles over Gaspard's speed limit. "Please, forget I even mentioned it."

"No, no, Wolfe, that's not how I meant it to sound."

"No? Because it sounded a lot like you'd rather sleep in Nosferatu's coffin."

Gaspard laughed, taking a step to him. "Did it?" He reached out for Wolfe's hand. "I just... I panicked."

"I can understand that." Wolfe pulled him closer and hooked a finger into Gaspard's belt. "But I'd never do anything you weren't completely comfortable with."

"It's not about *my* level of comfort," Gaspard said. "It's about yours."

"I'm perfectly comfortable with you sleeping in my bed," Wolfe said, his mouth touching Gaspard's. He could feel all of Gaspard's complicated defense mechanisms gearing up, yet, there was a fever in Gaspard's eyes. "I have no problem with that."

"And what if that turned out to be as far as I go?" Gaspard slipped his fingers into Wolfe's hair. "How long do you think you'd be okay with that?"

"I really don't care. Whatever you're willing to give me, I'll take."

"I don't wanna tease you, but I won't lie to you, Wolfe. I wanna stay tonight... I wanna lie down in your bed—"

"That's all I need to hear." Wolfe tugged on Gaspard's shirt, leading him to his bedroom. "Let's go to bed, okay?"

This time Gaspard didn't argue. In the bedroom, Wolfe pulled the blanket and sheet down and looked over his shoulder. "Are you gonna sleep in your jeans?"

"No… I'll take those off."

He tried not to be interested in Gaspard's awkward striptease, but Gaspard had really good legs and his thighs were perfect. Wolfe quickly jerked his own jeans off and unfastened the buttons of his shirt. Shirtless and clad only in his briefs, he climbed into bed, moving to the far side of it, near the window. In the dim light, Gaspard folded his jeans neatly over the edge of the bed's baseboard. "I'll iron them for you tomorrow morning," Wolfe teased.

"Sorry, just nervous."

"Come here."

"Maybe I should call Malena."

"She's sleeping."

"Yeah, you're probably right."

Wolfe leaned on his elbow, smiling up at Gaspard. "Come here. *Now.*"

At last, Gaspard climbed into bed, pulling the sheet up to his waist. He lay on his back but turned to look at him. "I feel like a complete idiot right now."

Wolfe inched closer, daring to put his hand on Gaspard's chest. For a moment, he tried seeing the situation from Gaspard's perspective. He remembered the first time he'd shared a bed with another man. Not a kiss. Or his body. But a *bed.* There was something exhilarating and strange about lying next to another man's body for the first time—to hear his breathing change as he fell asleep. To be close to him when he was at his most vulnerable. Wolfe lost his playful tone. "Gaspard, I want nothing from you right now," he said, feeling Gaspard's heart pounding under his hand. "It's been so long since I shared my bed with anyone, and maybe I'm nervous too. I've just stopped paying attention to my own fears a long time ago."

"Then, come here, Wolfe." Gaspard wrapped his arm around him. "Let me hold you."

IN THE morning light, Gaspard reached over for his jeans on the edge of the bed and searched his pockets for his phone. He glanced back at

Wolfe to see if the phone had woken him. No, Wolfe was sound asleep, on top of the blankets, with his arm thrown over his face.

How could this beautiful man let him so close to him so fast?

Gaspard answered Malena's call. "Hey, you," he said, as quietly as possible, getting out of bed. "Sorry I didn't call last night." He stepped out of the bedroom and half shut the door behind him, but to leave Wolfe, even for a moment, was difficult.

"Are you at Wolfe's place?" Malena sounded relaxed and cheerful. "'Cause when I saw your bed this morning, I figured you were. Are you?"

"I had a lot to drink, so we figured it would be better if—"

"Dad, you don't have to justify yourself to me."

"I know that," he said, going to the kitchen. Inside, he looked around for some coffee and coffee filters. "I just don't want you to worry that—"

"I'm not worried." She was eating something. "Listen, I'm gonna be out this afternoon, so when you come home, do you mind tossing the clothes in the dryer for me?"

In the cupboard over the sink, Gaspard found what he was looking for and started on making the coffee. "Yeah, sure. Where are you going?"

"It's a nice day, so we're gonna go hang out on the mountain."

"We?"

"Yeah, Zach and me." He could hear her moving around, opening and shutting drawers. "I'm getting a little picnic basket together here."

"Picnic?" He couldn't help laughing. "Funny, but I didn't picture Zach as the picnic type."

"Yeah, well, it was his idea, actually." She sounded tense again. "His favorite foster parents used to take him out for picnics when he was eight."

Gaspard held his tongue. Malena had always chosen her friends carefully. He'd have to trust her on this. But it was a challenge to sit on the sidelines and watch the game play out. "Well," he said, turning the coffee machine on, "you two have a good day. And I'll see you later, right?"

"Thanks, Dad." Her voice was sweet again. "I love you."

"I love you too." After they'd hung up, Gaspard held the phone tightly, trying to stay calm. She was so incredibly supportive of him.

Always understanding and patient. How could he let his own secret prejudice stop her from getting close to Zach? Should men like Zach not be allowed a chance to know his wonderful daughter?

Malena was a healer and had so much compassion for people. Ever since childhood, she'd always had a penchant for saving creatures others would have condemned to perish. He remembered the bird with the broken wing. The lost turtle. The many, many stray cats. The dog with the missing eye at the animal shelter.

But Zach was a man. A good-looking and immensely seductive man. He wasn't a pet in need of shelter. Would Zach hurt her?

"Hey, how long have you been up?"

Gaspard turned to see Wolfe walking into the kitchen. At the sight of Wolfe's smile, Gaspard set his cup down and immediately went to him. He had to touch him. "Not long," he said and then kissed Wolfe's forehead. Gently, he brushed his soft, wild hair away from his eyes. "Coffee?"

"Yeah, thanks." Wolfe sat at the kitchen table, folding his leg under him. He wore a white T-shirt over checkered pajama bottoms, and in the light, looked barely out of his teenage years.

All of last night's guilt assailed Gaspard once more. Last night, lying near Wolfe, he hadn't stopped thinking of their age difference. He'd held Wolfe but hadn't been able to make love to him. Those twenty-four years had tormented him, and he'd pretended to fall asleep, waiting to hear Wolfe's breathing change. Then he'd spent the next hours lying close to Wolfe, watching him sleep. He'd made promises to him. Silent oaths.

He'd even sworn to himself that he'd be gone by morning and stop this nonsense.

"I haven't slept this good since I moved here," Wolfe said, taking the cup from Gaspard's hand. "You were out like a light last night."

"Um, yeah, the wine, I guess." Gaspard leaned against the counter.

Wolfe reached his hand out. "Come here."

What was he doing here with this young man?

This could never go anywhere.

"Wolfe," he said, his own heart aching. "We need to talk."

Wolfe instantly looked down at the table, biting his lip. "What is it?"

"I don't know how to say this." Gaspard pulled a chair out and sat, close to him. "But honestly, you must know I'm way too old for you—"

"Why did you ask me out, then?" Wolfe's eyes were cold, as Gaspard remembered they could be. "You're the one who asked me—"

"I know." Gaspard leaned back in his chair. What an imbecile he was.

"Why did you ask me out, Gaspard? Why? Answer me."

"I don't know."

"Yes, you do." Wolfe leaned in closer. "Why did you ask me out?"

He couldn't hold Wolfe's gaze and lie to him. "Because I couldn't stop thinking about you. Because I told myself that age was just a number between two consenting adults. And because you're the type of man I'd have fallen in love with, if only I'd had the right to, a long time ago."

Wolfe took his hands in his. "I don't care how old you are," he whispered. "Maybe I should care, I know that. And maybe I have an absent father and need a father figure. Or maybe I have an old soul like my mother always said. Or maybe I need to be in control and you make me feel powerful. Or maybe, just maybe, I'm sick of the bullshit, Gaspard. Of the pettiness of most guys I've met. Of casual sex. Of being used and tossed over the side of the bed in the morning. Of playing cat and mouse. Maybe I just wanna give us a chance." He moved closer still. "Question is, can you do that? Can you give us a chance? Can you give *me* a chance?"

Gaspard was struck by the passion in Wolfe's voice. He'd never seen this side of him. There was so much left to discover in this man. And he wanted to dive into him. "Yes," he said, the excitement rising inside him. "I do, but I'm terrified, I'll tell you right now. I'm fucking terrified, Wolfe."

"I'm fucking terrified too." Wolfe stared into his eyes. "See, I'm a little like a door. I'm either closed or open. There's no in-between with me, and that's always scared me. But, Gaspard, I wanna trust you."

"You can. I promise."

Wolfe looked around the kitchen. "And I'm hungry."

Gaspard laughed. "I see."

"Let's go out for breakfast." Wolfe stood and stretched. "I have to eat. Like right now. Come on."

No one would know, Gaspard decided. They didn't have to announce anything. Malena didn't have to know all the details of their relationship. "Okay, sure. You wanna go out around here?"

"Yes, Gaspard, here. In the gay village, full of gay people doing gay things and eating gay food in gay restaurants." Wolfe winked and looked over his shoulder, walking out of the room. "Coming?"

Gaspard agreed, but his heart was in his mouth.

Wolfe stopped in the door. "It'll be okay, Gaspard," he said with a serious expression.

"Do you think it's pathetic how scared I am of even sitting in a restaurant with other queer men?"

"Come on," Wolfe said, coming back for him. "We'll sit there and order a big plate of sausages."

"Shut up."

"With a side dish of Swedish meatballs, of course."

CHAPTER TWELVE

THEY'D FINALLY made it through the restaurant's dining room and out onto the terrace, but as they sat down, someone accosted Wolfe again. This time, they were interrupted by a heavy woman carrying a cardboard box full of kittens. She stopped by the terrace's short fence, near their table, and grinned at Wolfe. Her toothless smile made Gaspard squirm in his seat. He quickly put his sunglasses on and picked up the menu. He couldn't believe how many people had stopped Wolfe during their short walk to the restaurant on Sainte-Catherine Street. He was trying not to be annoyed, but the woman wouldn't take any of Wolfe's subtle hints, and he suspected she'd probably be standing at their table for a while. Her kittens badly needed a home, and she was insisting Wolfe take them to the YBR center with him today.

With very frantic movements, the woman opened the box and showed him the litter squirming and climbing up the sides.

"Oh, wow," Wolfe said. "Hello there." He looked into the box and petted one of the kitten's little gray heads. He glanced up at the woman. "They're adorable."

"Aren't they?" She sniffed and looked around the street. She wasn't wearing a bra, and her huge breasts sagged under her brown T-shirt. Her hair was matted and hadn't been cleaned in a long time. She had blue-and-yellow marks, old bruises, on her neck and arms. "But I can't keep them, you know," she told Wolfe, shutting the box again. "There's no place for them where I'm living now. And the bed bugs would eat them." She swung back and forth on her heels, moving constantly. Something was eating through her. "So, what do you say? Will you take them? Will you?"

Until this morning, Gaspard had been under the false impression the people Wolfe helped were somehow all young and pretty, needing only a little pep talk or a pamphlet from him. Reality wasn't like that at all. The people who'd accosted Wolfe were mostly homeless men and drug addicts. On the corner of Saint-Hubert Street, they'd been stopped by a young man, obviously a hustler, coming out of a cheap hotel. Unaffected by the guy's jitters and overall countenance, Wolfe had spoken to him as if they were friends, taking the time to ask about his recent hospital stay. These were dirty and gritty people. Insane people too. One guy had been licking the top of a dumpster as they'd passed him in a side street. Upon seeing them, the man had looked up to say hello to Wolfe. His street name was Licky Luke, and softly, Wolfe had explained that the YBR often helped Licky Luke with getting his various medical prescriptions renewed.

The YBR wasn't supposed to be focused on this type of clientele, but with social services being cut every day and shelters overloaded, the YBR was like a patch in the system, and since his arrival in Montreal, Wolfe had been trying to figure out the neighborhood, getting to know the faces and cases, attending meetings, visiting hospitals, shelters, local food banks, and unemployment offices. He was beginning to get a clearer picture of what needed to be done in the next years to address the growing need for food, shelter, and therapy in the area.

The task seemed enormous and impossible, but Wolfe believed he could make a difference. He'd spoken so fervently about his plans that Gaspard could only listen in awe.

How much energy did Wolfe have, exactly?

"I really can't take them, Gloria," Wolfe said at last. "I'm sorry, but all I can do is put up an ad in the lobby. Or ask around and see if I can find a home for these little guys." He stood and took his phone out. "Let me take a few pictures of them, okay?"

She frowned and held the box to her hip, shaking her head. "I don't want you to take a picture of them." She looked over her shoulder and seemed to recognize someone. "No, they're already doing a secret story on me." She came closer and looked at Gaspard. "He's with them," she said and walked away, carrying her box full of kittens.

When she'd left, Wolfe touched Gaspard's hand over the table. "So sorry about that. She's been off her meds for a while. She's usually really sweet when she's following treatment." He frowned, scanning the menu. "So, what are you having?"

Gaspard was still dumbfounded by what he'd witnessed this morning. "How the hell do you do it?"

"What do you mean?" Wolfe sounded defensive. He frowned. "How I do what, exactly?"

Gaspard changed his tone and lost the confused look. Wolfe didn't want to be ridiculed or idolized for what he did for a living. No, what he wanted was to be understood. "Well, however you do it, you must be doing something right," Gaspard said, taking his sunglasses off. "Because these people obviously trust you."

Wolfe's face brightened. "I hope they do. That would mean everything. It would mean they could believe in the possibility of rebuilding an authentic relationship with another human being—something most of them have given up on. They've been hurt, but they've also hurt a lot of people in their lives, and sometimes I think it's not so much that they're protecting themselves from others, but more like they're protecting others from *them*."

Gaspard immediately thought of Zach. He hadn't dared bring his name up earlier, but now seemed to be a good time. "Is that why you hired Zach at the center?"

"Partly, yes. I thought he was a good candidate for the job. And I guess I wanted to actually help someone. Not on paper. In real life." Wolfe bit his lip. "But I'm not sure if my plan worked."

"A job doesn't fix everything. But it's a good start, right?"

"I got too close to him and mixed up all the cards." Wolfe lowered his voice, leaning in. "I feel terrible about it, Gaspard. I don't know how it happened, but I started flirting with him—"

"Did he fall for you?"

"I don't know," Wolfe whispered, his voice sad. "Maybe."

"And did you fall for him?"

Wolfe widened his eyes in surprise. He leaned back and stared at him but didn't say anything.

"He's a very attractive man," Gaspard said, playing with the corner of his napkin. "Hard to resist, I suppose."

"Well, I resisted, Gaspard. I *resisted* plenty."

"Yeah?"

Wolfe reached for his hand. "Look, it came real close and I almost crossed the line with him, but nothing happened and nothing will. And no, I don't have feelings for Zach. I was a little infatuated with him for a while, but that changed… when I met you."

Gaspard hadn't blushed in years, but he was blushing now. He picked up his glass and gulped down water.

"Look at you," Wolfe teased, but his cheeks, too, were a darker shade of pink. He ran a hand through his hair and laughed. "Did I fluster you?"

Gaspard tried to play it cool. "No."

"Oh, okay, because for a minute there—"

"Actually, yes, you did. I'm tongue-tied."

"Well, I can fix that." Wolfe rose out of his chair and leaned over their small table. "Come here. Come closer." He pulled on Gaspard's shirt collar and planted a soft kiss on his lips.

At that moment the waiter showed up. They both babbled out their order to the young man and watched him leave.

Wolfe fidgeted, obviously embarrassed. "My timing has always been terrible," he said, fixing his shirt.

"But your kiss makes up for it."

"So," Wolfe said before drinking water. "What were we talking about?"

"Zach. Has he ever dated women? Just curious."

"I'm not sure, why?"

"Malena and he have been spending a lot of time together."

"What?"

Gaspard wished he hadn't opened that can of worms.

"Zach and Malena hang out together?"

"You seem upset."

"Oh, and you're okay with this? You're fine with your daughter spending time with a man like Zach?"

"I shouldn't be?"

Wolfe looked away at the busy street, staring at the crowd.

"Wolfe, what's wrong?"

"I don't know why I'm reacting like this. I don't understand." Wolfe finally made eye contact with him. "It's like I wanna be *personally* responsible for everyone's well-being. That makes me sound selfish or hypocritical, doesn't it?"

"No, just afraid of being forgotten or abandoned."

Wolfe shrugged. "Story of my life. Every time I get close to someone, something changes in their life, and all of sudden, I'm a nuisance. Something that needs to go. A *problem*."

"I can't imagine you could ever be a nuisance or a problem for anyone."

"It still happens," Wolfe said, looking into his face. "Every time."

CHAPTER THIRTEEN

ON MONDAY, around noon, Wolfe hurried up the stairs to his office.

He'd been in meetings all morning, trying to get some official commitments from potential sponsors for the youth shelter. He'd met with two city officials, but it would take them months, perhaps even up to a year, to get any funds released for this kind of project. He just didn't have that time. He needed concrete evidence to prove to the board that he could come up with solid donors and corporate sponsors within the next three months. He'd met with a large corporation this morning, but their idea of plastering the YBR with their company logo and setting up kiosks with their merchandise inside the center didn't sit well with him. He'd taken their card, but he knew he wouldn't go with that kind of sponsorship. The YBR wasn't for sale.

Yet.

Preoccupied, Wolfe didn't see Astrid coming out of Talk-Talk's door, and she nearly spilled her coffee over him. "Whoa," she said, laughing. "You almost got a third-degree burn on your chest." She licked the hot coffee off her fingers.

"Are you okay?"

"Yes, I play guitar." She showed him her fingertips. "I feel nothing."

Wolfe took a few minutes to talk with Astrid and brought her up-to-date on everything. Astrid was always interested in what he had to say. She'd been the only one who'd accepted him as their new director, no questions asked. She was an ally he could depend on. He took out a copy of his presentation. "If you have the time," he said, handing it over. "This is basically what I'm going to be discussing tomorrow morning. I'd love for you to look at it."

"Thanks," Astrid said, glancing over it. "I'll read this tonight. For sure." She seemed to want to say something else but was hesitant.

"Well, I'll catch you later," Wolfe said, moving back to the stairs.

"Listen, Wolfe, I have to tell you something." She set her coffee down beside the door and gave him a nervous smile. "And I hope you won't be angry or upset with me. I don't think you knew this, but I lived out west, in Vancouver, a few years back, and well, I still like to read the local Vancouver papers online. To keep in touch."

Wolfe wasn't sure where she was going with this, but he suddenly felt a little trapped.

"Two years ago, a girlfriend of mine sent me an article, and that article really had an impact on my life. It was about this young man, a social worker in East Hastings, who'd gotten beaten up by two guys. Men he'd helped many times before.... And I remember how disgusted and disillusioned that article had left me. Me and my friend talked about it all the time. She was afraid for me. But you know what, when I read about how the young man went straight back to work after his recovery, well, I felt like if *he* could go through that and still want to help, I had no more excuses."

She knew, then. She'd known about his assault all this time.

"So," she said, "when the board announced they'd found a new director here, a young guy from Vancouver, a man named Wolfe, I knew it had to be you. Because I remembered your name. How could anyone really forget a boy named Wolfe, right? Anyway, I just wanted to thank you, Wolfie. For giving me that incentive. That benchmark I use to measure my own strength."

"Who else knows?" He'd finally found his voice. "Did you say anything to—"

"Nobody knows, I promise." She squeezed his shoulder. "I never said anything. I didn't want you to know I'd recognized you. That's why I never told you I'd lived out west."

"Is that why you chose that particular group for me?"

"Yes, Wolfe, and I hope you don't hold it against me. I just thought maybe you needed some support."

He couldn't be angry with her for trying to reach out to him. She was conditioned to. It was her job to try. To always try. No matter how impossibly hard to reach a person was. "You were only doing your job," he said. "What they pay you for."

"Not that night. That night, I was being a friend. And I should have talked to you first."

Wolfe cracked a smile. "I came to the session, didn't I?"

"Yes, you did." Astrid smiled back. "Now, question is, will you come again?"

Could he go back to that room? Hear those horror stories again? Could he share his own nightmare with those people? "Maybe," Wolfe whispered. "I'll think about it."

Astrid seemed satisfied with his answer and left, heading down the stairs for lunch.

Still shocked at being discovered, Wolfe watched the door for a while. Why did the possibility of others finding out he'd been assaulted bother him so much?

Because the assault said something about him.

He'd been caught off guard that night. He'd misread the very people he was paid to understand. And by pressing charges against them, he'd put two young men in jail.

How did that *help* them?

Upstairs, Wolfe went to his office but Clare stopped him on the way. "Mackay is sick again, huh?"

"He is?"

"Yeah, he didn't come in this morning." Clare stared at him, waiting for his reaction. "Look, Wolfe, it's becoming a problem around here. I was talking with Dominic, and he says some of the volunteers have been complaining about Zach's uneven behavior."

"Well, Dominic should come to me." Wolfe tensed, stepping toward his office. "And I'll handle it. In the meantime, Clare, please consider where we work and who we're trying to help."

"You're the boss," she said. Her voice had an edge as she turned away. "But remember what they say. One bad apple can spoil the whole damn bunch."

Wolfe wanted to retort but stopped himself. He stepped into his office and fell into his chair.

What was he going to do about Zach?

Seconds later, Malena was in his door. "Hi, how did the meetings go?"

"Fine," he said, his tone a little cold. "Encouraging."

"Busy, huh?"

"Yes, sorry." He glanced up at her. "Everything okay?"

"Sure. Just wanted to say hello…. Um, so how was your weekend with my dad?"

"Look," he snapped, in spite of himself, "I'd really appreciated it if we didn't discuss your father at work. It makes me really uncomfortable." He tried to relax and be more patient with her. "What I mean is—"

"I know what you mean, and I won't ask you again."

"Hey," he said apologetically. "I'm just really tense this morning."

"Wolfe, it's okay. I should know better, and you're right. It's weird for both of us."

"But, if you *must* know, my weekend with your father was fantastic." He winked. "Okay?"

"Cool!" She laughed as she came in. "Because, I have to tell you, he's been walking with his head in the clouds since yesterday. This morning, I found the milk in the pantry and the cereal in the fridge."

"Interesting."

"Indeed." She looked over her shoulder into the hall, and in a moment, her whole countenance changed. Wolfe knew she'd spotted Zach coming down the hall. "Oh, I've gotta run, but listen," she said, already stepping out, "I'll see you after lunch." She bolted down the hallway.

Wolfe stared out at the hall, waiting for Zach to come to his office. When he hadn't a few minutes later, he picked up his phone and punched in Zach's extension.

"Yeah?" Zach answered. "What's up?"

"Come see me, please," Wolfe said sharply. "I wanna talk to you." He hung up and arranged the papers on his desk, trying to calm down.

Now was not the time to blow his lid. He'd have to tread lightly. Be wise about it.

A minute later, Zach was in his door. "What is it?" he asked, not looking directly at him. "I just got in."

"You just got in now? It's almost noon, Zach."

Zach was obviously high, leaning awkwardly and defiantly on the door. He pulled a note out of his jeans. "I got a doctor's note and—"

"I don't need your note." He searched Zach's face. "Look at me."

But Zach sniffed and looked over his shoulder, down the hall. "I gotta go back to work, Wolfie."

"Look at me." How could he feel so helpless? He was trained for this. Why couldn't he take charge of the situation? "Look at me, Zach," Wolfe said again, but his voice shook.

Zach finally glanced up at him. "What?" He coughed into his hand. "I'm sick, man. I got the flu. My head's pounding and I've got this—"

"Oh yeah?" Wolfe stood and slowly walked to Zach, then put his hand on Zach's forehead. "Lemme see—"

"Your hand is cold." Zach quickly leaned back from his touch. "Like the dead."

His hand was frozen because he was panicked. "I just wanna see if you have a fever."

"I did, but the doctor gave me something for that." Zach's eyes were glassy and a little red, but from drugs or illness, Wolfe couldn't tell. "I just came to the office for the meeting with Graffiti for Change, and then I'm going home again."

"Are you being fair with me?" Wolfe stepped closer to Zach. "Are you?"

Zach backed away into the hall. His walk was a little off. "I'm sick, but it's nothing to worry about. I'm gonna do this meeting thing and go crash at home."

Before Wolfe could say anything else, Malena walked up to Zach and said something into his ear. Zach followed her into her office and quickly shut the door behind them.

From her office, Clare called out to Wolfe. "What's going on with Mackay?" she asked. As usual, her door was open so she could keep an eye on everyone. She peered around her computer screen and looked at the end of the hall. "He's okay?"

"Yes, he's got the flu, that's all," Wolfe muttered. Deeply concerned, he went back to his office, and for the first time since he'd started at the YBR, shut his door.

PACING THE living room, Gaspard listened to Curtis on the line. They'd been talking for nearly half an hour—a new record for them—and Curtis had finally opened up to him about what he was going through in New Orleans. Curtis was angry with himself, ashamed of his naïveté, cursing loudly about how much he hated Cassie's guts, but Gaspard knew better.

His son was heartbroken and his ego badly bruised.

"I swear to God," Curtis said, his voice harder than Gaspard had ever heard it, "I'm gonna get my money back from her. Ten thousand dollars, Dad. Can you believe that cunt—"

"Hey, whoa, watch your language there, Curt. And it's not your money. It's mine."

"Yeah, but you gave it to me."

"For school and lodging and food."

"Are you serious? You're gonna do this? You're gonna climb on your high horse and give me a lecture?" Curtis scoffed. "I don't think you're in a position to give anybody a sermon about responsibilities."

Hurt, Gaspard stopped pacing and sat on the couch, looking out the window. The sun was setting, and he thought of Wolfe, of seeing him tonight. In that moment, though, his excitement was no match for whatever anger Curtis threw his way. "Are you coming home?"

"I don't know… I still have some options down here."

"Like what?"

"Like a job. And I like it here. What do I have in Montreal, anyway?"

"You don't have your papers. What if you get caught?"

"Yeah, well, Todd, my boss, he says he can probably get me a work permit or something like that. Or I can try and renew my student visa."

"So you wanna stay down there." No matter how terrible Curtis could make him feel, he missed him. He missed him so much. "Can you come up for Thanksgiving next month?"

"I don't think I can take that chance. I won't be able to get back into the States after that."

When would he see his son again? How long would Curtis punish him for something he hadn't seen all those years ago? "Your mom's so worried. So upset. And I'm not saying this to manipulate you—"

"I know. I was thinking of calling her. And I will. I'll call her this week." Curtis paused and seemed on the cusp of saying something important, but didn't.

"I love you," Gaspard whispered, feeling the immense space between them. "I miss you."

"So, um, you seeing people these days or what? You know, like dating, I mean."

Why was Curtis asking him this now?

"Why do you wanna know?"

"Just curious. No need to be so defensive."

"I'm getting to know someone, yes." It was such a battle just to be understood by Curtis. Not loved or accepted. Merely understood. Curtis was always reading between the lines, often misinterpreting Gaspard's intentions or meaning. "But I don't think you're ready to talk about this right now," Gaspard added, checking the time again. He didn't want to be late for Wolfe.

"How about I tell *you* when I'm ready to talk about something, huh?"

"What do you wanna know, exactly?"

"Are you still going through your phase or not?"

"My *phase*. You mean, am I still bisexual?"

"Can you not call yourself that?"

"Look, Curtis, the bottom line is that I'm sometimes attracted to women, but as I grow older, I find myself more attracted to men, so what do you want me to call this sexual fluidity?"

"I don't know, but you're either straight or you're not. If you're not straight, you're a fag, Dad. Do you know what I mean? There are guys who fuck other guys and those who don't—"

"If you use that word again, I'm hanging up."

"Fine."

Gaspard fiddled with the corner of a fashion magazine on the coffee table. "Listen, I have to go."

"You have to *go*? Where are you going?"

"Will you call your mother this week like you said?"

"Will you send me the money you promised me last week?"

Gaspard stood and looked around the living room. He needed to hang up now. Needed to get out of here. Needed Wolfe. "I was just waiting for a check to clear, but yeah, I'll send it."

"All right, thanks, Dad." Curtis was being smooth again. "I won't ask you for any more. I got the job and everything, so I should be okay for a while."

"Don't hesitate, if ever you're in a fix down there—"

"Yep. I'll call you soon." Curtis hung up.

For a moment, Gaspard thought he'd throw something or punch a wall. Hot rage coursed through him, but he swallowed it down and grabbed his keys off the mantel by the door.

As he drove through town on his way to Wolfe's, all he could do to keep from yelling was blast the radio and clutch the wheel. But once in a while, he wiped at his eyes as bitter tears clouded his vision.

Curtis was right to punish him. He'd let his son down in a way that could never be forgiven.

And he wasn't done paying for it.

WOLFE RETURNED from the kitchen with a bottle opener. He opened their beers and sat down next to Gaspard again. "So we both had a terrible day," he said quietly and took a long sip of his beer. He clicked his bottle to Gaspard's. "Cheers. I'm glad you're here."

Gaspard drank a little and set the bottle down on the table. He leaned his arm on the seat and rested his head in his hand, watching Wolfe. Wolfe looked fantastic in his casual navy blue T-shirt, and Gaspard caught the subtle scent of freshly washed clothes. Wolfe's scent drugged him. "I'm glad I'm here too," he said.

"I'm sorry things are so difficult between you and your son."

"Yeah, me too." Gaspard couldn't talk about Curtis with Wolfe without feeling immensely guilty. "Sure you don't want me to have a talk with Malena and ask her what's going on with Zach?" he asked, changing the topic.

"No, if Zach wants to tell me something, then he'll have to tell me directly. Same goes for your daughter. I don't wanna have to go through you or Malena."

"I know, and you're right." Gaspard had to agree. "So you're ready for tomorrow?"

"I don't know… I hope so."

"Do you wanna give it a practice shot?"

"Here? With you?"

"Yeah… I can give you some feedback on your presentation." He squeezed Wolfe's knee and leaned in closer. "Come on, show me what you got."

"Oh yeah?" Wolfe pressed his finger to his lips. "Come here, and I'll show you what I got." Slowly, he ran his hand down Gaspard's chest and stopped just below his belt. "Or maybe you could show *me*," he whispered, skimming Gaspard's crotch with his fingertip. The delicate caress shot panic and lust through Gaspard, and he fought to keep control. But Wolfe's touch was more pressing now, and his breath was hot in his ear. "Relax," Wolfe said, kissing and nibbling his earlobe. "It's okay… just kiss me."

He kissed Wolfe, feeling Wolfe's young body hardening under him, demanding more. Wolfe was breathing faster now, kissing his neck as his fingers worked Gaspard's shirt open, but Gaspard still didn't know what he was capable of and how far he could go. Why was he always stopping himself before he even began? Wolfe must have sensed his hesitancy, because he slowed down and looked into his eyes. "What? No? Too fast?" His hand was inside Gaspard's shirt but he froze. "Okay… I'm sorry," he said, slipping his fingers out and sitting up.

"Why did you stop?"

Wolfe was clearly a little frustrated. "Something changed in you—"

"Yeah, but you can't take your cues from me."

"Who else am I gonna take my cues from? The neighbor?"

"That's not what I meant." Gaspard looked down at himself and quickly fastened his shirt up. If he wasn't careful, all of this would end badly. He couldn't tease Wolfe this way. Couldn't stop and go forever.

"Look," Wolfe said, more softly, "it's okay. I just got a little carried away there."

"But I want you to get carried away. Maybe what I need is for you to get so carried away, you end up carrying me with you."

"So what you're saying is, you want me to basically assault you—"

"No, but just force it a little."

"I don't know if I'm the type. Never been very aggressive, let's put it that way."

"Oh, I think you are very much the type," Gaspard whispered, knowing it to be the truth. "You just need to trust your instincts, *Wolfe*."

They watched each other for a moment. "You're very handsome," Wolfe said after a while. "You must have been devastatingly attractive in your twenties. You know what's funny? If you were my age today, you'd be way out of my league. I probably wouldn't even have a chance with you."

"You were exactly my type. You still are." Gaspard leaned in to kiss Wolfe, daring to put his hand on Wolfe's thigh, but somewhere on the cluttered table, a phone rang.

Wolfe glanced down at the phone, and his face tensed. "Oh, that's for me."

"Zach?" Gaspard asked.

"No, my dad."

Gaspard instantly leaned away from Wolfe. "Oh… shit."

Again he thought of Curtis.

"It's not like my dad can see you." Wolfe was watching the phone ring. "Oh, damn it, I have to get it." He picked up the call at the last minute and answered. "Hi, Dad," he said, stiffening up.

All Gaspard knew about Wolfe's father was that he was in his late fifties, spent a lot of time on his sailboat and was a retired architect. He'd done very well for himself, obviously. Wolfe had grown up in Victoria, on Vancouver Island, in a house worth more than all of Gaspard's savings and life insurance. As a boy, Wolfe had attended private schools, and later, he'd been groomed to follow in his father's footsteps.

Gaspard could only imagine the poor man's reaction the day he'd realized his youngest son preferred serving soup to homeless junkies to playing a game of tennis at Daddy's country club. He had to feel for the man.

But as he watched Wolfe's expression, Gaspard began to worry. Wolfe wasn't saying much and kept fidgeting, obviously holding back angry tears. "I know that, Dad," Wolfe said in a small voice. He was very different than his usual self. He seemed so insecure. "I… I told her that—" But he stopped and listened, his face reddening. "Yes, sir. I know. But—" Wolfe couldn't get a word in. He stared at his knees, nodding.

Gaspard rubbed Wolfe's shoulder for comfort.

Wolfe didn't look at him. He was too immersed in whatever his father was saying. He nodded again. "I can't. I really can't. I wrote you and told you about the meeting—" But again, he was forced to stop, and Gaspard watched Wolfe's hands clench and unclench on his knees. "I can't," Wolfe tried again. "I really wish I could be there with you guys." He seemed almost in pain for a moment. He listened for a while and bit his lip. "Yes, sir," he muttered. "But, listen, I—"

Then, shocked, Wolfe moved the phone away from his ear and stared at it. He looked at Gaspard. "He hung up on me."

"Hey, look, if it's any consolation—"

"The bastard hung up on me." Wolfe tossed his phone on the table and sat there, shaking his head. "He's a fucking adolescent, that's what he is."

"He probably just wants you to be there. He must miss you—"

"Are you taking his side?" Wolfe shot him a hard look. "He doesn't miss me, okay? He just can't handle my mother crying all the time, and he needs me to go over there and give her what he can't and never could. Love. Support. Understanding. Some damn attention." Wolfe picked up his beer and drank. "Not like my brother Xander is gonna take a minute to comfort my mother. No, he's too busy covering up all of his cheating and gambling to have time for anything else."

"So what you're saying is your father recognizes you're the only one who has the generosity and emotional intelligence to help your grieving mother through this."

Wolfe looked at him, holding the bottle to his lips, clearly a little surprised.

"I mean, think about it," Gaspard said, hoping he wasn't stepping into quicksand. "In his own way, your father is admitting that you're a better man than he is. Than your brother, even."

"Maybe...." Wolfe put his bottle down and turned to face Gaspard. "But maybe I don't want him to think I'm a better man. Or stronger than they are. Maybe I just want him to—" But Wolfe stopped—lost, it seemed.

"Maybe you just want him to give you a little comfort sometimes."

At the sound of those words, Wolfe's eyes filled.

"Hey," Gaspard soothed, pulling him closer. "It's gonna be okay. He'll have to man up and take care of your mom." He stroked Wolfe's hair. "You're doing the right thing, Wolfe."

"You really think I'm doing the right thing?"

"Yes, I do. Doing the right thing is like breathing to you."

"You make me feel really safe. And yes, I know it's weird or whatever. I mean, here I am, in your arms, complaining about my dad.... Talk about needing therapy, right? But I don't care. I feel good right now, and that's what counts. I feel like you're the first man who's ever really understood me. Am I saying too much?" Wolfe looked up at him. "Am I freaking you out with this whole dad thing?"

"A little. But I can't really make myself care right now. I just know I don't wanna let you go."

"Then don't. Just stay here tonight." Wolfe played with Gaspard's watch. "Please."

"You work in the morning. You have your meeting."

"Say yes."

Gaspard laughed and kissed Wolfe's hair. "I never had the intention of saying anything else."

CHAPTER FOURTEEN

THEY SAT in the car parked in front of a large nondescript building just off Papineau Avenue. They were quiet, watching the wipers swipe the rain. After a while, Gaspard put his hand on Wolfe's hand. "Is the coffee finally kicking in?" he asked.

In the passenger seat, Wolfe was pale and exhausted, chewing his nail and tapping his foot. "Yeah, but now I'm wired." He hadn't slept all night, and Gaspard had slept fitfully, constantly aware of Wolfe tossing and turning next to him. At last, around five a.m., he'd opened his eyes to see him finally asleep. But the alarm had woken them an hour later.

"Hey, are you okay?" He squeezed Wolfe's cold fingers.

Wolfe looked over at him and gave him a quick and nervous nod. "It's time," he said. "Thanks for the ride and for putting up with me last night."

"Putting up with you?" Gaspard smiled as best he could. Wolfe's anxiety was getting to him too. He was feeling more and more nervous about this meeting. He wished he could go in there and tell those people just how lucky they were to have a man like Wolfe at the YBR. He wished he could grab that Jacques guy by the collar and shake him up a little. What was wrong with these jerks? Couldn't they see the miracle Wolfe was? "Look," Gaspard said, livening up in his seat. "You're prepared. You've got the knowledge. The experience. The vision." He leaned in closer. "You go in there and you don't back down. You gotta let them feel that." He touched Wolfe's chest. "That fire you have in there. That magic."

Wolfe was responsive and listening.

Gaspard took his face in his hands. "Okay? You understand? This is *your* fight. *You* call the shots."

"Yes," Wolfe whispered. "I'll do whatever it takes to keep that place open." He moved away and took a long and deep breath. "Whatever it takes," he said again.

Gaspard could feel the change in Wolfe. He had an energy he'd rarely encountered before. The fire was hardly contained in Wolfe's small body. Watching Wolfe now, Gaspard was turned on in a way he'd never experienced until now. He wanted to channel the power Wolfe gave off. Wanted to feel it inside him. Flustered, he leaned back in his seat. "You should go," he said, his voice not quite right. "Or you'll be late." Wolfe's eyes contained a hint of mischievousness. "You really bring out something in me," he said, flirting. "I don't know what it is, or how you do it, but it feels like a thousand lights flicking on inside me."

Gaspard couldn't believe his timing. All night, he'd had Wolfe close beside him and had done *nothing*, but here he was, in this car, parked on a busy street, turned on and ready to tear Wolfe's clothes off.

"Gaspard... did you hear me?"

"Yes, I'm sorry." Gaspard tried to cool down, but his body was on overload. He shifted in his seat to conceal the bulge in his jeans. "I'm glad you feel that way—"

"Hey, come here," Wolfe said gently, moving closer. "Give me a kiss before I go."

But Gaspard moved back a little. "No, Wolfe, don't kiss me."

"Why? No one can see us with all this rain."

"It's not that," Gaspard whispered, reaching for Wolfe's hand. Slowly, he brought it down over his crotch.

Wolfe locked eyes with him, his cheeks darkening. "Now, Gaspard?" he teased him, squeezing gently. "God, now I really don't wanna go in there."

"Hey, I'm old, but not *that* old." Gaspard was getting his bearings back. "It's not like this is my last hard-on."

"Wow, you said *hard-on*." Wolfe laughed and nudged his shoulder.

"I'm familiar with the word, yes." Gaspard needed to say something. "You know, when I'm with a woman, I'm not like this... I mean, I'm not—" He stopped, not quite sure why he needed to justify himself.

"*Bashful*." Wolfe finished his sentence for him. "That's what you're trying to say, right? And I know that. I guess I like the idea of you being nervous and awkward, but look, Gaspard, I know you've had sex before. You've probably had more sex than I have."

"I've had my wild nights, yes."

"With your wife?"

"Yeah, with my wife. Who else?"

"So you had amazing sex with a woman for almost thirty years, and now you're curious about guys and wanna see what it's like on the other side."

"What?"

"I don't know, I just wonder sometimes."

"Wonder about what?" Gaspard made an effort to keep his tone warm. "Hm?"

"You know, about why you're doing this. Why you're with me."

Wolfe was entitled to answers. "I don't know what to tell you right now," Gaspard said. "But what I feel for you is real. And I'm not curious about *all guys*, Wolfe. I'm curious about *you*. You see, I was monogamous for thirty years, and yes, with a woman, but I was also very attracted to men. Just never acted on those desires. It's not all black and white with me. Do you understand?"

Wolfe's eyes were warm again. "Yes, I understand. I really do. And I'm being immature." He checked the time on the radio clock. "Oh shit, I really have to go. For real."

"I know. *Go.* Hurry."

Wolfe hesitated. "You're not mad at me, are you?"

He rubbed Wolfe's hair. "Go. Call me later."

"Bye, Gaspard... I love—" But looking embarrassed, Wolfe opened the car door and then his umbrella. "I mean, I'd love to see you later." He leaned in a little, standing under the shelter of his dark umbrella. "Yes?"

"Yes, absolutely."

Wolfe shut the door, and Gaspard watched him dash for the building.

What if they gave Wolfe bad news in there? What if things didn't turn out the way he wanted? Wolfe had such high hopes. He was so young still. So eager to prove himself to the world.

"Good luck, baby boy," Gaspard whispered as Wolfe entered the building. "Hope they don't break your golden heart in there."

IN THE empty conference room, still dumbfounded, Wolfe took another sip of water.

His mouth was dry. His ears were still ringing.

He couldn't make himself move just yet.

"Are you okay?" Adele, the board's vice president, touched his shoulder. She'd come back to the room. "I forgot my purse," she said, walking away to the end of the long conference table. "I'm so forgetful these days." She circled around chairs, talking nervously. "I guess it's menopause, huh?" She laughed, but it was a nervous laugh, and as she hurried by him, Wolfe caught the look of remorse in her eyes. "I'll see you soon," she said. "And thanks for coming today. Again, great job on the presentation."

He nodded and watched her leave the room, glad to be alone again. Jacques and the rest of them had left ten minutes ago.

They'd left him here, vanquished.

Across the table, black rain lashed the wall-to-wall bay windows, and Wolfe made himself look away, down at the letter on the table.

How could he have agreed to this?

He'd come in with guns blazing, but they'd shot down every single one of his ideas. They'd barely given him enough time to finish his presentation.

There was no money left, Jacques had said. Not one penny. Forget about the shelter. The fight now was to keep the center open for another six months.

Wolfe had argued with them. Quite vehemently, too. He'd surprised himself today. He'd stood there, alone, with nothing to offer but his guts and heart. Jacques had been moved by his plight, and for a second, Wolfe had believed he was winning, but in the end, it hadn't mattered what he said or how he said it. When he'd realized he'd lost, he'd sat in his chair, resigned.

They couldn't lower the center's expenses any more than they already had—all agreed on that point. Even he did. No, there was only one solution left.

One of the highest salaries had to go.

Wolfe had known right then and there: they wouldn't ask for Astrid's head and couldn't touch Antonio. Megan was a promising employee on her way to a management position, and she had many contacts in the field. As for Clare, she, too, was untouchable.

It had come down to Malena or Zach. And the board had made their choice with no hesitation at all. Besides, as Jacques had explained, with all the days Zachary had been missing lately, it was clear Zach was in over his head and needed an opportunity to seek help again.

Wolfe slid a fingertip across the letter, over Zach's name.

Two weeks' pay and a letter for unemployment purposes.

He was to meet with Zach this afternoon.

"What the fuck have I done?" Wolfe whispered, staring at his signature on the bottom of the letter. But hadn't he promised everyone he'd do whatever it took to keep the YBR open?

Whatever it took.

And *this* was what needed to be done.

INSIDE HIS kitchen, Gaspard poured a little more coffee into his cup." I'm glad you finally talked to Curtis," he said to Meredith over the phone.

"Yeah, maybe we could all get together at Thanksgiving."

Meredith still believed in miracles.

But Gaspard knew that would never happen. "We'll have to see, okay?"

"Yeah, well, thanks for letting me dream a little, Gatsby."

"Malena said you two are going to have a coffee or something?" The doorbell rang and Gaspard stepped out of the kitchen. "Oh, hold on," he said, crossing the living room to the door. "My lunch is here."

"You ordered in, wow. You're definitely living it up these days."

Gaspard grabbed his wallet on the mantle and opened the door, expecting a deliveryman.

But instead, he found Wolfe on his doorstep. "Did I come at a bad time?" Wolfe asked, looking ill. "I thought maybe you'd be home."

Gaspard pulled him in and shut the door. "Merry," he said, "I gotta go—"

"Something wrong?" Meredith asked.

Wolfe collapsed onto the couch. Clearly things had not gone well this morning.

"My friend just showed up," Gaspard said.

"Oh, you have a friend there?"

"Look, I'll tell you about it later."

"A woman or a man? That's all I wanna know."

The bell rang again, and Gaspard opened the door and pushed money into the delivery boy's hand before grabbing his lunch. He shut the door again. "Does it matter?"

Wolfe dashed past him, stumbled into the washroom, and shut himself in.

"Merry, I really have to go—"

"It's a woman, isn't it? That's why you don't wanna tell me."

Gaspard dropped his lunch on the coffee table. "No, I'm not seeing a woman. All right? Can I hang up now?"

"Oh my God!" she cried happily, and to his surprise. "You've finally done it! What's his name? What's he like? Where did you meet him? What's he do?"

"Look, he's had a very bad morning and he's locked up in my bathroom right now. Can I go and see about him, please?"

"Oh... yes, sure."

"Thank you." Gaspard tried to be patient. "I'll call you later."

"Wait, wait, one last thing. Is he cute?"

"Leave me alone." Smiling, Gaspard hung up. He tossed his phone on the couch and went straight to the bathroom door. He knocked gently. "You okay in there?"

"No." Wolfe's voice was close to the door. "I'm fucking *not okay*."

"Open the door." Gaspard tried the handle. "Come on."

"No, I'm too ashamed."

"Why, what'd you do to my bathroom?" Gaspard hoped he could make Wolfe laugh.

But Wolfe was quiet and slid something under the door. "Read that."

Gaspard looked down at the paper and picked it up. It was a job-termination letter. For Zachary Mackay. He understood immediately. "Wolfe... I'm so sorry—"

"That's why they hired a guy from Vancouver," Wolfe said, still not opening the door. "Someone outside Montreal. A guy with no ties here. No loyalties. Some young guy they could manipulate easily. A puppet, Gaspard. That's what I was, all this time." Wolfe hit the door, causing Gaspard to jump back. "A fucking puppet! I'm the cleaner! The guy who does their dirty work!"

"Baby. Just open the door."

Wolfe finally cracked the door open. "I worked so hard," he said, on the edge of tears. "You know? I believed I was doing something. That I was *building* something. That my work counted. But all this time—"

"Hey. Hey." Gaspard grabbed his hands. "Everything you did counts. Nothing you did was in vain. I saw it with my own two eyes, Wolfe—"

"I have to fire him, do you understand? *I* have to fire Zach. *Me.* His friend. What do you think this is gonna do to him?"

"I don't know," Gaspard whispered. "And I'm sorry."

"I never saw this coming. Just like that night. I never saw it coming, and I stepped right into it. I just stepped right into it."

Gaspard put his arms around Wolfe. "It's not you. It's them. Do you understand? And it's not that you're too trusting, baby, it's that people aren't trustworthy."

"No, I should have told them to go fuck themselves." Wolfe looked up at him, searching his face for an answer. "Do you think it's okay to take something from a man in order to give to many more?"

"Yes… I do believe in sacrificing one life for the greater good, if you wanna put it that way."

"See, I never did believe in that concept." Wolfe leaned back, shaking his head. "That whole idea of one life to save a thousand. I think every life is equal and worth saving."

"Yeah, well, live another twenty years, and you might see it differently."

Wolfe locked eyes with him, and for a moment, Gaspard thought they were going to have their first fight. But Wolfe looked away. "They say the biggest cynics were once the most fervent idealists. Is that what life does to us? Wears us down until we just give up and stop trying to make a change and start trying to make a living instead?"

"You inspire me."

"Do I?"

"Yes."

Wolfe pressed his hand to Gaspard's chest. "You know, you were the first face I wanted to see, after I came out of that awful meeting."

Gaspard touched Wolfe's face. "You're so beautiful," he whispered, his heart racing. "So good, and I never thought I'd fall this hard again."

Their kiss was like a wildfire.

He wanted Wolfe. Had to have him.

Roughly, Gaspard tore at Wolfe's tie and then started on his shirt. Wolfe wanted this too. He could feel him losing control. Wolfe licked into his mouth, jerking Gaspard's belt and pants open.

"Bedroom," Gaspard managed to say, pushing Wolfe's shirt down his shoulders and arms. Wolfe's skin made him crazy, and he gripped Wolfe's thighs, then lifted him up and off the ground, knocking him up against the wall. Wolfe pulled his hair, wrapping his legs around his waist, groaning his name in his ear. Charged with desire, Gaspard half carried him to the bedroom.

They fell back on the bed, and Wolfe slipped his hot hand into Gaspard's open pants. "You won't stop me, will you?" he whispered.

Gaspard reached down and slowly unfastened Wolfe's belt. "No," he said, bending his mouth to Wolfe's. "And this time, I won't stop myself, either."

CHAPTER FIFTEEN

WHEN GASPARD pulled up in front of the YBR center, Wolfe felt sick. He rolled down his window, and the cool morning wind helped a little.

With nervous hands, he unfastened his seat belt and turned to look at Gaspard's face. In spite of what awaited him this afternoon, Wolfe smiled.

"What?" Gaspard asked, smiling back. Gaspard's hair was a little messy and his shirt wasn't properly buttoned. He'd skipped a few buttons in a hurry to get here.

"Just thinking what they say is true. Older men *are* better lovers."

Gaspard looked away, grinning devilishly.

"Well," Wolfe said, leaning in closer for a kiss. "I gotta go."

"You're gonna be okay?"

"I don't know how he's gonna take it. I have no idea. I don't know how anybody is gonna take this." His anxiety was back in full force. "Not even Malena."

"Let me worry about her."

It was coming on two p.m. He needed to go back to work. Wolfe popped the car door open and looked out at the building. "Maybe he'll understand," he said. "Who knows? We're friends."

"Yes, and that's what scares me. His reaction might be more emotional because of the nature of your relationship."

"Try not to worry too much... I'll call you." He kissed Gaspard's lips and climbed out of the car. When they'd made plans for the evening and said good-bye, Wolfe shut the door and watched Gaspard drive off. Then he faced the YBR and fixed his jacket and tie. Clutching his briefcase, he entered and stared up at the long, narrow staircase.

He began his climb, but on the second floor, something made him stop. He glanced over at the door and without thinking walked into Talk-Talk's lobby. He looked around for Astrid but couldn't spot her. She was probably in the back room with a group.

"Hey, boss," she said, coming out of her office. "I was just gonna call to ask how the meeting went."

Her friendly face made him want to burst into tears, but Wolfe showed nothing. "I need to talk to you, Astrid. If you have a minute."

"Yeah, sure," she muttered, looking down the hall. "Come into my office. They don't expect me for a few more minutes."

Once inside, Wolfe gestured for her to sit down and pulled a chair up close to hers. They sat face-to-face, their knees almost touching. "I'm gonna fire Zach this afternoon," he said, looking into her eyes.

"Is that what they want? What were your choices? Was I one of them?"

"No."

"Megan, does she stay?"

He nodded, looking away at the window behind her.

"Why Zach?"

"For all the obvious reasons." Wolfe glanced back at her. "The shelter is staying closed."

"I see." She took her glasses off and rubbed her eyes. "All right, okay. What else?"

"I hate myself."

She slipped her glasses on again, putting her hand on his. "Look, we all knew these personnel cuts were coming. Eric knew it. Yvan knew it—"

"You guys knew I was just here to clean—"

"No, Wolfe, that's not what I—"

"Why didn't you say anything to me? Why did you lead me on to believe I was part of the solution?"

"Because I didn't know how it would all play out, okay? Nobody really knew. Well, maybe the old-timers did, but I had faith. I still have faith. Do you?"

"Yes, but right now, I have to go upstairs and tell Zach today is his last day at the YBR."

"You should have asked Jacques or Adele to do it."

"No," Wolfe said, standing. "I wanted to be the one." He turned for the door. "I don't want Adele or Jacques telling him he's not welcome here anymore."

"Look, Wolfe, for what it's worth, you're the best director we've ever had. And it's really a pleasure working for you."

Wolfe stopped and looked over his shoulder at her. "Thank you, but I don't think I'm gonna be very popular in a few minutes."

Upstairs, he found an empty lobby. Tuesdays were quiet. Everyone was in their office.

How would he do this?

Malena was coming down the hall. "That must have been quite a meeting you had. What's going on?"

"I'll... I'll tell you all about it later." Could he count on her support? Would she quit on him this afternoon? "Is Zach in?"

"Yeah, he's in his office."

"Alone?"

"Yeah, why?"

Wolfe walked away without answering her. Zach's door was half-open, and he paused, looking in.

Zach was at his desk, typing on his computer, but soon glanced up. "Wolfie," he said, smirking. "Well, well."

He couldn't do this.

He couldn't do this to Zach.

Zach frowned. "Bad news this morning? Are they coming in with the wrecking ball?"

"Zach... I need to talk to you." Wolfe shut the door behind him and sat on the other side of Zach's desk, leaning in. "There's no money left, Zach. The shelter's not gonna reopen—"

"Oh, Wolfie, I'm sor—"

"No, please. Don't say you're sorry." Wolfe ran both hands down his face. "They need to cut down on the salaries." He took a sharp breath and looked Zach deep in the eye. "Do you understand?"

Slowly, Zach's face grew pale. "Okay," he said, quietly. "You're firing me."

Wolfe had to look away. "Yes. Yes, I am."

Zach rose and threw a set of keys on the desk. He opened a drawer and took out a pack of cigarettes, a paperback, and his silver lighter. He shut the drawer and walked over to the window. He grabbed two pots.

"Zach—"

"Say one more word to me." Zach shot him a look so full of hatred and anger, it left Wolfe mute. "One more fucking word and I swear...." He sniffed. "You owe me two weeks' pay."

"Yes," Wolfe muttered, his face burning up. He rummaged through his briefcase for that letter. "I have this for you to—"

"Give." Zach tore it out of his fingers, and in the process, cut Wolfe's finger with the corner of the paper. Wolfe brought his finger to his mouth and tasted blood.

"There." Zach dropped the flowerpots on his desk, sending dirt flying all over, and furiously signed his name on the line. He pushed the form into Wolfe's chest. "Fuck you and good-bye." But he frowned when he noticed Wolfe's mouth. "You have blood on your mouth—"

"I... I just cut myself with the paper."

Zach looked down at the form. "I cut you?"

"It's fine. I'm fine." Wolfe sucked on his finger for a second. "It's just a stupid paper cut."

"Let me see." Roughly, Zach grabbed Wolfe's hand and forced it up, staring at the blood on Wolfe's fingertip.

"I'm fine, Zach," Wolfe whispered, seeing the pain and anguish on Zach's face. He couldn't take it. "I'm sorry," he blurted, reaching out for Zach's shoulder. At his touch, Zach seem to come apart and allowed Wolfe to slide his hand around his neck. Wolfe pulled him closer and hugged him. "You know I didn't wanna do this—"

"Fuck off, Wolfie." Zach pulled back, tumbling backward to the door. "Honestly, go fuck yourself."

"Damn it, Zach!" Wolfe bolted out of his chair and into the hall.

But Zach spun around, standing taut and defiant in the lobby. His voice carried through the whole floor. "You'll never see my fucking face again. I swear to God."

"*What's going on?*" Malena yelled, stepping out of her office.

"Wolfe just fired me." Zach turned to look at her with fierce eyes. "Just now. I gotta go."

"You fired him?" Malena's face was red with anger and emotion. "What's your problem? How can you fire him when I've been here much less—"

"It wasn't my choice, Malena."

"Ah!" Zach mocked him. "Weak words. Your *choice*. We always have a *choice*." He laughed and stepped back, looking at Malena.

And Wolfe knew she was going to take off with him. "Malena, listen," he said carefully, "you've got a good thing here and—"

"Malena." Zach reached out to her. "He's the one who has a *good thing* here with you. He's fucking your dad, and he doesn't want you to leave—"

"Who are you?" Wolfe stepped closer to Zach. "This is not like you at all. What are you on?"

"Malena, are you coming or staying?" Zach moved back, cocking his head, watching her with a terrible gleam in his eye. He quickly turned away and was out the door and down the stairs before she could even answer.

She turned to Wolfe. "I can't let him leave alone," she whispered. "He needs me." She looked back at her open office door and then at Wolfe, panicked. "I can't just—"

"Go," Wolfe said, spent and confused.

"You won't fire me, right?"

He shook his head. "No… just take care of him." He struck off for his office, passing a few people who stood in open doors with shocked expressions. "And call your father!" he shouted before slamming the door in everyone's face.

CHAPTER SIXTEEN

THE YBR was a very different place in the evening when everyone had gone.

Inside its silent walls, Gaspard could feel the remains of what had happened here today. Climbing up the stairs to the third floor, he thought of Zach, and what it must have been like for him to walk out the front door, knowing he could never come back here again.

Marooned and exiled from a place whose very motto was *Welcome to all*.

But though Gaspard felt terrible for Zach, he couldn't forgive him for taking Malena with him this afternoon. She'd called him up in tears an hour ago, confused and upset, and Gaspard had convinced her to come home. He'd fixed her a cup of tea and tried talking some sense into her, but she'd been too emotional to hear him out and had shut herself up in her bedroom.

She'd been asleep when Gaspard had left for the YBR.

Upstairs, he found Wolfe alone in his office.

Wolfe stood by the window, staring out at something. Very aware of the tension in the room, Gaspard approached him carefully and put his hand on Wolfe's shoulder. "What are you looking at?" he whispered, then kissed Wolfe's earlobe.

"See that tree there?" Wolfe didn't look at him or respond to his touch. "It just stands there and takes it. The wind. The rain. The cold. The sun. And do you know why?" Wolfe glanced over at him. "Because it doesn't have a *choice*. It's a stupid tree." He smiled bitterly. "Zach was right. We always have a choice. And I could have saved his job, but maybe I didn't want to."

"Maybe." Gaspard stepped back and leaned on the desk. "But it was still the right choice."

Wolfe turned to look at him. He was clearly exhausted and miserable. "You just hate him because Malena took off with him."

"I don't *hate* anyone, Wolfe," Gaspard said in a hard voice. "All right?"

"No, of course not." Wolfe looked back at the window. "Because you're perfect," he grumbled.

Gaspard couldn't let Wolfe get away with that last remark. "Yeah," he replied. "I'm perfect. So perfect, I have a son who won't talk to me because the very idea of me disgusts him, and maybe he's got a point there, and I have a daughter who's so lost, she thinks love means complete and utter self-abnegation, and not to mention my wonderful career, right? My career has taken the kind of nosedive you only see on shows like *Caught on Camera*."

Wolfe was trying not to laugh.

"Yeah?" Gaspard raised a brow. "Funny?"

"Not funny," Wolfe whispered, coming closer. "Not funny at all." He leaned his head on Gaspard's chest. "I'm sorry."

"Yeah, well, I'll make it through." He put his nose in Wolfe's hair. "And so will you."

"Yes, I know." Wolfe stepped back and seemed to reconnect with his surroundings. "Anyway, I did a lot of damage control today, and people get it. I think some of them, Clare and her colleagues especially, are relieved. Question is, who's gonna take over all of Zach's projects."

It was time Wolfe understood what was really going on. The board was dismantling the YBR, and nothing less. They'd do it slowly, piece by piece, in hopes of distracting the staff from their final and lethal move: shutting down the center.

It was only a question of time before Wolfe would be out of a job.

How could he bring Wolfe to see that?

Wolfe looked over Gaspard's shoulder. "Hey," he said to someone behind him, "I didn't even know you were still in the building."

Gaspard turned to see a heavyset man with friendly brown eyes standing at Wolfe's office door. "Didn't know you had someone here," the man said, taking a small step back.

"No, it's okay." Wolfe gestured for him to come in. "Please, come in, Antonio." He looked at Gaspard and smiled a little nervously. "Gaspard, this is Antonio. He runs the CPLHIV."

Antonio immediately offered him his hand. "Hi there."

"This is Gaspard," Wolfe said, and cleared his throat. "My... my boyfriend."

Antonio was clearly shocked. His face darkened a little. "Oh, I didn't know you had a boyfriend."

"How was your day?" Wolfe asked Antonio, changing the subject.

"Um, it was... well, it was probably better than yours, I bet." Antonio stepped a little closer to the desk. "I just came up here to see how you were doing." He glanced over at Gaspard. "But I see that you're okay."

"It's been a rough day," Gaspard said. "It's nice that you came up to see about him."

Antonio squinted. "Do I know you? I feel like I know you from somewhere."

Wolfe fiddled with some papers on his desk but didn't say anything.

Gaspard decided to be blunt and honest. "You've met my daughter. She works here. Malena."

"You're Malena's father?" Antonio looked him up and down. "No way. That's impossible. Unless you had her at nine years old." He chuckled and looked back at Wolfe, serious again. "Look, Wolfe," he said, his tone changing. "I gotta tell you something, all right? Yesterday, a man came in, a young guy I've seen a few times already, and well, come to find, he's Zach's friend. Not exactly a friend, mind you, but more like an old lover. He still sees Zach once in a while."

"What did you find out?"

"A lot of things. Things I don't like." Antonio pulled a chair out. "You wanna sit down?" They sat around Wolfe's desk, and in a quiet voice, Antonio told them what he knew. Gaspard listened with an open mind, but the more Antonio talked, the more trouble he had keeping his hands from clenching on his knees. Antonio had found out that, while Zach had resisted heroin up until now, he'd been drinking cold syrup like water, taking codeine, Vicodin, Percocet, Oxycontin, whatever painkillers he could get his hands on in order to keep his body in control, and then perking up on "black beauties"—a mix of amphetamine and dextroamphetamine and liters of black coffee—which explained his uneven behavior. His mood swings were less and less easy to hide. He was two months behind on rent and hadn't seen his doctor for months. For Antonio, the most alarming news in all this was that Zach was off his antiretroviral drugs.

Gaspard stared down at his shoes. What had Malena gotten herself into? No, what had *he* gotten his daughter into? He'd let her get closer and closer to Zach and never really put his foot down with her. Why?

Because he was afraid to. Because he still felt ashamed of his choices. Of his lifestyle. Of his identity. And he'd preferred not confronting her than hearing what she really thought of her queer father but was too considerate to say.

Hearing Antonio recount Zach's last turbulent months, Gaspard realized just how irresponsible he'd been with his two kids. He'd said he trusted them, but trust wasn't what they needed from him. It was a guiding hand. *Strength.* They were both lost and looking for love in all the wrong places. He'd been too busy with his own self-discovery to see his kids were being led astray in their own.

"What do I do?" Wolfe was pale and shaken by Antonio's words. "Tell me."

Gaspard thought of Malena. Of everything that could and *would* go wrong if he didn't intervene soon.

Antonio touched Wolfe's hand. "You've been doing this long enough to know what the score is. He needs to get back into recovery."

"I gave him a chance. And then I took that very chance away from him." Wolfe remembered the first time they'd met. Zach had walked into his office for an interview, and from the moment he'd looked into Zach's dark and clever eyes, he'd felt drawn to him. He'd wanted to give Zach the opportunity to bounce back. To make a real contribution. He recalled how nervous Zach had been, but as the interview had progressed, they'd talked more freely, and Zach had relaxed. He'd even shown Wolfe his drawings, telling him about his dream to help people through his art. Zach had seemed a perfect addition to the YBR staff.

If only Zach had believed in himself a little more. He had so much to offer the world.

"You're wrong, Wolfe. Zach just wasn't ready for that chance yet, but that doesn't mean he won't be." Antonio turned to look at Gaspard. "Hey, are you all right?"

Without thinking, Gaspard stood and stepped toward the door. "I have to go home. I have to talk to Malena.... Now." He stared into Wolfe's eyes. "Okay?"

"I'm coming with you."

"No." Gaspard's instincts told him Malena had gone to Zach this evening. She wouldn't be home. Yet if he showed up there unannounced, he knew Malena would think he was being unreasonable and he'd lose his chance at trying to talk some sense into her tonight. "I have to do this alone, Wolfe. I have to get Malena on the phone, talk to her, and hope she'll come home on her own." Gaspard took another step to the door. "Baby, please, okay?"

Wolfe searched his face, clearly worried.

"I'll call you," Gaspard said, turning away and heading for the stairs. "I promise."

"Let him go," he heard Antonio say somewhere behind him. "Let him do what he's got to do."

WOLFE STARED down at the empty stairs, but Antonio pulled him back again. "Come on," he said into Wolfe's ear. "Let him go see about his daughter."

"I brought chaos into Gaspard's life," Wolfe said. "As if he needed more complications."

"Hey, chaos can be nice."

"Not this kind." Wolfe looked down at the stairs again. "He's such an amazing man, Antonio. You have no idea." He looked back at Antonio. "He's devoted and warm. And just so honest. I've never met anyone quite like him."

"How long have you two been together?"

"Not very long."

Not long enough to say the words he was dying to say to Gaspard.

"Is he married?"

"Divorced. Two kids. And his son is my age."

Antonio whistled. "That's tough right there."

"And I think I'm Gaspard's first... male lover."

"Really?"

"Never thought I'd be anyone's first *anything*."

"Shit. He sure took his time."

Wolfe had to see about Gaspard. "Can you close up for me tonight?"

"You're gonna follow him, even after he asked you not—"

"Yes, Antonio. Yes, I will. Because it's what I do. Because it's in my nature to chase, all right?"

Antonio grabbed his shoulder. "Then go get him."

AT GASPARD'S front door, Wolfe knocked and waited.

What was he doing here?

What if Gaspard asked him to leave and never come back?

Gaspard opened the door. The first thing Wolfe noticed was his eyes. They were a little swollen. Had he been crying? He couldn't imagine Gaspard coming undone enough to shed tears. Gaspard was always so calm and grounded.

"Hey," Wolfe said softly, daring to come closer. "I couldn't stay away."

Gaspard was guarded, barely opening the door wide enough to show himself. "You shouldn't have come here," he said.

Wolfe knew he was blushing. "I know that," he muttered.

"Look, I just got off the phone with my ex-wife, and it was pretty horrible. She can't understand how I could let Malena get into this dangerous relationship, and she's got a point—"

"Malena? Is she here? Have you heard from her?"

Gaspard wouldn't look at him. He was so closed off. Caged in his fears. "She's staying at Zach's tonight. I couldn't change her mind. I couldn't make her see. She's with him, doing God knows what."

"Listen, I know where Zach lives, and we could go there right now—"

"No, she told me if I showed up there, she'd be furious. She's not a baby anymore. I can't just go over there and drag her out." Gaspard sighed. "Just go home, Wolfe. Please. I need to be alone."

"But, Gaspard," he tried weakly, "I think we should talk—"

"No, go home. I'll call you later." Gaspard shut the door in his face.

Shocked, Wolfe stepped down to the path and looked back at the closed door. How could Gaspard shut him out this way? He fastened his jacket against the cool September wind and gazed down the street. It was endless and bleak. He walked fast, against the wind.

"Wait," Gaspard said, touching his arm. He was out of breath. Wolfe turned to him. "Oh, please, wait. I shut you out because that's what I do. I've done it all my life." He slid his hand down Wolfe's arm. "But I can't do it anymore, you know? I can't do it anymore because I'm breaking down, Wolfe. Piece by piece. Like that damn center you work in. And I'm so scared, okay? I don't know how to hold it all together."

"You don't have to hold it all together."

"Yes, I do. I'm their father—"

"You're their father, Gaspard, but you're also my lover. And I'm not gonna let you do this alone." Wolfe could see the boy in Gaspard's face. The setting sun erased the passage of time in his features. Gaspard's blue eyes were incredible in this light. "You're more than just one thing," Wolfe whispered. "You're a thousand different men, Gaspard, and I—" But he couldn't say those three words just yet. Not here. Not on a sidewalk. "Can we go back inside?"

"Yeah, but listen, the apartment, it's a bit of a mess." Gaspard scratched his head, looking embarrassed. "I don't know what got into me. I just went wild. I couldn't stop myself."

"You broke things?"

"Yes."

"Then, let me give you a hand, okay? I'm good at that. Cleaning up messes. You could say that's what I do in so many ways." Wolfe winked and was relieved to see Gaspard's sexy smile finally making an appearance. They headed back to the apartment, and inside, Wolfe assessed the damage. He slipped his jacket off and rolled up his sleeves. Gaspard had apparently thrown shoes and umbrellas across the living room and knocked down plants by the window. Soil and leaves were everywhere. He'd overturned a chair and broken a wineglass. "I've seen worse," Wolfe said, looking around with his hands on his hips. "My ex-boyfriend once threw my dog against the wall."

Gaspard was crouched by the window, cleaning up, but stopped to look up at him. "Your *dog*?"

"Yeah, my dog." Wolfe remembered that terrible evening. Sawyer had accused him of sleeping with a mutual friend of theirs and gone into a rage. He'd yelled, cursed, and thrown things, but nothing had satisfied him.

Until his hands had landed on Wolfe's dog.

"Did he kill him?"

"No... I don't know why I brought that up." Wolfe shook the memory off. The dog had survived. He'd survived too. "Come on, let's get this place cleaned up and have some dinner or something."

"He threw your dog against the wall."

"Yeah."

"You never talk about him. Your ex."

"There's nothing to say." Wolfe sighed. "I was young. I was trying to impress my parents with my mature and posh boyfriend. Funny thing is, they still miss him. They loved the guy. He made me miserable and ruined my life for years, but they still ask about him."

"Parents can be idiots." Gaspard looked around the living room. "I don't know why I did all this."

"You're under a lot of pressure." Wolfe put his hand on Gaspard's shoulder. Then he bent down and helped him gather up the broken pieces of a pot.

"What if she sleeps with him tonight?" Gaspard didn't look at him when he spoke those words.

"Look, it might happen, but I'm sure Malena would know to be safe."

"Would she? In the heat of the moment, would she?"

Wolfe thought about it. "I don't know about Malena, but I do know Zach would never, and I mean *never*, risk her health." He was sure of it. He'd overlooked certain details about Zach in the last months, but he did know the man's heart, Wolfe realized. "You can trust him. As strange as that may sound."

Gaspard looked over at him. "Thank you for coming tonight."

"I had to know you were all right."

"You're always thinking of other people," Gaspard said, taking his hand. "Do you ever think of yourself?"

Wolfe looked down at the mess around them and summoned his courage. He needed to speak what was in his heart. "Gaspard," he said quietly. "I don't know if you've noticed, but I'm falling for you pretty fast here. Do you know what I mean?" He didn't wait for a reply. "And I can fight it if you want me to. I can be reasonable and sensible about this, but it would be so extraordinary if I could just let go." He dared to look at Gaspard's face. "If I could just free-fall and not be scared of where I'm gonna land."

Gaspard's features tensed. "I know, that would be great," he said, and nothing else.

That was not the answer Wolfe had been hoping for. "We need a bag for this," he said, standing, needing to get away for a moment. "Kitchen?"

"Yeah, under the sink, by the garbage can." Gaspard's cheeks were red and he avoided Wolfe's eyes. "Thanks."

In the kitchen, Wolfe poured himself a glass of tap water and made himself drink. Obviously he'd jumped the gun on this one. Gaspard wasn't ready to hear the words Wolfe was aching to say. Gaspard was freshly divorced after all. Just spreading his wings. Why couldn't he have been more patient and careful? Did he really have to open his big mouth tonight?

Wolfe grabbed the garbage bags from under the sink and went back to the living room.

Gaspard stood and took the bag from him. "Thanks," he said, his tone uneasy. "Why don't you sit down and relax. I can do this. It's my mess anyway."

"Sure, why not." A wave of coolness moved over Wolfe. His heart seemed to shrink back into his chest. He gave Gaspard a cold look and sat on the couch. He took out his phone and clicked into his e-mail. He couldn't help himself, couldn't let Gaspard see just how lost he felt.

Gaspard busied himself with cleaning up, but he seemed just as lost.

Too proud to say anything, Wolfe typed into his phone, hating every minute of silence passing between them.

GASPARD SAT at the edge of his bed, staring at the half-open bedroom door.

It was 2:00 a.m. and he couldn't sleep.

How could he rest knowing his daughter was out there with a man on the brink of self-destruction?

Behind him, Wolfe stirred and mumbled in his sleep, and Gaspard turned to look at him. In the darkness, he could see the pale outline of

Wolfe's naked shoulder. Gaspard felt a surge of love so great, it hurt him in a place he couldn't even name or reach. He wanted to touch Wolfe, whisper words in his ear. But he looked away instead, back at the sliver of light he could see between the door and the wall. That opening taunted him.

Wolfe was that half-open door slowly closing himself off to him.

Carefully, Gaspard rose and walked out of the bedroom.

What was he going to do about Wolfe? How could he be falling in love again so soon with a man half his age? Was this real, or some kind of midlife crisis?

At the living room window, Gaspard stood looking out at the street. What would he tell Meredith when the time came? And Wolfe's parents? What would they think of their baby boy dating an old software engineer with more of his life behind him than ahead of him? What could he offer that young man in his bedroom?

"Gaspard? What are you doing?" Wolfe was standing in the hall, dressed in boxer briefs and one of Gaspard's T-shirts, which was too big for him. "Are you out here torturing yourself?"

Gaspard smiled sadly. "Yes...."

"Why don't you come back to bed? You can torture yourself in there just the same." Wolfe turned and walked back to the bedroom.

Gaspard couldn't resist following. In the bedroom, he climbed into bed and turned on his side, facing Wolfe. The words came easily, or maybe he just couldn't fight them anymore. "I know I hurt you before, when I didn't say anything after you opened your heart to—"

"No, don't worry about—"

"Wolfe, wait, let me finish." He moved closer, until he could feel Wolfe's breath in his hair. "I guess I'm still shocked at how much of my life was buried before you. I feel like, every day, I dig up something new. And it just keeps getting deeper and deeper, and it's not supposed to be that way. I mean, I should know all of this by now."

"Know what?" Wolfe's voice was soft. "Are you talking about your sexual identity?"

"No, I'm talking about... I'm talking about falling in love, Wolfe."

Wolfe seemed to stop breathing. His face was still on the pillow.

"I don't know if I should be saying these things to you." With a fingertip, Gaspard touched Wolfe's mouth. "Is it right to say these words?"

"I don't know. You haven't said anything."

"I thought I had."

"Not quite."

Gaspard leaned into Wolfe's ear. "Okay, then, I'm gonna say it now," he whispered.

"Say it." Wolfe laughed quietly into his shoulder. "Say it, I'm dying here."

Gaspard pressed his mouth to Wolfe's ear. "I love you," he said, the sound of his own words rocking through him.

CHAPTER SEVENTEEN

IN THE shower, Wolfe quickly rinsed the shampoo out of his hair and turned the water off. He was going to be late if he didn't hurry up. He grabbed one of Gaspard's towels from the rack and wiped down the mirror, looking at his reflection, catching the gleam in his eye.

Gaspard had finally given him everything last night.

"Wolfe, baby, you better get a move on," Gaspard said, close to the door. "It's almost eight."

"Yeah, I'm getting dressed." Wolfe looked around for his clothes. He'd forgotten them in the bedroom. "Gaspard, can you get—" But he stopped, listening.

Gaspard was talking to someone. Seconds later, Wolfe heard Malena's voice. She sounded upset.

Gaspard knocked on the bathroom door. "I have your clothes."

Wolfe cracked the door open. "Malena's here?"

"Yeah, in the living room." Gaspard was a little pale. "Get dressed, please." He walked away.

Anxious, Wolfe dressed, and ran a hand through his wet hair. He looked back at the door. This was a complicated situation, but not an impossible one.

He could do this. He could help Gaspard get through this.

He stepped out and walked straight into the living room. "Good morning," he said to Malena. She sat close to Gaspard, holding his hand. Her hair was undone, falling over her red-rimmed eyes.

"Hey, Wolfie," she said in a weak voice. "You look nice." She looked at her father. "I'm so sorry, Dad," she blurted out.

"No, it's okay. It's okay. I'm just so glad you're here. I was so worried about you."

"I know. But I was caught up in the moment and I just couldn't leave Zach last night." She met Wolfe's eyes. "He's so sorry, Wolfe. So embarrassed. You don't know how ashamed he is of how he acted and what he said to you."

Wolfe fell back into the armchair at the side of the sofa. Since yesterday afternoon, he'd been trying not to think of Zach's dark eyes, but now he realized how much he cared about him, and how intensely he needed Zach in his life. He missed him already.

"He didn't mean to lie to you," Malena said. "He was only trying not to disappoint you. You gave him a job and your trust, and Zach worships the ground you walk on."

"I'm not worth his admiration. I fired him. My job was to stand up for him. To get him help."

"He wouldn't have taken it," Malena insisted. "He told me. Not from you. Not from anybody there. He knew his days were numbered at the YBR. He doesn't blame you."

"What's he gonna do now?" Gaspard asked. "Did he tell you? Because he can't keep seeing you if he's gonna be falling off a cliff."

"You know, I don't appreciate the way you've been acting lately. Zach is going through so much right now and I'm just trying to be there for him. Didn't you teach me that, Dad?"

"Okay, okay, maybe I haven't been handling all this very well, but you know I'm a worrier, and Zach is a recovering addict with—"

"But he's my *friend*, Dad."

"It feels like he's more than that."

"We don't have a sexual relationship, if that's what worries you." Her tone was agitated. "It's completely platonic. Dad, he's barely functioning right now. Sex is the last thing on his mind."

"Why him, huh? Of all the guys in the world, why Zach? Why couldn't you get close to Cory, the way you are with Zach?"

"Because I'm not interested in people like Cory." She looked at Wolfe for approval. "You understand what I mean, don't you?"

Wolfe didn't want to agree with her, but he understood perfectly. He locked eyes with Gaspard again, trying to read him.

"I get that you like the people who walk close to the edge," Gaspard said. "I get that. But it seems that with the years, they just keep getting closer and closer to that edge, and I don't know if it's because you're trying to prove something to yourself or—"

"It's not that they're so close to the edge, Dad. It's that you're further and further away from it."

Wolfe saw Gaspard's jawline tense. Malena had clearly offended him. But though he wanted to come to Gaspard's rescue, he decided not to intervene.

"Yeah, maybe I do play it safe," Gaspard said at last. "Maybe I've always played it *too* safe. But you weren't there the night I heard my sister was dead. You never met your aunt, but Gisele was just like you. Passionate. Empathic. Especially keen on saving people. She used to say she was a magnet for loners and the marginalized. And she was. She loved life so much.... And sometimes I think it's the lust she had for life that caused death to come down on her with a vengeance."

"I'd never do something to put my life at risk," Malena said softly.

"That's what she thought."

Wolfe had to say something. "After your sister passed away, you were all your parents had left. That must have put a lot of pressure on you."

Gaspard looked at him and tilted his head. "Yes, you're probably right.... I was seventeen when Gisele died. But that year, I put all childish things aside and became a man overnight."

"Dad, you've always done everything for everyone. When are you gonna start thinking of yourself for a change?"

"Funny," Wolfe said. "Your father was asking me that same question last night."

Malena took Gaspard's hand in hers. "Look," she said, "I promise I'll be nothing but careful, and you promise me that you'll—" But a phone was ringing.

"Is that mine?"

"No," Gaspard said, taking his phone out. "It's me." He looked at the phone, and his mouth opened.

"What? Who is it?"

"It's your brother." Gaspard stood and walked away, going into the bedroom. He didn't look back at Wolfe.

Wolfe watched him leave, feeling a little nervous.

"My brother calls a lot," Malena said. "He's kind of in trouble down in New Orleans."

Wolfe glanced over at the bedroom door. "Your dad told me." He looked back at Malena. "So is Zach gonna get help? Is he going back to rehab?"

"Not right now. But he will. He will. He doesn't want an intervention, okay? He just needs a few more days." She leaned in a little "He has feelings for you, you know? Intense ones."

"He told you this?"

"Oh, Wolfe, last night, he cried himself to sleep."

"I never wanted to lead him on or for him to fall for—"

"I gotta go," Gaspard said, coming out of the bedroom. He went straight to the entrance closet and grabbed his jacket. "Malena, you're gonna go to work with Wolfe, okay?"

Wolfe jumped out of his chair and walked up to Gaspard. "What's going on?"

"I gotta go, baby." Gaspard looked over Wolfe's shoulder at Malena. "Your brother's at the airport."

"Airport?" Wolfe searched Gaspard's face. What was happening here?

Malena was on her feet in an instant. "You mean here, in Montreal?"

Gaspard zipped his jacket up. "Yeah. Look, Malena," he said, opening the door. "Something happened down there, and he wouldn't tell me what, but it sounded pretty bad and I gotta go get—"

"I'll come with you," she said.

Wolfe took a step toward Gaspard. "So will I."

"No." Gaspard held his hand up. "You two just go to work, and I'll take care of this." He walked out the door.

Wolfe stood in the entrance, watching Gaspard run down to his car.

"Oh shit," Malena said, coming to him. "My brother's back."

Wolfe turned to look at her. "He just… he just left. Just like that. Just grabbed his jacket and left."

"Oh, I'm sorry, Wolfe, but my dad gets like that when it comes to my brother." She sighed. "It's like the whole world just disappears and all he sees is Curtis. Been that way since we were kids."

Wolfe still couldn't believe how quickly Gaspard had left. "What's he like, your brother?" he asked, aware of how insecure he sounded.

"Curtis? Well, hm, let's see, he's tall, blond like my dad, and has the same blue eyes, except his are—"

"No, no, I mean, what's he like? Laid-back? Open-minded?"

"Curtis? Hell no. He's uptight, moody, and definitely not open-minded."

Wolfe blew out a hard breath. "In other words, I'm screwed."

"DAD, I'M walking out of the terminal right now." Curtis said over the phone. "Where are you parked?"

"I'm in the parking lot. First floor. Just next to the pay booth. Look, let me come to—"

"No, no, I'll be right there. Just stay in the car. You still have the Jetta, right?"

"Yeah." The line went dead and Gaspard hung up. Feeling guilty, he thought of Wolfe. He'd left him in such a hurry, without even saying good-bye. But Wolfe would understand. He had to understand.

Gaspard drummed his fingers on the wheel, jumping every time someone walked by his car. Minutes passed, and he waited, sitting there with his heart beating in his ears, wondering what was to come after this.

Someone knocked on the passenger window, and Gaspard turned to see his son leaning close to the glass. Cuts and bruises covered Curtis's face.

Curtis opened the door and climbed in. "Hey," he said, a little breathlessly. "Thanks for coming to—"

"What happened to you?" Gaspard grabbed Curtis's chin and turned Curtis's face to his, looking him over. "Your eye. Your lip—"

"Dad, Dad, please." Curtis pulled away and jerked his seat belt over his shoulder. "I'm fine. Just got banged up a little." He shot Gaspard a quick look. "Can we go?"

Gaspard stared at Curtis's face, overcome with relief. He was here. He was finally here. In one piece. Bruised, but alive and well. "You're different," he said, taking in the details of his son's features. Curtis was the most beautiful thing he'd ever made. Those piercing blue eyes could cut ice. "You've grown up since I last saw you."

"And you look younger or something." Curtis sniffed and looked away at the dashboard. "Can we go?"

Gaspard started the car. "Do you wanna grab some breakfast, and maybe you can tell me why you left New Orleans in the middle of the night and who beat you up? Was it the husband?" Out of the corner of his eye, Gaspard saw his son's expression darken. "Hey, listen, I know you went through—"

"Dad, I'm hurting real bad right now." He turned his face to the window a little more. "I just don't wanna talk."

"Your face hurts?"

Curtis shook his head, biting into his lip, and for a moment, he was his little boy again. "No, Dad, not my face."

Gaspard couldn't help putting his hand over Curtis's. "Okay, I won't say another word."

"I fucked up, Dad."

"It's all right, we'll fix it. I'll fix it." He squeezed Curtis's fingers. "You're home, that's all that matters now. I don't care what you did. I really don't."

"I don't know what I'm gonna do. I don't even have a place to stay."

"Don't worry about that." Gaspard drove out of the parking lot into the bright light of day. Again, he thought of Wolfe. "You can stay with me and Malena for a while."

"Yeah?"

"Of course. It'll be like the old days."

"Except Mom won't be there. Did you tell her I was in Montreal?"

"I didn't have time. You can tell her later, after breakfast. I'm sure she'll be thrilled to know you're back."

"Yeah… right. Anyway, do you have a room for me at your place?"

"I do. We have an office-type room I can turn into a bedroom for you."

"I don't wanna put you out or anything, but thanks. That would be cool. Just for a little bit."

"You can stay as long as you like." Gaspard glanced over. "Okay?"

Curtis nodded, playing it down. "What about your boyfriend?" he asked out of the blue. "The guy you're seeing."

"Who told you I was seeing someone?"

"Malena."

"Oh, I didn't know you two were talking about me."

"We do. We talk about you all the time. And your little secret slipped out during one of our late-night talks."

Gaspard waited for more, his stomach tightening.

"He's her boss, right? She said he's pretty young too. So what's that about?"

"Look, I don't know what your sister told you, but we're not seeing each other. We're just friends." The lie burned his tongue. It choked him. But he couldn't stop himself.

"So you're *not* having sex with a guy my age?"

Gaspard fought back the nausea. "No," he said, chuckling. "No, absolutely not."

Curtis relaxed, cracking a smile. "She was probably just trying to get a reaction out of me—"

"Probably." He cast Curtis a nervous glance. "It sure worked, huh?"

"Well, I didn't really believe it. I mean, you're not a pervert."

Gaspard struggled to keep his face from showing the shame he felt. He'd betrayed Wolfe.

"Hey, can we go to that place we used to go, the one in the Mile End?"

"Sure," Gaspard said, his voice sounding foreign to him. "We can go wherever you want." He stared at the brake lights on the car ahead of him, thinking of the things he'd done to Wolfe last night. Of the words he'd whispered in his ear.

Words he shouldn't have said so soon.

CHAPTER EIGHTEEN

WOLFE TAPED the box up and set it by the door. That was the last of Zach's things.

He looked around at Zach's white and vacant office, and its bare walls reminded him of everything he'd lost in the last three weeks.

He was hemorrhaging, and no one could even see it.

"I'll bring this down to the van," Malena said, picking up the box and a pile of rolled-up posters. "Thanks for lending me the van, by the way. I promise to bring it back in perfect shape."

"That piece of garbage?" Wolfe said. "After you're done with it, you can push it into the Saint-Laurent River, for all I care."

"Hey, you just said 'Saint-Laurent.'" She winked at him in the door. "You didn't say 'Saint-Lawrence,' like you used to. You're turning into a real Montrealer, Wolfie. Careful there."

He tried to laugh but didn't have it in him.

Malena stepped back into the lobby. She was obviously concerned for him. "I'll call you later, all right?"

Wolfe shut the light off in the office but stayed in the door. "Hey," he called out to Malena before she'd made it to the stairs. "I'd like to see him before he leaves tonight." Zach was checking into the Pennington Treatment Center this evening, of his own volition. It had taken him three weeks to make the commitment, but he was doing it tonight. Wolfe had tried to reach him, but Zach wouldn't return his calls.

"He doesn't want you to see him the way he is now. Look, you're sort of like his motivation. He has it in his head to go in there, get clean again, come knocking on your door, and then you two—" She stopped.

"We walk into the sunset together," Wolfe said without a trace of sarcasm. Maybe he should have gone for Zach instead of Gaspard. At least he had a chance with Zach. But he wasn't in love with Zach. Gaspard was the one he was dying for every night. Every minute of the day.

"Wolfe, Zach knows it's not gonna happen, okay? He knows you don't feel the same way about him, and it's just this thing he does to keep himself motivated. You're like his magic talisman or something."

"Yes, well, tell him I miss him." Wolfe crossed his arms around himself, holding everything back. "Tell him I believe in him. That I know he'll kick it for good this time."

Malena watched him for a moment. She seemed hesitant to speak. "Listen, Wolfe, my dad's been so miserable and I want you to know that—"

"Don't." The pain ripped through him again. "Please. Don't say anything."

"If you knew just how much he's hurting—"

"Malena, I can't. I have work to do. I have to... I have to concentrate."

"I'm sorry," she whispered and turned away. "So sorry about you two." Seconds later, she was gone.

Wolfe made himself move. Made himself take that first step to his office. For the last three weeks, he'd been in survival mode, trying to make it through the day without breaking down. He barely slept. Couldn't eat. Nothing made sense anymore.

In his office, he sat behind his desk and stared at his computer for a while. What was that thing he'd told himself not to forget this morning? He couldn't remember now. He picked up the Graffiti for Change file on his desk and opened it. He read the correspondence between Zach and Michael, Zach's contact there, but nothing stuck. The letters formed words, which in turn formed sentences, but the sentences then vanished somewhere inside his exhausted brain, never to be remembered or understood.

"Hey, can I talk to you for a second?" Antonio stood in his doorway. "It's important."

With a hand gesture, Wolfe asked him in and waited until Antonio had sat down. "What is it?" he asked, not really caring one way or the other.

"I don't know how to tell you this, but by the looks of you, I'm not sure you give a shit anymore." Antonio leaned in closer to the desk. "What's wrong?"

"Nothing."

"Wolfe, I know you're taking all this pretty badly, but you'll find the right place. I have no worries about your career—"

"What is it you need to tell me?" His career. What career? He'd invested a year of his life in this place. And for what?

Antonio stared at him with kind eyes. "You've got all this pressure on you, and sometimes I forget you're just a kid—"

"I'm not a *kid*." That word. He couldn't hear it one more time. "I haven't been a *kid* for a long time."

"No, I know, but you're so young still, and this place is old and set in its ways. And it's dying, you know that." Antonio's voice wavered and he looked away at the window behind Wolfe. "I've been here for fifteen years. Can you believe that? And now they're gonna turn this old place into something new. Give it a facelift. Seems like that's all they ever do with aging buildings in this city." He looked back at Wolfe.

And Wolfe frowned, hoping to hide just how painful all this was. He loved this building. It was like a home to him, but a real-estate promoter had made the board an offer they just couldn't refuse. The YBR would be renovated and turned into condos. Wolfe's opinion had been heard, but dismissed. Astrid and the girls were relocating next month to a community center just off the Atwater metro. The support line would be merging with another hotline in the coming weeks. Yvan's program had been canned. The place was being torn down from the inside, bit by bit, and he spent his days making phone calls and writing e-mails, arranging the closing of the very center he'd been asked to save.

Antonio fidgeted in his seat. "We're leaving, Wolfie," he said. "The committee and the Blue Bird Foundation. We're gonna be working out of the AIDS Foundation offices for a while, you know, until we find ourselves a new home. We should be out of here by the end of the month."

Wolfe put his own sorrows aside for a moment. "I'm sorry I couldn't deliver," he said quietly. "I really thought we'd make it through—"

"No, please. Please don't do that to yourself. You did everything you could. I know that. Astrid knows it too. And so does Clare."

"What pisses me off the most isn't losing my job," Wolfe said, sitting up in his chair, feeling that old familiar heat burning slowly in his chest. "It's the fact that we're all being scattered across the city, and that the people who need us the most won't be able to access us the same way they used to." They were a team, all of them, and should have been kept together, under one roof. But what was that to the board? To the city? To the government?

"You can still make a difference," Antonio said. "Astrid says you're thinking of going back to Vancouver? Why, Wolfe? There's still so much left for you to do here—"

"No, I have nothing here."

"What about your boyfriend?"

"I don't have a boyfriend." Wolfe had to look away. He wasn't going to come undone in front of Antonio. "He dumped me three weeks ago. It's over."

"Oh shit, I had no idea. I don't understand, you two seemed so—"

"Antonio, I can't talk about this."

Antonio stood. "Look, Wolfe, I know you don't wanna hear this from me right now, but I'm gonna say it anyway. In my line of work, I see a lot of injustice and a lot of pain, and I see guys your age having to come to terms with shit they shouldn't be thinking of at twenty-five. So, listen to me: You've got your health. You're as cute as they come, and you've got a solid head on your shoulders. Bottom line? You've got more than most people do. It's your responsibility to be grateful for it and spread the love."

Wolfe had never enjoyed sermons, but Antonio had a right to lecture him. The man had sat by too many hospital beds to let him get away with self-pity. "I know.... It's just so much all at once."

"Sometimes life hits us with a wrecking ball, and leaves us with this giant hole, but when all is said and done, we end up with a lot more room to build something new." Antonio stepped back to the door. "I know how much a broken heart hurts. And I'm sorry, Wolfie. I really am. It's too bad. There was something about the way he looked at you that made me think you guys had something special."

Those words were too much for him. Wolfe quickly picked up some papers on his desk and shuffled them. "I need to get back to work," he muttered.

Without another word, Antonio left.

Alone again, Wolfe dropped the papers on his desk and put his face in his hands. What was he going to do now? Run back to

Vancouver with his tail between his legs? Go back to Daddy and Mommy? Admit they were right?

"God," he moaned. "What are you so fucking scared of, Gaspard?" He sat back in his chair and slipped his hand inside his pocket, feeling the letter there.

No, he wouldn't read it again.

Every time he read that awful letter, it hurt him more than the time before.

But he couldn't resist taking it out. It was all he had left. This one-page letter that Gaspard had left in his mailbox three weeks ago.

Carefully, Wolfe unfolded the paper and read Gaspard's words.

Dear Wolfe,
Letters are life in slow motion....
And I wanted this good-bye to be as slow as I could make it.

I wish I was twenty-five years old again. I wish I could get in my car right now and take you for a road trip across the country. I wish we could discover things together. The world around us. Ourselves.

I've done all the discovering I can handle. Every new turn terrifies me now. I thought I had it in me to start again. Throw away the map. Rewrite a different route. But I don't, Wolfe. I don't have it in me to shake everything up. I'm a coward, I know.

I know it, Wolfe. I know it.

But that's no consolation to you, now is it, my love? No, it isn't.

Your light burns, baby. It's a slow and wonderful burn, and I'll miss it.

I'll miss it more than I can say here. Even to myself.

I made choices a long time ago. Choices I can't undo now. My son found out about us and has made it clear to me: he'll throw me out of his life if I choose to continue seeing you. Whatever grandchildren I may have, he told me, I'll never see.

Wolfe, in ten years, I'll be sixty years old. You'll be thirty-five.

I can't imagine a life trying to hold on to you.
No, that's a lie.
I wish I could hold on to you until my last breath,
but that's a fantasy, and one I'll have to lock up inside,
with every other lost dream I've ever dreamed.
How do I end this letter?
With this.
I end it with this.
Baby boy, know this, and please know it forever....
You have been loved, wholly and completely.
Gaspard

Chapter Nineteen

DASHING ACROSS the street, Wolfe skipped over a puddle of rain and quickly entered the coffeehouse. Inside, he shook his umbrella, looking around for Astrid.

She was sitting at a table by the window, and upon seeing him, jumped out of her seat. "Oh, Wolfe," she said, moving to him, then hugging him tightly, "I'm so happy we're finally meeting outside of work." She leaned back and looked at him. "It's nice to see you."

It was nice to see her too. Of all the YBR staff, Astrid was the one person he'd missed the most. Her and Zach. "How you been?" he asked, sitting down across from her.

They hadn't seen each other in over a month, since Talk-Talk had moved out of the building to their new western location.

"Me, well, I've been all right," she said. "It's different where we are now. We share the space with a lot more groups, but I guess, in some way, it also helps to network, and I've been busier than ever."

"And how's Malena?" He hadn't spoken to Malena since she'd left the YBR, choosing to follow Megan and Astrid to their new location.

"Oh, she's good. Her project is taking form, and I'm helping her with that."

"Zach? How's he doing?"

"Still in treatment." Astrid touched his hand over the table. "But I heard he's sticking it out like a pro. So, um, Clare and her staff left last week?"

Wolfe looked down at the menu. Was it too early for liquor in his coffee? "Everyone's gone," he said, thinking of the YBR's long, empty halls.

"You're alone in there? When are you leaving? Or do you intend on staying until the construction crew shows up?"

He glanced up and forced a smile. "I'm leaving on Monday, actually."

"Tell me you got some kind of salary compensation. They're giving you something, right?"

"They've been fair," Wolfe said. "I'll be fine, don't worry."

"Look, you know Nancy was absolutely serious about her job offer, and so am I. There's an opening in the training program at the Open-Hands Center—"

"I'm not staying in Montreal."

Before Astrid could say anything else, a waitress was at their table. She took their orders and left.

They sat in silence for a moment. "So," Astrid finally said, "you're really leaving? Why?"

The waitress set their cups down on the table and left again, and as she did, Wolfe stared out the window for a while, watching people scurry out of the rain into shops and restaurants.

He'd agonized over his decision in the last weeks, but he couldn't find a reason to stay here anymore. His mother had begged him to come home and swore his father was willing to change his point of view on social work, if that meant having him back again. Xander had even called him, to Wolfe's surprise. His brother wanted Wolfe to consider a job with his advertising firm, as an intern. Xander believed Wolfe needed to get "a taste of success and rise to a position worth his status." After all, his brother had argued, being around poor, helpless, and troubled people could take its toll on a man, and wasn't it time for him to step up and out of the dirt for a change?

"I guess I need to go home and see about my life," Wolfe said, answering Astrid's question. "Maybe I took a wrong turn somewhere."

Or fell in love with the wrong man.

Astrid watched him closely, stirring her coffee. "Malena told me about Gaspard and you," she said softly. "And I'm sorry. I think you two should have—"

"I really don't wanna talk about it."

"But it seems to me that you need to."

He couldn't tell his mother the real reason why he was so downhearted. He couldn't talk to his brother about it, either. He hadn't been able to reveal the true motive behind his decision to come home, not even to his old friends. Especially not them. They were all young and hitting the clubs on weekends, looking for the perfect male specimen to add to their long list of conquests. They'd never understand why he was in love with a man twice his age.

"You know what's disgusting," Wolfe couldn't help saying. "I judge him for not being able to stand up to his family, but yet, when my friends back home asked if I was seeing someone, I didn't have the guts to tell them about Gaspard."

"Well, I don't know what that says about your so-called friends."

"They wouldn't understand. They're twenty-five years old. They're kids—" But Wolfe stopped himself, realizing just how ridiculous he was. "Look, I don't blame him. I don't blame myself. And I don't blame anyone who doesn't understand. I just miss him. I miss him like crazy."

"Has he called you?"

"No, he believes he's doing the right thing."

"Do you think he is?"

"Doing the right thing?" Wolfe sighed and drank some of his coffee. "It's true that in ten years he'll be sixty and I'll be thirty-five. It's not like I haven't thought of that. But right now, in this moment, all I want… is him."

"Then why are you leaving? Why not stay and fight a little?"

"Because that's all I've been doing in the last year. Fighting. Or chasing something. Someone. I don't wanna have to convince him we have what it takes to make it. I don't wanna have to make an argument for our love."

"You're just gonna give up, then."

A surge of anger went through him. "He gave up on us when he put that letter in my mailbox."

Astrid looked away at the window.

"What?" Wolfe was annoyed. "Say it. It's obvious you wanna say something."

"No offense, but you sound just like a little boy not getting what he wants."

"Well, maybe I am a fucking kid like everybody says." He pushed his cup and crossed his arms, leaning back in his chair. "So what? Maybe I'm tired of trying to be reasonable all the time. Maybe I want what I want when I want it, for a damn change."

"And what do you want?"

The answer shot out of him like a bullet. "I want him to go to bed wondering how he'll make it through another night without me. I want him to walk down the street and look for my face in the crowd. I want him to hear my voice everywhere he goes. I want him to miss me so bad, he starts thinking he'll go crazy, and then I want him to come *get* me. I want him to choose *me* over everything else. That's what I want. It's selfish and despicable, but it's the truth and it's all I have."

"Is that all?" Astrid smirked.

"Yes, that's it." Wolfe looked down at the dessert menu. "That and a caramel sundae."

Chapter Twenty

On Sunday evening, Wolfe stood at his kitchen window, watching the small courtyard darkening under the cover of dusk. He was thinking of tomorrow.

His last day at the YBR.

Tomorrow, he'd be inside that old building for the last time.

It had fallen apart so fast.

He'd been a fool to believe in happy endings. Being an idealist didn't pay well these days. He'd be better off in his new job, in downtown Vancouver. The job required nothing of him but to show up and handle his case load. Paperwork and meetings, that's all he had to look forward to.

No challenge. No defeat.

He'd be home in two weeks. His mother had already moved her sewing machine out of his old bedroom. He was to stay with his parents until he found a place.

Stay with his parents. In that house he'd yearned to escape the minute he'd hit puberty.

The doorbell rang, and Wolfe spun around, looking at the front door.

Could it be Gaspard?

With his heart speeding, Wolfe went to the door and checked the peephole. "Oh my God," he breathed. "Finally."

It was Zach.

Quickly, Wolfe opened the door and found Zach standing there, smiling brightly. "Hey," Zach said, chewing gum. "Am I disturbing you?"

Wolfe couldn't believe how great Zach looked. His eyes were fierce and clear, and his face had filled in a little. "You look so amazing," he whispered, grabbing Zach's arm to pull him in. "Get in here."

Zach laughed and ran a hand through his hair. "Yeah? You think?"

Wolfe shut the door. "How do you feel?"

Zach opened his hands, grinning. "I feel pretty fucking good, actually." He winked. "You know, *clean*."

"Do I get a hug or what?"

"I don't know... maybe." Zach laughed, throwing his head back. Then he moved closer. "Come here, Wolfie."

"I'm so proud of you," Wolfe said. "Zach, you amaze me."

"Thank you," Zach whispered, his voice sinking a little.

Wolfe made himself pull away from Zach's arms. He was lonely. Yearning for affection. Zach's body felt too good.

Zach moved back, looking down at the couch. "Can I sit down?"

"Yes, please. Do you want anything to drink? Coffee or—"

"I'm off the caffeine for a while." Zach gestured for him to sit. "I'm good, just sit down here a minute." He waited until Wolfe had settled in next to him and looked him straight in the eye. "I came here 'cause I wanna make amends with you. And it's not just 'cause it's part of the program, but 'cause I wanna do it. All right?"

"You don't have to—"

"Wolfe, I'm sorry I lied to you the whole time I was working with you. And I'm sorry I messed around with your head sometimes. But most of all, Wolfie, I'm sorry if I sort of fucked things up between you and Malena's dad. That wasn't right of me, dragging her into it, but I gotta tell you, I love the girl, and I'm not sure what that means yet." Zach smiled a little nervously, scratching his temple. "I mean, I don't know if I'm bi or what, but I do have feelings for her, and we just don't know what we're gonna do about it. But that's not what I wanna say. What I wanna say is I know I muddled everything, and I'm here to say I'm sorry for that."

"You're not the only one who's sorry. I made a lot of mistakes with you, and I should have been much more vigilant and supportive."

"All right, whatever, so we're cool?"

"Yeah, we're cool."

"Now what's this bullshit about you moving to Vancouver?"

"Who told you?"

"Nancy, at rehab. Is it true? You're gonna leave us?"

Wolfe squeezed Zach's hand. "It's just something I need to do."

Zach looked around, his eyes clouding. "You do what you gotta do. But I'm gonna miss you."

"You know I care about you, don't you?"

"I know that, Wolfe, okay? You and me, maybe we could have had something, but I'm not the man for you. You're everything that's right with the world. You're the solution. The balm over the wound. And if I was gonna fall in love with a guy, well, I'm glad it was with you. Now, I want you to go to Vancouver, do what you do best, and forget about ol' Zach here."

"No."

"Listen to me," Zach said, taking his face in his hands. "I want you to be the one that got away.... Do you understand? I want you to be that guy I never had."

"Promise me you'll take care of yourself," Wolfe finally said. It was over. Everything done. "Promise me you'll stay the course. That you'll make it to a hundred years old and write your memoir."

Zach smiled a little. "Shit, who knows."

"Give me a kiss good-bye."

But Zach turned away, walking to the door. "I'll kiss you in my dreams," he said, winking. But his wink was just a front.

"Bye, Wolfe. I'll see you around." He opened the door and stood there for a moment.

"Be good to Malena," Wolfe said, thinking of Gaspard. "For me. For Gaspard."

"And you, you be brave, Wolfie."

"Will I hear from you?"

"Through the grapevine."

"You're something else, Zach Mackay. I'm glad I hired you that day."

"You and me will never find a place like that again. It was like going home."

Wolfe stepped up and kissed Zach's mouth. "Under all that tin, you've got a whole lot of heart," he whispered.

Zach gave him a sexy grin. "Now, listen to me, Wolfie boy, you better click those heels of yours and get out of this crazy town."

CHAPTER TWENTY-ONE

REVIEWING HIS notes on the new client he'd met today, Gaspard sat in his car, listening to the radio. He was parked at the end of the street, and once in a while, he anxiously glanced up at the YBR's doors.

He could see the building from here, but his car was far enough down the street to remain inconspicuous.

Gaspard checked the time again. It was coming on seven p.m. Wolfe would be out any minute now. In the last month, Wolfe had started leaving work earlier and earlier, and he'd had to adjust his schedule in order to catch Wolfe coming out of the building.

There had been a few close calls. Last week, Gaspard had sworn Wolfe had finally noticed him, but he'd been mistaken. Wolfe rarely turned his head in his direction. No, every evening, Wolfe would step out of the building, quickly climb down the steps, and set out for his home without looking in either direction. Gaspard would wait until Wolfe had reached the end of the street, and then, when he felt it was safe enough, he'd drive off and slowly follow Wolfe home. He never drove right up to his door but got close enough to make sure Wolfe made it into his apartment without incident.

It was absolutely unacceptable behavior.

He was stalking him.

But Gaspard couldn't make himself care.

On the passenger seat, his phone vibrated, and he looked over at it, seeing Curtis's number flashing. What did he want now? "Hello," Gaspard answered, turning down the radio.

"Hey, Dad, listen, I'm out the door right now, but I was wondering if I could take the hundred-dollar bill in the pot and—"

"That's for the cleaning service tomorrow."

"No, I know, but I'm not getting paid until Thursday, and me and Chloe are going out." Curtis lowered his voice. "Look, Dad, I promised her we'd go see a movie—"

"A movie? That's an expensive movie you're seeing."

"You know what? Never mind."

Distracted, Gaspard checked the YBR doors again. "Take it, it's all right."

"Thanks." Curtis was quiet for a moment. "So, how are things going with your new contract?"

Gaspard had told the kids he had a new client who only allowed him access to his network from six to eight p.m. and demanded he be on site. "We're making progress," he said uneasily. "You and Chloe, it's serious?"

"I'm crazy about her, actually."

Curtis had met Chloe two weeks ago. Before that, he'd been *crazy* about Eliza. Curtis hadn't been popular with the girls in high school, but he was definitely making up for lost time now.

"I'll see you later, Dad," Curtis said. "Thanks for the little gift."

Curtis would never use the word *money* when it came down to asking Gaspard for cash. Everything was a *gift, donation, advance, loan,* but never actual money. "You're welcome," Gaspard said, trying not to sound too short. "Have a good night. Don't forget you work tomorrow morning."

"Yeah, yeah, I know. Bye, Dad."

Curtis had found a job as a sales coordinator, but the salary was low, and with the debts he'd accumulated in the last year, he still depended on Gaspard's help. Meredith had offered to take Curtis in, but Curtis was too smart to move in with his mother. Why would he? He had a good thing going with Gaspard. Gaspard knew he was being manipulated, but every time he summoned the nerve to confront Curtis, he'd look into those cool blue eyes and see all of his own shortcomings and failures. How could he ask Curtis anything, after what Curtis had gone through all those years ago? And right under his nose.

Gaspard raised his eyes to the YBR again and caught sight of Wolfe stepping out the front doors. As usual, Wolfe didn't look in his direction, but only straight ahead. He climbed down the steps, and Gaspard got ready to follow.

But tonight, Wolfe stopped and stood in front of the building, looking up at it.

While Malena had kept him up-to-date on the closing of the center, Gaspard still wasn't certain what day it would close its doors for good. Looking at Wolfe now, he suddenly knew. "Oh, baby," he whispered. How could he let Wolfe do this alone? With his heart in a vise, Gaspard watched Wolfe saying his last good-bye to the YBR.

Then slowly, as if he'd sensed someone watching him, Wolfe turned his head in Gaspard's direction.

Panicked, Gaspard immediately leaned back in his seat, but Wolfe tilted his head, searching the end of the street.

Gaspard waited for his next move.

Within seconds, Wolfe had struck off in his direction. He came right up to his car and paused, looking at him through the windshield. "What are you doing here?"

Gaspard stepped out of the car and up on the sidewalk but stayed a safe distance from Wolfe. "I could lie to you, but I'm not going to. I've been following you home, Wolfe."

"What?"

"Yeah… every night. I just wanted to make sure you were all right—"

"That I was *all right*?" Wolfe's smile was bitter as he looked away. "I don't understand—"

"I know, I know it's crazy—"

"Gaspard, you can't do that. I mean, you dumped me, remember? So, no, I'm not *all right*, and following me home won't fix me." Wolfe studied him. "Every night? You've done this every night?"

"Yeah."

"I never saw you."

"You never looked my way."

Wolfe sighed. "How are you?" he asked in a gentle voice.

The question felt like a slap. How was he? "I'm all right," Gaspard whispered, lying.

Wolfe bit his lip. "Glad to hear it."

"Was today your last day?" Gaspard didn't know what to say anymore. He couldn't think. Or even breathe.

"Yes, and I'm moving back to Vancouver."

"What?" He felt the blood drain from his face. "No, what?"

"In two weeks, actually. I got a job there."

"Wolfe, no, what are you say—"

"What? You thought I'd stick around here and wallow in self-pity?"

"What are you doing? Why are you going back so soon? I thought—"

"You thought you had time to make up your mind."

He did. He'd convinced himself that he'd slowly work things out with Curtis and Meredith, and then, when everything was smooth again, he'd call Wolfe and announce he was ready to begin.

Ready to start their love.

"I took it for granted that you'd stay," Gaspard said, his legs feeling a little shaky. He leaned back on the driver's-side door. "My God," he breathed, staring at the ground. "What have I done?" He looked up at Wolfe and held out his hand to him. "I'm sorry. I'm so sor—"

"I know, Gaspard, I know. I'm not angry with you."

"Please, I'm so sorry," Gaspard said again, grabbing Wolfe's hand and pulling him near. "Please don't go, Wolfe," he said into his hair. "Please don't go to Vancouver. Don't run away. Stay. This is your home—"

But Wolfe pulled away. "I can't stay here. I can't be here in this city, so close to you, and not be able to see you. To touch you—"

"I love you." He tried for Wolfe's hand again. "Oh, God, please, Wolfe, I love you—"

"I have to go," Wolfe said, stepping back, shaking his head. "I have to go. Just let me—"

"No—"

"Gaspard! Let me go, okay? Just fucking let me go!" Wolfe yelled, on the edge of tears. "I can't stay here! I'm not as strong as you are."

"Strong? You think I'm strong? I'm nothing—"

"You have your family. You made your choices." Wolfe's voice was calmer now as he stared him down. "Now, let me make mine."

"I'm supposed to just let you go?"

Wolfe walked up to him and stopped close. "You wanna be with me?"

"Yes, you know that I do, but—"

"But?"

Gaspard could feel himself being ripped apart, and by his own hands. "But I have to consider my son in all this, and right now—"

"Then good-bye." Wolfe quickly turned around and walked off.

"Wolfe!"

"No!" Wolfe spun around, and the look in his eyes struck Gaspard down. He couldn't go after him. He had no right to. "No, Gaspard, do you hear me? *No.*" Wolfe held his hand up. "No more. Let me go. Just let me go."

Defeated, Gaspard stepped down to the street.

But as Gaspard opened his car door, Wolfe grabbed his arm. "Why is it so easy to let me go?" he asked in a broken voice. "Why is it always so easy for people to let me go?"

"No, baby, no, it's not—"

"Fuck you!" Wolfe was crying now. "I gave you everything I had! And maybe it wasn't much, but it's all I had, and for what? For what, Gaspard?"

"I wasn't deserving of it."

"Oh, don't you dare give me that."

"Okay. Okay." Gaspard was desperate to find the right words. Wolfe needed him right now. He needed his guidance. "Look," he said quietly, daring to step closer to Wolfe. "What I mean is—" But he didn't know anymore.

He had no idea what he meant.

"I'm so lost, Gaspard. So lost without you."

"Come here."

Wolfe pressed his face against Gaspard's shirt, letting his defenses down. "Hold me," he whispered. "Just hold me for a little while."

Gaspard stroked Wolfe's hair. He'd hurt this man enough. It was time to let him go. "You're gonna be okay, Wolfe," he said close to his ear. "Everything's gonna work out, you'll see. Everything's gonna be okay."

Wolfe leaned back and looked up at him. "I don't know anymore."

"Shh." He kissed Wolfe's forehead. "I promise you. Go back to Vancouver. Pick up your life where you left it. Time will heal you, and before you know it, you'll be moving on." With every word, Gaspard's pain intensified, but he wouldn't let Wolfe see it. "You'll meet someone," he said, his heart breaking inside. "And fall in love again."

"But what about you?" Wolfe wiped his nose. "You're gonna sacrifice yourself again?"

"Oh, I'll be fine. Don't worry about me. Please. I just… I want you to be happy."

"Without you?"

"Yeah, without me." He needed Wolfe to go before he broke down. "Okay?"

"This is what you want? You want me to leave you?"

"Yes." Gaspard moved back, going for the door handle. He climbed into the driver's seat and looked at Wolfe. "I don't want you to stay."

"You're full of shit." Wolfe leaned in and gave him a sad smile. "Don't you think I know what you're doing?"

"Please go now," Gaspard said, staring back at the wheel. "Please."

Wolfe hesitated, watching him. "This is how you want us to say good-bye. With a lie?"

"Wolfe, go. Please. Now."

"I love you, Gaspard," Wolfe whispered, leaning in to kiss him. He pressed his mouth to Gaspard's lips but pulled away before Gaspard could kiss him back. "And you're a fool to let me go." Wolfe jumped into the street and walked away with his head hung low.

Wolfe never turned back.

WHEN GASPARD entered his apartment, he found Malena reading in the living room. She looked up at him and immediately understood. "You saw him tonight, didn't you?" she asked, putting her book down.

"How did you know?"

"I can see it on your face."

"Malena, tell me the truth. Do you really think it's okay for me to be in love with a young man your brother's age?"

She sat up straight. "Oh, Dad," she cried. "I love you! I'm so sick of seeing you like this."

"He's going back to Vancouver. In two weeks. He's leaving—"

"Fuck that." She blushed. "Sorry. I mean, I know that he is, but can't you change his mind?"

"It's not up to me."

"You're just gonna let him go? Really? Just like that? I don't understand. Dad, Mom's living with Karen. Curtis is not interested in us at all. He's just doing his thing, and pretty soon, he'll be shacking up with some girl, and trust me, he won't need *your* approval, and I'll be moving out eventually, so what then? What then, Dad?"

"I don't wanna lose my son. I can't lose my son."

"Maybe you'll lose him for a little while, yeah, but maybe, with some distance, and some time, Curtis will grow up. Will learn to miss you. Will learn to understand what you mean to him—"

"And you? Your mom?"

"Why are you worried? And Mom? *Please.* She's over you and living with someone else. Why do you care so much what she thinks? Did she care what you thought when she started her affair with her best friend?"

Gaspard's heart beat faster as he looked around the apartment. Could he? Could he really make that decision? "You always make me feel so strong," he said, looking back at Malena. "Just like she used to make me feel. Gisele."

"Maybe there's a little of your sister in me."

"There's a lot of her in you. But I need to think about all this, and most of all, I need to talk with your brother."

"Why do you always need Curtis's validation? Why isn't mine enough?" She rose and picked up her book. "He'll never give it to you, and you'll never stop trying to convince him you're worthy of it."

"You're angry."

"I'm tired of the way you let him walk all over you. I mean, what is it about Curtis, anyway? I love him, you know that, but I don't like him very much."

"Don't say that—"

"You're always protecting him, Dad! No matter what he does. No matter what he says. And I've been trying to figure it out all my life. It's like you care more about him than you do me."

"No, that's not true—"

"Yes, it is!" She threw her book on the couch. "Don't deny it to my face. At least let me have that. The truth. I give you love and support and my time and devotion, but he gives you nothing, and yet, he's your favorite child."

"Malena, honey, you've got it all wrong." He would have to tell her. But telling her meant thinking about it. And thinking about it meant remembering it. It was buried so deep inside him, yet he could summon it so easily. He always knew where it was, that image. The image he could never forget. "I… I wasn't there," he said, sitting on the couch and looking at his hands. "I wasn't there to protect him."

"What? You've always protected us."

"No, Malena, sit down." Meredith had made him swear never to tell their daughter, but he'd always felt it was wrong. That secret between them. "Come on, come over here."

"What is it?" she asked in a small voice. "It's about Curtis, isn't it?"

"Yes."

She sat by him. Her face was white. "Something happened to him."

"Yes, when he was—" But Gaspard stopped. He hadn't spoken about this, to anyone, in so many years. "When he was eight."

"Dad, don't tell me." She briefly shut her eyes, as if to shut the thought out. "Please. Don't."

"I won't, if you don't want me to."

"Tell me. Tell me now. Who was it?"

Donny, their neighbor's son, had been seventeen that summer and had taken an interest in Curtis. He'd shown him the car he was working on. They'd spent afternoons together. Donny was a loner. A bit of a strange young man, but a kind and caring boy who often stopped by the house to take Curtis for a bike ride. Gaspard had looked into Donny's eyes. He'd trusted him. Absolutely trusted him. It was great to see Curtis smiling. The two seemed to share a bond, and Gaspard had even been relieved to see his son was capable of forging a relationship with another boy, no matter his age. Curtis had no friends at school. He wasn't interested in sports and spent a lot of time in his bedroom, reading comic books. Donny had seemed to be a gift to him.

Donny.

They'd never seen it happening.

"It was Donny, our neighbor."

"Oh, God, Dad, what did he do to him?"

One afternoon, the day that had changed his life forever, Gaspard had walked into Curtis's bedroom and found him playing with his wrestling figures. One of them was the same figurine Gaspard had seen in Wolfe's apartment.

"What are you doing?" he'd asked his son that day. "What's he doing to him?"

But he'd known right there and then.

"Making his penis spit," Curtis had answered, "like I do to Donny's."

At the sound of those words out of his boy's mouth, Gaspard had clutched the dresser, seeing black.

"You never told me. You and Mom, you never told me."

"Malena, don't hold it against me. Please." Gaspard reached for her hand. "Please."

"Is that why Mom sent Curtis to Louise's every Sunday afternoon? For therapy?"

"Louise was, *is* a great child psychologist, and we thought because your mom—"

"Curtis was in therapy. He wasn't going there to help her mow the lawn."

"No."

"So many lies."

"Do you understand why he can't, and will not, ever accept who I am and who I love."

"It's not the same, Wolfe is an adult—"

"In your brother's mind, it's the same thing." Gaspard was finally understanding the immense void between Curtis and himself. "I should have been more present. More vigilant. I should have—"

"I don't even know how to feel. Or what to say."

"Do you forgive me? Because I really need you to understand. You of all people. I can't bear to—"

"There's nothing to forgive, Daddy." She burst into tears. "I can't believe how much you've suffered."

They held each other for a long time, whispering to each other, and Gaspard tried to answer all of her questions as candidly as he could. As they spoke, his anger and pain receded back into the place inside him that he rarely visited. Finally, he released her. "Look," he said, regaining his composure, "your brother came out of it okay. I know it was hard for him, during his teenage years, and maybe that's why I stayed away during that time, because I didn't wanna remind him of what I knew about him, but he came out of it okay. In his own way, Curtis is pretty happy. I think the only time he's reminded of it is when I'm around—"

"Does Wolfe know? About Curtis?"

"No." Gaspard rose and went to the bookcase for the Jameson bottle. "I need a drink. You?"

"Oh yes."

He poured them both a stiff one and sat down again. "You're not gonna talk to him about it, are you?"

"Curtis? No, I won't. I'd never do that to him." She took a sip and grimaced. "But I hope one day he'll tell me about it."

They were silent, sipping their whiskey for a while.

"I'm glad you told me," Malena whispered at last. "Because it explains a lot about Curtis, and it makes me love him a little more."

"I wish I could have stopped it before it began."

"You're an amazing father, but you're not perfect."

"And my mistake cost my son his innocence. One day, if you have a child, you'll understand what that feels like." Gaspard finished his drink and stood.

"Where are you going?"

"For a walk."

"Are you okay?"

"Yes, but I need to think." Gaspard opened the door. "I've got some decisions to make."

Malena watched him from the couch, and Gaspard remembered that morning, the morning he'd set out for the gay village. The morning he'd met Wolfe Byrne.

He'd turned back for Wolfe that day.

He'd gone back for him.

CHAPTER TWENTY-TWO

IT WAS nearing midnight when Gaspard finally headed down the mountain and back home. He'd spent the evening walking around Mount Royal. Later, he'd stood on the Belvedere, watching the city lights glitter below. Somewhere in that city, Wolfe slept alone. Many times during the evening, Gaspard had wanted to walk down to his car and drive to Wolfe's home to beg him to stay. He'd forsake it all for Wolfe. He'd change his life. His address. Anything.

But he'd done nothing of the sort.

Tired, and at peace with his decision, Gaspard entered his apartment.

Curtis was in the living room watching television.

"You're still up," Gaspard said, hanging up his jacket. "You should be in bed."

"Where were you?" Curtis asked, glancing over at him.

"On the mountain, walking. How was your night?"

"Good." Curtis looked back at the television. He was watching an old episode of *Saturday Night Live*.

They watched the sketch for a while, but Gaspard needed to speak before he lost his nerve. "Listen, Curt, I wanna tell you something, all right?" He leaned in, trying to keep from clenching his hands. "Something important."

Curtis's profile tensed, but he didn't look his way. "What? What is it?"

"I'm only gonna bring this up once, I promise you, but what happened to you, when you were eight, with Donny—"

"I'm going to bed." Curtis made a move to stand, but Gaspard put his hand on his arm.

"Wait," he whispered, stopping Curtis. "Just wait a minute. Let me say this—"

"No. Absolutely fucking not—"

"Curtis, sit down and listen to me." Gaspard waited, staring Curtis down. "Please."

Finally, Curtis sat, but remained poised on the edge of his seat, ready to pounce. "I don't understand why you had to say his name to me."

"Because it's very relevant to the rest of what I have to say. Look, I'll make it quick." Gaspard took a moment to get the words right. He'd thought about this all night. He knew what to say. "I'm sorry... I'll start with that." He tried making eye contact with Curtis. "I'm sorry I didn't see it. I'm sorry you had to go through something like that and right across from our house. And we didn't see it. We didn't do anything to help you—"

"I can't hear this—"

"Curtis, I fucked up." Gaspard struggled to remain calm. "I never meant to, but that doesn't count for much to an eight-year-old boy hoping someone will see he needs help."

Curtis turned his cool eyes his way.

"I let you down," Gaspard went on. "You were my responsibility, and I let you down. And I don't wanna say I'm sorry anymore because those are just words. So, this is what I wanna say to you instead. I need you to know that."

"What? What do you wanna say that's so important you have to bring all this shit—"

"I love Wolfe. Do you understand? I *love* him." Gaspard watched his son's expression darken, but he went on. "Every day I spend without him is like a day I spend in a grave. It's the same thing to me. Cold. Bleak. Lonely. And fucking pointless."

"Pointless? That's nice." Curtis shook his head, looking down at his knees. "What about your family? Hm? What about me and Malena—"

"Let me finish." Gaspard held his own. "Now, I'm willing to pay that price. But I'm telling you right now, without Wolfe, I'm half the man I could be. And maybe the man I could be, would be a man you'd like to know, but that's not up to me anymore. So, Curtis, the bottom line is, we're even now. You can't hate me anymore. You can't manipulate me anymore." He touched Curtis's cold hand where it rested on his knee. "I let you down once and it changed your life. Now I'm letting myself down."

"You think that makes us even?"

"It makes us both broken."

"I'm not broken—"

"No?" Gaspard moved closer. "You're not?"

"Fuck no."

"Then why are you still acting like a victim?"

Curtis's blue eyes lit up with fury, and Gaspard knew his words were having the intended effect. He'd been playing it close.

"You think I act like a victim?"

"Yes, most of the time—"

"And you don't?" Curtis scoffed. "Please. Here you are, telling me you're willing to sacrifice your life, blah, blah, blah—"

"In order to have you back. To have your love again. Your respect—"

"My respect? You let Mom walk out with her best friend and did nothing. You gave her the house—"

"Is that what all this is about?"

"You're a fucking coward, Dad!"

"And you're not a man, you're a child!"

"Yeah? Well, at least I'm not in love with one."

The words hit Gaspard hard, and he stared at Curtis, the blood pounding through him. This conversation would be fruitless. Nothing would come of it. But at least he'd said what he'd wanted Curtis to know. "Okay," he whispered at last. "I'm done. I've said what I had to say." There was no talking to Curtis. It was impossible. "I'm not seeing him anymore. Wolfe is moving back home, to Vancouver. It's over between us."

"Good." Curtis stared up at him.

"Yeah, well, try telling him that." Gaspard turned away from the living room.

"That's it? You're going to bed—"

"Yeah, good night."

"Whatever, Dad. Honestly, I don't understand you."

"And I don't understand you. But I still love you." Gaspard went to his bedroom and shut the door, shutting himself in again.

DOWNHEARTED, WOLFE watched the dark clouds rolling in.

That was all he needed now: rain.

"Guys, we really need to get a move on," he said, looking out from the back of the U-Haul truck.

Astrid and Dominic were carrying the last of his books to the truck. They'd been at it for two hours, and he was tremendously grateful for their help.

"All right," Dominic said, sliding a box in, "there's about five boxes left in there and the two carpets you wanted to keep."

Wolfe jumped out of the truck and dusted his jeans off. He looked around at the street, seeing it differently. "I never thought I'd be leaving this place so soon."

"You can still change your mind," Astrid said sadly. "I really wish you would."

He leaned in and kissed her cheek. "Yeah, I know."

"Don't kiss me, you little tease." She blushed and flustered, stepped back to the open door of his apartment. Two of his neighbors were standing on their balconies, watching him pack his things up. Funny how he was interesting to them now that he was leaving the building. From the sidewalk, Wolfe waved at them. He didn't even know their names.

He went back inside and helped Dominic with the rolled-up carpets. He'd be storing his things until he figured out the next step. His mother had insisted on paying for everything, and Wolfe realized just how quickly he was regressing back to being her helpless little boy. He dreaded the first night in his parents' home. His mother had spent the last year caring for her ailing father, and now that she had no one to look out for, he'd be her new project. He could see himself sitting at the dinner table, forced to eat his greens at every meal.

Dominic took the carpet off Wolfe's hand. He had a sad expression on his face. "Let me do it," he said. Dominic hadn't taken the news of Wolfe's departure very well. Actually, all of his YBR colleagues and many Montreal acquaintances were depressed about him leaving so soon. Dominic pushed the carpet into the back of the truck and wiped his brow. "Well, that's the last of it. You're all set."

"Thank you so much." Wolfe squeezed Dominic's arm. "For everything. I'm really glad you decided to continue volunteering—"

"I don't understand, Wolfe. Are you really leaving everything and everyone because of a guy who's, like, your father's age or something?"

Wolfe flinched at the remark but stayed composed. He shut the back door of the truck and looked Dominic in the eye. "Yes, I am."

"Why? You can have any guy in the world. You probably don't know this, but everyone in the field, who's either met you or heard about you, wants a chance with you, male or female—"

"Oh, that explains the lineup at my door on Saturday nights." Wolfe winked.

"I'd have gone for you." Dominic grumbled, turning away.

"What's wrong with him?" Astrid asked, passing Dominic on the sidewalk as she came down to Wolfe.

"Nothing, he's just upset—" But his phone vibrated and Wolfe quickly checked it. "Oh my God," he cried, seeing Gaspard's text. "He just wrote me."

"Who, Gaspard?" Astrid clutched his arm. "What did he write?"

"He wants to talk." Adrenaline rushing through him, Wolfe read Gaspard's short message. "Wants to meet near his apartment." He looked back at the truck full of his belongings. "That's all he says."

"You're leaving in three days. Do you think it's wise to see him?"

"I don't care about wise or not." If Gaspard asked him to stay again, if he said the same things he'd said that other night, he'd bend to Gaspard's will this time. He wouldn't leave him. He'd stay and be his secret love. He'd live in a hotel room with a toothbrush as his only possession and be Gaspard's lover. That would be enough. "I have to hear what he has to say. He wouldn't ask to see me if it wasn't important."

"I guess you're right." She touched a strand of his hair and studied his face for a moment. "You have very beautiful eyes, Wolfe. Especially when you're thinking of him."

Wolfe looked down at his phone and quickly typed his reply. Seconds later, Gaspard wrote back. They'd meet at the diner near Gaspard's home in half an hour. They'd never been there before, but Wolfe knew the place. "I have to bring this truck back by two this afternoon—"

"Then you better hurry up. *Go.* See what he wants—"

"Hopefully me."

"Please don't get your hopes up."

"I know." Wolfe looked down at himself. He was full of dust and his hair needed a wash. "I have to jump in the shower real quick. Do you think you and Dominic could park the truck somewhere in the back and—"

"Absolutely."

Wolfe ran up the steps but stopped and turned to look at Astrid. "You know, you're a really good friend, and I think I'm gonna miss you the most."

"Yeah, and if I only had a brain, I'd follow you to Vancouver and start my life again."

"Then why don't you?"

Astrid shook her head. "Because I've sworn off falling in love with gay men." She reached her hand out. "Now, throw me the keys and ask Dominic to get out here."

BARELY ABLE to sit still, Wolfe fiddled with the place mat, the cutlery, his thumb ring. He checked the street through the window and watched the diner's entrance.

"More coffee?" The waiter was already pouring it into his cup. "Are you ready to order—"

"Not just yet," Wolfe said, his mouth dry from the two coffees. "Thanks." He gave the waiter a quick look. "I'm okay for—" His heart jumped. A tall, blond man had entered the diner and was scanning the room with cool blue eyes. Wolfe was seeing Gaspard, twenty-five years ago. The resemblance was indisputable and allowed no doubt. This was Gaspard's son.

This was Curtis.

What were the odds he'd be here this afternoon? What would Gaspard do when he came face-to-face with his son?

Curtis's icy stare moved around the tables and booths and finally came to rest on Wolfe's face. As Curtis made eye contact with him, Wolfe knew he wasn't meeting Gaspard today.

He'd been set up. Quickly, he looked down at the menu, buying time.

But Curtis was at his booth, looking down at him. "You're Wolfe?" His voice was different from his father's. His tone, even more so.

"And you're Curtis," Wolfe said, raising his stare. "I thought I was meeting your father."

"Yeah, well, I didn't know if you'd show or what, so." Curtis slid into the seat across from Wolfe and leaned back on the torn red leather. He watched him for a while. "So you're the guy."

Wolfe wished he could be calm and collected, but his face felt hot, and he was completely unprepared for this confrontation. What did Curtis want from him?

"Are you guys ready to order?" The waiter was back again, oblivious to the tension between them. He scribbled something on his pad and stared back at them. "Obviously not," the man said after a few seconds of uneasy silence. "Tell you what, holler if you need me." He left them in a hurry.

When he had, Wolfe cleared his throat. "How are you, Curtis? It must be nice to be home again."

Curtis squinted a little, clearly surprised. "It's all right," he muttered, his cold demeanor changing slightly. He shifted in his seat. "I guess you'll be finding out how that feels soon enough."

"I guess so." Wolfe clenched his hand under the seat but smiled. "In three days, actually."

"That soon—oh." Curtis frowned and looked down at the menu. "You're in a big hurry."

"Well, considering I lost my job and the man I love, yes, I'm in a big hurry to leave Montreal." Wolfe looked down at the menu as well. They were speaking in harsh tones but avoiding eye contact. This was a showdown and he was ready for it.

"I guess that's what happens when you go after an old man with two kids."

"No, that's what happens when you go after a mature man with an immature twenty-five-year-old son."

"A son who's your own age."

"A son who's willing to stand in the way of his father's happiness."

"And you know what makes my dad happy? Please, you've known him for what, four months?"

"I've known him long enough to know he's not the man you think he is." Wolfe dared a glance up.

Curtis's stare was unflinching. "You know, he doesn't have that much money."

Wolfe's mouth opened, but he was too stunned to speak.

"Yeah," Curtis went on, "he's actually going back to work full time next week. So, for your information, he isn't as loaded as you might think he—"

"You think I'm after your dad's money?" Wolfe found his voice again. "Oh, you have no idea who you're talking to, do you? If I was after money, I'd have stayed in Victoria and continued to be Daddy's little boy."

"So, you're one of those, then." Curtis's tone was disgusted. "Looking for a father figure or whatever they call it."

"What do you want, Curtis? Huh? Why did you come here?"

"I wanted to see your face." Curtis shrugged and looked out the window at the rain. "I wanted to see what the big deal was."

"Well," Wolfe said bitterly, "I'm sure I've disappointed you enough. Now can I leave? I've got a move to plan."

"So you're really leaving." Curtis's voice was softer, his blue eyes warmer but still hard. "Just like that?"

"Your dad made his choice and I wasn't it." Wolfe drained his coffee and put his hand on his jacket. "I have to go now."

"Fine, go." Curtis looked back at the window again, his features tensing. He was very attractive, but so stern and cold. Wolfe could see why Gaspard was constantly trying to reach his son. It must have been very painful for Gaspard to raise a boy whose whole personality seemed built around an iceberg. Curtis turned his face to him. "Maybe you don't deserve my dad after all."

"What?" Wolfe paused, standing by the table with his arm halfway inside his jacket's sleeve. "What did you just say?"

"Nothing." Curtis looked away.

For a moment, Wolfe just stood there, confused and furious. How could Curtis say that? Gaspard had been the one to push him away. How much of a fight was he supposed to put up and for how long?

Curtis slipped out of the booth and stood. He was a head taller than Wolfe, as Gaspard was. "Have a nice life, Wolfe," he said, stepping back to the entrance. Moments later, he was outside.

Without a second thought, Wolfe tossed some money on the table and ran out into rain after Curtis. "Wait a minute!" He grabbed Curtis's arm. "Why did you come here? Huh? And don't lie!"

Curtis jerked his arm away and wiped the rain off his face. "I don't know."

"No, that's not true."

"I'm telling you, I don't know why I wanted to see you." Curtis ran a hand through his wet hair. "Okay? I don't know." He walked off. "Just leave me alone."

Soaked and queasy, Wolfe couldn't hold back from shouting at him. "I love your father, you little shit!"

Curtis spun around and threw his arms out. "And he loves you!" He turned around again. "You little shit!"

Chapter Twenty-Three

GASPARD STEPPED into the deli and quickly shut the glass door behind him, keeping the cold out. He wiped his boots on the welcome mat and waved at the woman behind the counter. The store was empty. He was the only fool out in the storm, it seemed.

But he had a dinner party to plan and shop for.

He'd just started ordering some cold cuts when his phone rang. It was Malena again. Gaspard slipped his leather glove off and answered, trying to stuff the glove into his coat pocket while holding on to the phone. "What is it, honey?" He set the bag down by the counter. "I'm ordering—"

"I just remembered I forgot to ask you to buy some napkins and candles." She was nervous about tomorrow, constantly checking up on him.

They were throwing Zach a surprise party for his ninety days of sobriety. Astrid and Megan would be there. And so would Clare, Yvan, Dominic, and Antonio. Everyone from the YBR.

Everyone except the one man they all missed the most.

"I'll get those last, on my way home." Gaspard showed the woman behind the counter what he needed. "Thank you," he whispered. She was very attractive, in her forties, with curly brown hair and smart brown eyes. "Mal, listen, sweetie, everything's gonna be all right. Relax, okay?"

"I know, Dad. Mom says you're the king of dinner parties."

The woman went to the cash register and rang everything up, but kept glancing his way.

"I have to go," Gaspard said, walking up to the cash register. "I'm almost done here, and I'll be home in about an hour. Is your brother home?"

Curtis had been spending most of his nights at Chloe's apartment. The two were very much in love, and the relationship was having a great effect on Curtis. He was a little more relaxed around Gaspard. But

Curtis was barely home anymore, and even talking about moving out. Malena and Astrid were also thinking of sharing a place near the center where they worked. There was no way he was going to stay in an apartment in the middle of the student ghetto if both kids left in the next months.

"He's sleeping at Chloe's tonight again," Malena said. "Oh, I have to go, Zach is here." She quickly said good-bye and hung up.

"That'll be fifty-seven forty." The woman raked her fingers through her curls, waiting for him to cough up the last of his cash.

"This is a nice place you have here," he said, being polite. He paid her and stuffed everything in the bag. "My daughter told me about it."

"Well, that's nice of her, and I hope you'll come back." The woman smiled seductively. "Soon," she added.

She was flirting with him. Lately, he'd been getting a lot of attention from women. He couldn't walk through the office without being accosted by a female colleague wanting to talk with him. Of course, the guys made fun of him, but he could tell everyone at work was trying to figure out what his "deal" was.

He was in love with a boy half his age who lived two thousand kilometers away.

That was the deal.

But to anyone at the office, he was a handsome divorced man with two grown kids.

Available and straight.

"Have a good evening," Gaspard said, stepping back to the door.

From behind the cash register, the woman waved. "Bye," she said, frowning at him, obviously trying to figure him out too.

Outside, Gaspard hurried to his car and tossed everything in the backseat. He drove out slowly, trying to see through the snow. The wipers were no match for the storm, and as he drove carefully through the vacant streets, he came to his exit but didn't take it.

No, he headed east instead.

At Plessis Street, Gaspard turned left and drove up and into the gay village. He hadn't dared to come back here since Wolfe had left Montreal, more than three months ago.

Gaspard parked the car and sat in silence, watching the old building across the street.

Yes, there it was. The YBR.

He stepped out, cringing from the cold. "Hello, old friend," he said, his voice getting lost in the wind. "Look at what they've done to you." The building stood proudly before him, sealed up in protective nets, surrounded by dormant machines and scaffolding. Its face was torn, ripped open, showing him the depth of its structure, and Gaspard's heart pounded as he stared at the place Wolfe had wanted to save. The place Wolfe had loved and fought for. The place he'd been forced to abandon and leave.

They were restoring it. Turning it into condos. Homes.

Homes.

Gaspard blinked and looked over at the white trailer on the terrain. The real estate promoter was advertising that the units would be available in the spring. One of the units was the *penthouse*, as they called it, a large, two-bedroom, loft-size apartment covering the left part of the third floor.

Gaspard looked up at the window on the third floor; Wolfe's office. He looked back and over his shoulder at the tree there. Its branches were bare and heavy with fresh snow, and Gaspard stared at it for a moment, remembering Wolfe's words so many days ago.

"It just stands there and takes it. And do you know why? Because the tree doesn't have a choice."

A powerful chill shook him, and Gaspard looked back at the white trailer.

Choice.

He took his phone out.

CHAPTER TWENTY-FOUR

ON SATURDAY afternoon, Wolfe stared down at a piece of chocolate cake.

His birthday cake.

He felt someone tugging at his sleeve and looked over to see his nephew Collin staring up at him. Collin had chocolate icing in his hair, and his little nose was running. "Come here," Wolfe told him, picking him up and cleaning his face with a napkin as best he could. Collin elbowed him in the stomach, jumped off his lap, and ran out of the room. The child didn't like him very much.

Wolfe looked around the table. Everyone was engrossed in a heated conversation, talking loudly and over each other. The table was cluttered with food and drinks and the remnants of his cake. He tried following what they were saying, but wasn't all that interested anyway. Xander and his father were arguing about the economy and the European Union, and next to them, Xander's best friend Ryan and his wife were discussing the day-care system.

Wolfe took a sip of his white wine, gazing around the table. These were the people he'd grown up with. They shared genes. He could see that he had his father's hair and his mother's mouth. He and his brother had the same eyes and expression. Collin looked like him when he'd been two years old. They were related. *Related.* He thought about the word. What did it really mean? To be related to someone. Linked? Bound?

Obliged?

"Honey." His mother touched his head. "Are you done?" She picked up his plate and kissed his hair. "Happy birthday, baby."

He smiled up at her. "Thank you."

She was thrilled to have him here. And he hated every minute of it. It wasn't her fault. It wasn't anyone's fault. For the last weeks, he'd been scouring the city for a place of his own, but Vancouver was way more expensive than Montreal, and he couldn't afford most of the neighborhoods his parents approved of. There was no way they'd let him move out anywhere near where he wanted to be.

Again, Wolfe tried joining the conversation, but they'd already moved on to something else, and because he didn't know much about tennis anymore, he refrained from commenting. They spoke quickly and loudly, while Collin played with the television in the background, turning the volume up and down.

Everyone's voices swelled against the loud television, but they were too focused on their conversation to notice anything else. Wolfe felt queasy. He'd had too much wine. Too much food. Too much of everything. He drank some water, hoping to get a grip, but under the light of the chandelier, everyone's face seemed to glow bright pink, while their mouths laughed and chewed and yelled out words he couldn't make out anymore.

The room was spinning around his head.

Collin was crying over the sound of blaring cartoon voices, and Wolfe clutched the table, feeling dizzy.

He was caught in a twister of noise. Spinning out of control.

No one paid him any attention as he rose from his chair and stumbled out of the dining room.

ON ABBOT Street, Wolfe stepped off the bus and put his hands in his pockets, heading off for the halfway house where he used to work. His mother had called twice. She didn't understand how he could just leave his own birthday celebration and take the next ferry off the island. She was upset with him. She suspected something. Had asked him about drugs. Men. HIV. The typical questions. How could he tell her about Gaspard? She, of all people, would never understand. And his father?

He'd probably want Wolfe to see a psychiatrist if he ever found out about Gaspard.

Walking with his head low, Wolfe made his way to the place he hadn't visited for more than two years. He reached it soon enough and stopped, looking at the house. They'd fixed the porch light. He walked back a few steps and stood in the exact spot he'd been standing when Aaron had called out to him that night.

He remembered that the first blow hadn't knocked him down, but the pain had shocked him. He'd stumbled backward and held his ear, still trying to understand what had happened. But when the second punch had hit him, he'd understood. That was when the fear had gripped him in a way he couldn't forget. Not even now. The fear of pain. Of death. But still, he hadn't fought back. There wasn't any time for that. It had happened so quickly.

On the sidewalk, Wolfe stared down at the cracks in the cement. He'd bled right into those cracks, but the blood was gone now.

Along with everything else.

Emotional and still tipsy from the wine, Wolfe touched the phone inside his pocket. Up until now, he'd resisted calling Gaspard, but he couldn't fight it anymore. Why should he? Why couldn't he speak to the man he loved?

He took his phone out and dialed Gaspard's number. He didn't know what he'd say to him, but it didn't matter.

Not today. Not on his birthday.

"Hello?" Gaspard answered.

Wolfe suddenly remembered he'd changed his number and hadn't listed it. Gaspard couldn't know it was him. "Hi... it's me," Wolfe said, moving to stand by a street lamp. "It's Wolfe."

Gaspard was quiet for a second. "Oh my God," he whispered after a moment. "Wolfe? How are you? Is everything okay?"

What could he say? "I just.... Well, it's my birthday today and—"

"It's your birthday? I had no idea." Gaspard's voice sank. "Then, happy birthday."

Wolfe stared at his boots, trying to keep it together. "So how's everything? How's Malena? How's Zach? Well, how are *you*, first of all?"

"I miss you, Wolfe. I miss you so much. Can I say that?"

The quickness and sting of his tears surprised Wolfe. "I hate it here. I hate being here—"

"What's going on? You don't like your job? Are your parents being nice to you?"

"I don't know if I can make it without you."

"Of course you can. Okay? Yes, you can, and you will."

"But I don't want to." Wolfe turned his face from the sidewalk, hoping to conceal his tears from people passing by. "I don't want to, Gaspard."

"Shh, don't get so upset. It's okay. It's gonna be all right."

"No! It isn't! And stop telling me it is. Because none of this is okay."

"What do you want me to tell you, Wolfe?" Gaspard's tone was gentle. "I don't know what to tell you. You're over there. I'm over here."

"Do you still love me?"

"Oh, baby, yes, with all my heart."

"Then how can you do this to me?"

Gaspard was silent.

Wolfe wiped his eyes, looking back at the halfway house. "I never thought I'd hurt like this again," he said, feeling all of his old wounds opening up. "Always thought I'd seen the worst of it." How could he ever get over this? "Everything is slowly fading to gray around me, and I can't even remember the last time I laughed. I don't even know if I wanna try anymore."

"Wolfe, what do you want from me?" Gaspard asked sharply. His voice had a new strength to it. "Tell me, and I swear to God, I'll do it. I'll do anything for you. Do you understand me? I don't give a shit anymore. I don't care if I lose everything down to the clothes on my back. I'm ready to go all the way. I'm ready, Wolfe, and you just say the word. Just say the word, baby."

"I'll say four words to you and that's all I'll ever say."

"Tell me. *Anything.* Just tell me."

Wolfe took a deep breath and closed his eyes. "Come and get me."

FOR A moment, Gaspard was speechless, listening to the silence on the line.

Come and get me.

He looked around the kitchen, excitement surging up inside him.

Zach raised an eyebrow at him. "Well, what did he say? What the fuck is going on?"

"Dad? Hello." Malena touched his arm. "Say something."

Gaspard looked at their expectant faces and let out the air in his lungs. "It's his birthday today."

"Shit, I didn't know." Zach scratched his head. "Damn it, maybe I did. Yeah, I remember, he's a Capricorn boy." He looked over at Malena. "We should have called him."

"Dad," she said, concern on her face. "Did you mean it? That you're willing to lose everything? Did you?"

Gaspard met Malena's eyes. "He needs me."

"*We* need you."

"Malena," Zach said. "Come on now."

"What? You think I want my dad to move to Vancouver?" Malena grabbed Gaspard's hands. "Dad, you can't. I'd miss you too much!"

"Who says I'm moving to Vancouver?" It was time he told her what he'd done. "Look, Mal, I need to tell you something."

"What are you guys doing?" Astrid walked into the kitchen, followed by Dominic. "We were thinking it was time for your sobriety gift, Zachy boy."

"I hope you got me ninety-nine bottles of beer."

Malena and Gaspard were silent, exchanging glances.

"What? What is it?" Astrid asked, losing her smile.

"Wolfe just called," Zach said. "I don't think he's doing too good out there."

"Oh." She came closer. "Yeah, I spoke to him two days ago, and he didn't sound so cheery, let's put it that way."

"He doesn't like his job?" Gaspard asked, leaning up against the sink behind him. They stood in a circle, speaking softly. "What's it like?"

"Well, it's sounds pretty awful, actually. It's a private clinic, so the clientele is very different from what he knows. It's all the people he tried to escape, I guess. Rich people. The country-club-type addicts."

"But I thought he was going back to social work," Zach said, confused.

"That didn't work out. Supposedly they didn't like his ideas."

"Wolfe... in a private clinic." Malena shook her head. "I don't see it. I can't imagine him working in a place like that."

Gaspard's heart would burst if he didn't say something soon. "He doesn't belong over there," he whispered. "He belongs here, with us."

"We all agree on that, Gaspard," Dominic said, looking around at everyone's face. "It's very weird not having him here today."

"He's the one who got me the job," Malena said. "And introduced me to you." She pinched Zach's arm. "My own Dallas."

Zach was serious. "He gave me a chance when I needed it the most."

"He fought for us." Astrid said. "All of us."

Gaspard knew they were looking at him for an answer. "Listen, guys, I guess now's as good a time as any to tell you about my plans." He winked at Malena. "You ready for this, little girl?"

"Shoot."

"I bought a condo unit in the old YBR building. The top floor, right where his desk used to be."

Astrid shoved him. "What! Really?"

"Oh, you son of a bitch," Zach said, grinning. "No way. For real?"

Malena only stared at him, and he wasn't sure what she thought. "For you… and him?" she finally asked.

"Yeah, if he wants to." Gaspard blew out a short breath. "God, I really hope he wants to."

"Did you tell him?"

"No, he doesn't know. I signed with the bank last week."

Zach laughed. "Shit."

"What are you gonna do?" Astrid was excited. "I mean, are you just gonna get on a plane and show up at his doorstep or something?"

"That would be completely insane," Malena said. "What if he says no?"

"I have to agree," Zach said. "That's a long trip to make. Not to mention expensive."

"You guys didn't hear me…. I don't care if it's insane, expensive, risky, or doomed."

"You're gonna go get him," Malena said, clapping her hands. She looked over at Zach. "He's gonna go get him."

Zach winked at Gaspard. "Is that the plan?"

"That's the plan."

"What about Curtis?" Malena asked, speaking everyone's thoughts. "You know he's gonna be very much against the idea."

"I'm aware of that. And Curtis will just have to deal with it, that's all."

Gaspard thought of the choices he'd made. He'd lived with the consequences for so long. And for who? For what?

But the great thing about choices was, you could always make new ones.

"So this is it, then," Astrid said, looking around. "We're gonna be a family again."

"That's if he says yes."

He'd never done anything so irrational. So spontaneous. He'd used a good chunk of his pension fund as down payment for the condo. He'd have to work full time, and clear into his seventies, if he ever wanted to pay off the mortgage.

But if Wolfe said yes, if he came home to him, Wolfe would keep him young.

And he'd do it all over again. Gaspard longed to feel that fire inside him once more.

He yearned for Wolfe's magic.

CHAPTER TWENTY-FIVE

BLEARY-EYED, Wolfe sat behind his desk, hoping the coffee would kick in soon.

It was Wednesday morning, but the week was dragging on like a bad movie.

He looked up at his computer screen and clicked into his schedule again. He was to sit in for a few group discussions, *finally*. After three months of working here, they were showing him a little trust. He'd been filing and typing long enough. He needed some action. Some human contact. He'd take Gloria and her box of kittens, or even Licky Luke, over this bureaucratic crap.

"Wolfgang, hi." Diana, one of the counselors, poked her head in his door. She was tanned, blonde, with arresting green eyes and absolutely no personality. He'd noticed how everyone at the clinic seemed to be on the same pill. They were apathetic on their good days. "William is coming in again around one."

William was a frequent flier here. As were many of the clients. They didn't come for recovery. They came to clean up long enough to set their affairs straight and calm the wife or husband down. It wasn't rehab. It was a little break between cocaine lines.

And he was a participant in this charade.

"Can you make sure his room is ready?" Diana was flipping through the mail in her hands. "Thanks."

"Sure, I'm the bellboy here."

"Okay, thanks again." She hadn't heard him. Or maybe it was simply that she cared about him as much as she cared about the wallpaper in the hall.

Wolfe looked back at his screen. If he didn't get out of here by the end of the month, he'd lose his mind. No, first he'd lose his soul, then his mind.

He blinked a few times, trying to perk up, but needed another coffee. As he made his way to the small employee cafeteria, he passed a few rooms, glimpsing bored faces or sleeping bodies. This was definitely not as exciting as reality TV made it look.

There was no Doctor Drew here.

Inside the empty cafeteria, Wolfe poured himself another cup of coffee from the pot they all shared. He put on a new one and left. Walking back to his office, he was stopped by Ron, the guy at the front desk. "Someone is at the front gates for you," Ron said. "Some dude. Told him we can't let him in or anything, so." Ron's face twitched a little. He had all sorts of nervous ticks. "You know you're not allowed any visitors—"

"Not even my dealer?" Wolfe gave Ron a caustic smile. "Kidding. He's my brother, by the way." Xander had mentioned he'd come by one of these days and they'd have lunch. But it was nine a.m. Wolfe took his phone out and dialed Xander's number.

"Wolfie... what's up?" Xander was out of breath.

"Did you run all the way here?" Wolfe grabbed his heavy winter coat in the office and walked to the front doors. "It's a little early for lunch—"

"What?"

Wolfe opened the front door and peered down the long path leading up to the security gates. He couldn't see his brother. "I'm coming down to you right now."

"Yeah? Cool." Xander's voice jumped. Apparently he was still running. "I'm gonna be here for another half hour, I think—"

"What do you mean?"

"Well, I'm on the treadmill right now, but I'm gonna hit the weights in ten minutes—"

"The weights?" Wolfe stopped, halfway to the gates. "Where are you?"

"What do you mean where am I? I'm at the gym, where else? Where are you?"

"I'm... I'm outside the clinic." Wolfe looked around, his heart beating faster and faster. "They said that you were here," he whispered, staring at the gates.

"Wolfie, are you high?"

"No... sorry, I made a mistake." He took a step forward. "Let me call you back, okay?"

"You all right, man?"

"I'm fine. But let me call you back." Wolfe slipped his phone into his coat pocket and slowly made his way down to the gates. He looked out the wrought-iron bars.

Gaspard stood a few feet off to the side.

"This is a little different than the YBR," Gaspard said, smiling nervously. He wore a black wool topcoat, and against the white winter sky, his eyes were bluer and more beautiful than ever. "They've got you caged in here, huh?" He stepped up to the bars and put a gloved hand to them. "You're locked up."

Wolfe moved closer to the bars. Close enough to catch the scent of Gaspard's cologne in the wind. "What are you doing here?"

Gaspard shook the iron bars, smiling. "I came to break you out."

"What are you saying?" Wolfe stuffed his hands into his pockets, frowning at Gaspard. What was happening? What did this mean? "How did you know where to find me?"

"Astrid."

"You flew here?"

"Yes, in a hot air balloon."

"Gaspard, are you crazy? Are you insane?"

"No."

Wolfe slipped his hands out and put them over Gaspard's hands. He leaned his head on the gate, feeling a little dizzy. "Why did you come here?" he whispered.

"You said, 'Come and get me.'" Gaspard folded his fingers over his. "So, here I am."

"And I'm supposed to do what now? Just leave?"

Gaspard looked away, at the path.

"Oh God, Gaspard, how could you spend all that money and come all the way here without even checking with me first? What were you thinking? How could you not call me or—"

"I don't know... I don't know what I was thinking." Gaspard looked back at him, and his eyes burned like blue flames. "I just bought a condo in the YBR building and told everyone I was coming to get you and we were gonna live together." He shut his eyes and shook his head for a moment. "Wow... you're right. I'm fucking crazy."

Wolfe wasn't sure he'd understood correctly. "You bought what?"

"A condo unit. You know, a home. On the third floor of the old YBR building. Where your office used to be."

"You bought it. It's done?"

"Yeah." Gaspard cleared his throat and laughed quietly. "I can always sell it—"

"For us to live in?"

"Yeah, that was the plan."

The head rush made him nauseous, and Wolfe stepped back from the gates. "Can you give me a second?" he asked, putting his head between his knees. "Just hold on, okay?" He straightened up and looked back at the clinic. That terrible hellish place he hated.

"Hey, don't take it so bad," Gaspard whispered, paling. "Do you wanna go out for a coffee or maybe—"

"Can you give me a minute? I just gotta go in there for a minute." Wild with excitement, Wolfe ran back to the clinic.

WHEN WOLFE had disappeared through the front doors, Gaspard stepped back from the gates and leaned against the wall there. His legs were a little weak.

Wolfe was more beautiful than he remembered. Those gates had kept Gaspard from touching him, but he'd endured the pain. He deserved it anyway.

Gaspard looked at the iron bars again.

Those bars held captive everything he'd ever wanted, but he'd been the one to lock Wolfe up. He'd trapped him inside a life he wasn't meant to live.

So they'd go for a coffee and he'd be kind to Wolfe. Then, if he was lucky, Wolfe would want to make love one last time before he left. They'd go back to his hotel room. Have a drink.

Say good-bye all over again.

Tomorrow, he'd be on a plane, homeward bound, with only an empty seat beside him to remind him just how close he'd come to having it all.

"Okay… let's go." Wolfe was at the gates. His cheeks were red and he looked agitated. He nervously punched in a code and opened the gates. "Come on, hurry up. I really don't wanna deal with them right now." He glanced back at the clinic.

"They're angry with you?" Gaspard wanted to pull Wolfe into his arms but couldn't take that step yet.

"Yeah, they're angry." Wolfe quickly shut the gates. "Let's go."

"Don't you get a coffee break or something?" Gaspard followed down to the street. "I'll have you back in fifteen minutes—"

"No, I doubt that." Wolfe looked around. "Where's your car?"

"That one right there."

"Good, let's go."

"Okay… where's the nearest coffee place we can go to?" Gaspard popped Wolfe's door open and went around the car. "Or do you wanna wal—"

"Get in the car. Let's drive."

Inside, Gaspard turned the engine on and looked over at Wolfe. Wolfe was still rosy-cheeked and out of breath. "So, where to?"

Wolfe turned his eyes to him. "I just quit, by the way."

Gaspard couldn't speak.

"I need to stop by my house," Wolfe said, fastening his seat belt. "To pack. You won't come in. You'll just wait. Yes, you'll just wait around the corner."

"Are you saying…? I mean, are you—"

But Wolfe leaned in and stopped his babbling with a kiss. "Drive, Gaspard. Get me out of here."

"Are you fucking serious?"

Wolfe grinned and kissed him again, his lips lingering over Gaspard's. "I missed you," he said, leaning his head on Gaspard's chest. "Let's go home."

Gaspard took a moment to enjoy the feel of Wolfe in his arms. The scent of his hair. "Your parents. What are you gonna tell them?"

"I'm gonna say a friend just showed up and someone died in Montreal and I have to go."

"Someone died? Hm, I don't know about that." Gaspard leaned back in his seat.

"Well, someone did." Wolfe smiled very tenderly. "In so many ways. Look, if you and me put all our fears in a coffin, how much do you think the thing would weigh?"

"Are we having a *fear funeral*?" Gaspard winked and his heart soared with joy.

Wolfe kissed his hand. "Just drive."

Stunned, Gaspard gazed out at the iron gates. One of them was swinging in the wind. "Hey, baby, you didn't close the fence properly," he said.

"Let it be."

Gaspard drove out, but as he passed the clinic, he slowed down a little and watched the swinging gate.

There was an opening there.

It was an opening allowing loss and mistakes. Enough of a space to let someone out.

But it was also all the space needed to allow someone in.

EPILOGUE

THERE WAS a hand in his hair. Warmth on his face.

Wolfe heard voices around him and slowly opened his eyes.

He was in bed. Sunlight flooded the room.

What time was it? How long had he slept?

Why was everyone around his bed?

"How long was I out?" Wolfe asked, hitching himself up on the pillows.

Zach smiled down at him. "You don't remember? You were out in the sun all day, handing out rubbers and pamphlets. You got a fever. A real bad one."

"You have sunstroke, Wolfe," Malena said, touching his forehead.

Astrid held out a glass of water to him. "Your fever is gone now, but you gave us quite a scare. We thought we'd lost you there."

"Oh, I don't remember... I mean, I remember it's Pride Day, right? And we had to hurry, because I was late, and you were there, right?" He looked up at Zach. "Or were you?"

"Yeah, Wolfie, I was there with you all morning." Zach glanced over at Malena and back at him. "Don't you remember? I told you you'd get sunstroke."

"Yes... I remember that." Wolfe sat up a little more. It was all coming back to him now. All of it. He gazed around the bedroom. "Wow, I had this dream, and it was so real. So lucid."

"That happens with a high fever," Astrid said. "What was it?"

"I'm not sure anymore... but you were all in it. All of you." Wolfe could feel the emptiness in the room. Someone was missing. Someone he needed above all others. "I was back on the West Coast, and I really wanted to get back here, back to you guys."

"You were talking in your sleep." Malena stood and stepped back to the door. "It was kind of cute." She left the room.

"You should get more rest," Zach said, patting his leg. "We still have a lot of cooking to do today. Maybe if you feel better later, you can help."

Astrid kissed his forehead. "I gotta go back to the kitchen, actually. Dominic is in there, probably making Antonio nuts." She touched his face. "I'm so glad you're back in the world, Wolfe."

When they'd stepped out, Wolfe stared at his hands on the sheet. Then his eyes strayed to the window. His heart leaped.

There was the tree.

He knew that tree. He was in his office. No, he was in his bedroom, in what used to be his office.

Wolfe looked back at his open door.

"Hey, baby," Gaspard said, walking through it. "You're awake. How you feeling?" He put his hand over Wolfe's forehead. "Good, your fever's gone."

"Where were you?" Wolfe whispered, still not quite sure of anything.

"What do you mean? I was right here. In the kitchen—"

"You were always here. You never left."

"Where would I go?" Gaspard watched him closely. "Hey, listen, I want you to take a break from work, like we agreed. Just a few days. Can you do that for me?"

"I work at the Open-Hands Center."

Gaspard laughed. "What's going on with you?"

"We live here together."

Gaspard bent to him and kissed him gently. "Drink some water. Rest. I'll bring some food in a minute, all right?" He stood and paused by the bed, looking down at him. "Are you sure you're okay?"

"Yes. I'm okay now."

Gaspard tilted his head and winked at him from the door. "I love you, baby." He turned away and left. "I'll send some food to you."

Wolfe was remembering everything. It was July. They'd moved in together in spring. He faced an exciting challenge as head of the youth outreach program at the Open-Hands Center. Gaspard was doing well as chief consultant for Crystal Telecommunications. They were planning a road trip out east this summer.

After Curtis's engagement party.

That's why they were all in the kitchen. They were planning the party.

"Oh, too bad, you're still alive."

Wolfe looked up to see Curtis standing in his bedroom door.

Smirking, Curtis carried a plate to him. "Here, sandwich. From my father."

"You mean you didn't make it for me?" Wolfe picked up the ham sandwich and tore a huge bite into it. He was starving.

Curtis sat by him, at the edge of the bed. "If I had, I would have put a *special* ingredient in it."

"I bet," Wolfe said with his mouth full.

"Anyway, are you all right?"

Wolfe nodded, chewing.

"You sort of freaked everyone out."

Wolfe swallowed and drank some water. "Sorry," he said quietly. "I don't know what happened."

"Yeah, well, you should be more careful. Only an idiot stands in the sun all day."

"I'll try and remember that, Curtis." Wolfe wiped his mouth with the napkin on the plate. "And thank you for calling me an idiot."

"You're welcome." Curtis cracked a smile. He was quiet for a moment, still a little uneasy around him. But they were working on that, slowly, day by day. "Anyway, hurry up and get better because we have a hundred cupcakes to decorate and there's no way I'm gonna be dashing sprinkles on cakes all afternoon."

"So I'm the sprinkles guy."

Curtis smiled, and it was a boyish smile that warmed Wolfe's heart. "Yeah," he whispered shyly. "I guess so." Soon he was up and out of the room.

For a moment, Wolfe stared at the open door, taking the time to revel in the sweetness of the moment. Curtis was coming around to him. It was a beautiful gift he hadn't expected, and he cherished it.

Still a little weak, Wolfe leaned back into the pillows and turned his face to the window, watching the green leaves sway gently in the summer wind.

The food made him sleepy, and he fought to stay awake.

But the bedroom was cooler now, the sunlight fading out.

Across his window, the leaves danced their wingless flight, and as
he listened to the voices coming from beyond his open door, Wolfe
closed his eyes, drifting back to sleep.

He dreamed it was Pride Day in Montreal.

And running late, he hurried up the stairs to his third-floor office
at the YBR center....

MEL BOSSA is a Lambda Literary and Foreword Book Award finalist who gave up a career as a chef to pursue her dream of writing. She lives in Montreal's gay village with her partner and three kids, where she volunteers for a crisis center and help line.

As a queer Franco-Italian feminist raised in a patriarchal family, she's felt like The Other for a great part of her life and finds peace in dreaming up worlds where grace wins over fear.

A bit of a hermit and an avid reader of French and German philosophy, she sometimes has to let off a little steam, and that's when you'll find her at the local karaoke bar, singing her favorite Janis Joplin songs.

Chasing the
Swallows

JOHN INMAN

http://www.dreamspinnerpress.com

Just the Way You Are

E E MONTGOMERY

http://www.dreamspinnerpress.com

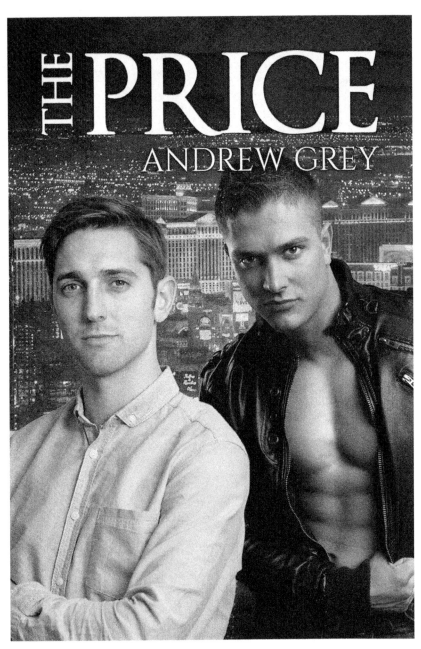

THE PRICE

ANDREW GREY

http://www.dreamspinnerpress.com

soufflés
at sunrise

M.J. O'Shea • Anna Martin

http://www.dreamspinnerpress.com

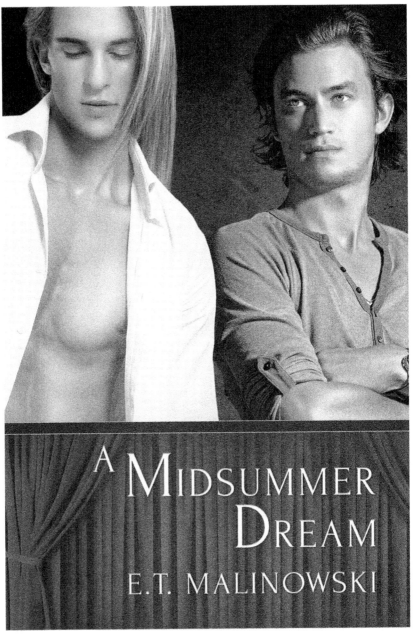

A Midsummer Dream

E.T. Malinowski

http://www.dreamspinnerpress.com

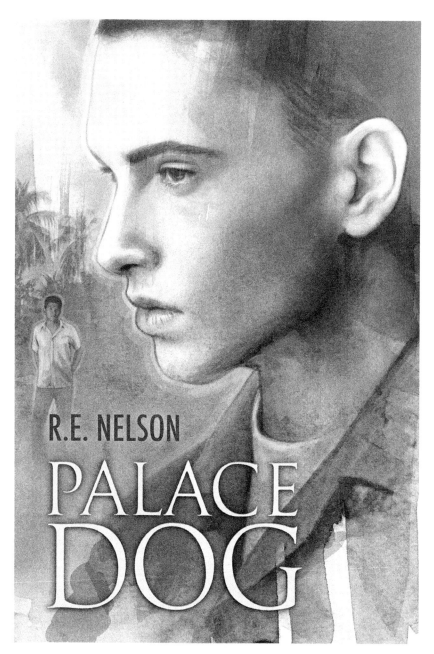

R.E. NELSON

PALACE DOG

http://www.dreamspinnerpress.com

FOR **MORE** OF THE **BEST GAY** ROMANCE

REAMSPINNER
PRESS
dreamspinnerpress.com

CPSIA information can be obtained at www.ICGtesting.com
Printed in the USA
BVOW07s0127150615

404095BV00010B/171/P

9 781632 169303